THE
LOVE
CON

Titles by Seressia Glass

Sugar and Spice novels

SPICE

SUGAR

THE LOVE CON

THE
LOVE
CON

Seressia Glass

Jove
New York

A JOVE BOOK
Published by Berkley
An imprint of Penguin Random House LLC
penguinrandomhouse.com

Library of Congress Cataloging-in-Publication Data

Names: Glass, Seressia, author.
Title: The love con / Seressia Glass.
Description: First Edition. | New York: Jove, 2021.
Identifiers: LCCN 2021022683 (print) | LCCN 2021022684 (ebook) |
ISBN 9780593199053 (trade paperback) | ISBN 9780593199060 (ebook)
Subjects: GSAFD: Love stories.
Classification: LCC PS3557.L345 L68 2021 (print) |
LCC PS3557.L345 (ebook) | DDC 813/.54—dc23
LC record available at https://lccn.loc.gov/2021022683
LC ebook record available at https://lccn.loc.gov/2021022684

First Edition: December 2021

Printed in the United States of America
1st Printing

Book design by George Towne

To my fellow blerds: This one's for us

CHAPTER ONE

Welcome back to *Cosplay or No Way*. Our three remaining contestants are fighting for the opportunity to make it to the final round where one of them will win $100,000 and the chance to work in costuming for a major motion picture!"

Kenya stared at Mark as the host recapped the competition so far. Being in the final three had her mentally bouncing with excitement. She'd read enough online comments after last week's show, the first to broadcast live, to know that a lot of people thought she was there simply to mark a diversity checkbox. *Please.* She'd worked her ass off to stay in the competition.

"As you know, this round's theme is cosplay mashups. Kenya, tell the judges about your cosplay."

Kenya smiled as she stepped forward, buoyed by the audience's applause. "For my cosplay mashup, I chose Dora the Milaje Explorer. In my vision for this, Dora's mother is a powerful warrior who instilled in her daughter all her skills and a desire to explore, learn, and grow. Dora's prized possessions are her digital helper Boots, her mother's gauntlets, and a map to Wakanda."

Based on the audience's reaction, she'd done an excellent job on her mashup. Using the fabrication skills her best friend, Cam, had shown her, she'd recreated Shuri's panther-headed gauntlets, complete with blue glow-lights to simulate energy beams. She'd sewn her battle costume in General Okoye's style but with Dora's pink and yellow colors. A black panther–shaped backpack holding a map of Wakanda and Dora's signature brown bob completed her look. Everyone had instantly known what she'd done. When you didn't have to explain your cosplay, you were already a step ahead. That didn't stop the anxiety fluttering in her stomach.

"Thank you, Kenya." Mark turned his good looks to the panel. "Judges, do you have any comments you'd like to make about Kenya's cosplay?"

Kenya tightened her hands in her gauntlets, almost wishing she could bite her nails. This was the part she hated most, facing the judges. Not because she didn't want their opinions—they were some of the best in their fields—but because one judge seemed to have it out for her.

On cue, Rebecca leaned forward, concern drenching her features. "Kenya, do you really feel that you *embodied* the blending of Dora the Explorer and a Dora Milaje?"

She bristled at Becky's use of the word *embodied*. Throughout the competition, Rebecca had taken issue with her size, her race, and her assertiveness, but Kenya hadn't made it anywhere in life by being anything other than true to herself. Today was not the day to change.

"It's plural, not singular."

"Excuse me?"

"It's *the* Dora Milaje, not *a* Dora Milaje. They are a group, a sisterhood, never alone. Like Dora, who has many adventures and discoveries with the help of her friends. Neither Dora nor the Dora Milaje apologize for who they are or what they do. They simply are, and people accept that and move, or they will be moved."

Applause washed over her. She lifted her chin. She'd refused at the start of the competition to wear the Angry Black Woman mantle, and she wasn't about to cosplay that caricature now. That didn't mean that she wasn't going to stand up for herself.

"You've been a dark horse this entire competition," Rebecca said. A murmur rose from the audience. Rebecca had made herself the judge people loved to hate, with good reason. "Your cosplay choices have been extremely risky, considering your limitations."

Dark horse? Limitations? Kenya fixed her face in the automatic flat expression that all Black women perfected before puberty. She had no idea if Becky meant her size, her color, or her skill, but she'd be damned if she would consider any of those limitations. She was fat, Black, and had been cosplaying since she'd first dressed as Sailor Moon for Halloween as a kid. She knew what she was, but she also knew what she was capable of. Her parents hadn't raised her to be ordinary.

Knowing she had nothing to lose at this point, Kenya squared her shoulders. "With all due respect, Rebecca, I don't know what you mean by limitations. I believe I've met every challenge with grace and ingenuity. I refuse to limit myself so someone else can be comfortable." *Including you. Especially you.*

The crowd applauded in support, and Kenya nodded at them, gratitude welling in her chest. Their opinions mattered the most, since they could boost her popularity at cons and help her costuming business get off the ground.

"That's what I like about you, Kenya," Leon said, a ghost of a smile curving his lips. "You don't allow anything, or anyone, to hold you back. I've enjoyed your unique spin on each of the cosplays you've presented to us over the last two months, especially today's. I know you have a lot of people who see you as a role model and who are rooting for you. I look forward to seeing what else you have up your sleeves. You have my vote."

"Thank you," she mouthed. *One vote in my favor. I only need one more.*

All eyes focused on Rebecca. Kenya knew her vote before she opened her mouth. "I'm sorry," Rebecca said, her tone declaring she was anything but. "I think Amanda delivered the better cosplay this week."

Amanda had chosen the Cat in the Hat Woman for her cosplay. She'd had another meltdown on set because she'd run out of glue for her glue gun, as if it was someone else's fault she didn't have extra glue sticks in her supply kit. The crying jags had become a daily occurrence; they just didn't know what would set her off. Kenya hadn't minded giving the other woman support, but she wasn't there to help someone else win. The longer she stayed in the competition, the more exposure and publicity she received. During the brief times they'd been allowed to use their phones, she'd discovered that she'd gained tons of new followers (along with some new trolls) on all her social media streams, but that wasn't all she wanted. The winner would get the chance to work in the costuming department of a big-budget live-action fantasy film. She hadn't come to the show to be runner-up, and she sure as hell hadn't come to be number three.

Kenya's stomach bubbled as she focused on the last judge, Caroline. The perky blonde flailed her hands. "Oh my God, I can't believe it's up to me! Both of you have done an amazing job week after week. I've been so impressed with how each of you have risen to every challenge we've thrown your way."

Mark stepped forward. "Unfortunately, only one can move forward into the *Cosplay or No Way* final round. So, Caroline, who will it be? Will it be Amanda, or will you choose Kenya?"

Dramatic music swelled as the audience chanted both their names in a muddled cacophony. Caroline looked at them each in turn. Kenya reached out to clasp Amanda's hand, awkwardly squeezing the other woman's trembling fingers in an effort to steady her own. The other woman had already started the deep breaths that presaged tears.

"This is so hard . . . and I'm really sorry that I have to do this," Caroline began.

Silence fell, thick enough to choke on.

"Kenya."

Her eyes flew open as ice raced down her back, her shocked gasp echoed by the audience. Surely that didn't mean . . . ?

Caroline stared at her for a long moment before finally breaking into a smile. "Welcome to the final round."

"Oh God." Relief nearly buckled her knees as the audience rose in a standing ovation. She covered her open mouth with her gauntleted hands, smothering the gasp that wanted to become a scream. She had the presence of mind to turn to hug Amanda before the other woman sprinted from the stage. Blowing out a breath, she pulled back the panther on her left gauntlet, then straightened her shoulders to face the judges.

The host set up a commercial break as Ben, the other finalist, returned to the floor. He gave her a smile and a hug before joining her in facing the panel.

"And we're back with our two *Cosplay or No Way* finalists, Ben and Kenya!"

The audience cheers washed over Kenya. Euphoria zapped through her, nervous energy making her bounce on her toes as she vacillated between disbelief and elation. The final round! She was in the final round! She almost pinched herself as the reality of being a finalist began to settle in. The grand prize was close, so close. Just one more cosplay away.

Mark turned to them with a smile. "Congratulations, top two. You've fought long and hard to make it here, and each of you deserve your place in the finals. However, there's no time to rest on your success. In fact, in this final round we want to see how you design and create your cosplays on your home turf."

She and Ben exchanged glances. Home turf?

"That's right. The next part of the competition will follow the two of you as you return home to make your final-round costumes. A production crew will film you in your element. We want to see how you craft your creations in your personal space!"

Excitement and anxiety faced off in her nerves, ready to duke it out for the top spot. Her personal space was her bedroom in the apartment she shared with Cam, her best friend. She couldn't imagine trying to fit a camera crew in there. Besides, it was her bedroom, and she tended to be a bit messy during the design phase, creating several sketches as she finalized her concept. Maybe Cam would agree to let her use their dining area since they usually ate at the breakfast bar or in front of the television.

"I'm sure everyone is wondering about the final-round challenge. For that, we turn to our judges. Leon?"

Leon regarded them, his smile stuck somewhere on the road between heaven and hell. "Contestants, you've consistently brought your A game for every week of this competition. Now, we want to see your A-plus work. Your final challenge will be iconic duos."

Duos? After they'd just finished mashups week? If that's what they wanted, she wasn't going to complain. She could do a gender-bent Two-Face, or one of the gem fusions from *Steven Universe*.

"That's the good news," Caroline said, "but you know we have to step it up for this final round. With that in mind, your iconic duo must be a pairs cosplay."

"What?" Ben whispered, looking as confused as Kenya felt. Did that mean making two costumes?

"That's right." Rebecca surveyed them. "Not only do we want to see how you juggle cosplaying with your normal life, we want you to create two costumes: one for you, and one for your cosplaying partner."

Kenya's mouth dropped open. Two costumes? Cosplay partner? Her mind raced. Did they need to create them from scratch or could they source parts? Most importantly, how much time did they have to create two costumes?

Caroline leaned forward. "We all know that cosplayers do everything from making their own cosplays to commissioning full costumes from someone else. You're probably wondering what's allowed for you in this final-round iconic duo cosplay challenge. So here are the parameters.

"First of all, both costumes must be at least fifty percent handmade. Of course, the more handmade the costumes are, the more points you can score. Secondly, we know there's a lot of pressure to make two costumes, so you're allowed to have help from your cosplay partner. However, seventy-five percent of the work has to be yours. You'll also need to recap your work at the end of the day with a video diary entry."

Rebecca gave them a smile Kenya instantly mistrusted. "This is all about being the best, which means testing and stressing you. That's why you and your partner will have four weeks to complete your costumes before you return here to cosplay for the live audience."

The shocked murmurs of the audience echoed the shock that

swept through Kenya. There was no way they could expect two costumes to be finished in four weeks, especially with that fifty-percent-handmade requirement. And with one person doing the bulk of the work?

She looked at Ben, who looked as floored as she felt. "What?" he whispered. "Are they serious?"

"We're very serious," Leon answered. "Just as you should be, especially about who you'll pick as your cosplay partner. Remember, your partner can do up to twenty-five percent of the build, and they'll need to cosplay with you in the finale."

"Who will our finalists pick as their cosplay partners?" Mark asked the audience. "We'll find out—right after this."

Kenya's mind raced as everyone waited for the commercial break to end, imagining and discarding all the duos that immediately came to mind. With four weeks to work, it would be nearly impossible to do any costume with a great deal of detail work, and certainly not two.

Then there was the matter of picking her cosplay partner. Who could she get to help her? Her mind instantly went to Cam, but her best friend had his hands full running the fabrication shop, especially since she wasn't there to handle logistics and order intake. Her parents were out. Neither one understood her obsession with the geekery of anime and gaming or adults running around in costumes outside of Halloween, and even then they deployed maximum side-eye.

Besides, they'd been against her doing the show from the start. They wanted her to "give up this foolishness" and use her engineering degree they'd paid for. Her brother was off in the air force and her sisters were busy with their families and their careers on opposite sides of the country. Janelle might have been willing, but her other best friend didn't even own a sewing kit. Bringing Janelle on board meant Kenya would wind up doing one hundred percent of the work. What was she going to do?

"Welcome back to *Cosplay or No Way*," Mark announced as he was counted back in from the commercial break. "Let's recap the parameters of the final round."

Dramatic music and lighting rolled across the stage as the jumbo screen lit up, bold white letters spelling out FINAL ROUND RULES on a purple background. "First, conceive of an iconic duo cosplay that you and your partner will showcase during our live finale. Second, at least fifty percent of each costume must be handmade. Third, your cosplay partner can help you, but you must do seventy-five percent of the work. Each of you will have a production crew following your progress, and of course we want to continue seeing those video diaries. Judges, anything else?"

Leon spoke. "You're going to have your hands full in this challenging round, but overcoming challenges is part of what being a *Cosplay or No Way* champion is all about. I would suggest you choose your cosplay partner carefully."

"Ben," Mark said. "Who will you choose to partner with to help you become the *Cosplay or No Way* champion?"

Ben, who'd done an excellent mashup of The Stay-Puft Michelin Man, smiled. "My husband, John. He's as into cosplay as I am."

Crap. She knew from their conversations that Ben's husband was an active cosplayer and did set design for their local theater. Acid churned in her stomach. The choice gave him a huge advantage. She needed to level the playing field, which meant she needed someone who not only cosplayed, but could help make their costumes without Kenya having to supervise every step.

Her thoughts returned to Cam. They'd been best friends for half their lives and had cosplayed together since they first attended

Dragon Con during their senior year of high school. He also knew his way around a 3-D printer and an X-acto knife. But she couldn't take him away from the shop. Yes, Mack and Javier were there, but since she ran the project management software, she knew just how lean the shop ran. Taking her off the schedule was a pain, but manageable. Taking Cam out of production . . .

He would do it, she knew. Cam was the reason she'd heard about the competition. He'd helped her prepare her audition video, sent encouraging texts and a good-luck video with their game night friends. He'd supported her every step of the way. This . . . this might stretch the bonds of their friendship to the breaking point.

"Kenya, it's now your turn," Mark said, his voice snapping her out of her spiraling thoughts. "Who will be your cosplay partner in the final round? Who will you choose to help you create an iconic duo cosplay that will win you $100,000 and the title of *Cosplay or No Way* champion?"

The musical tension increased as the audience fell silent. Kenya was sure they could hear her gut churning. She glanced at the judges, trying not to let Rebecca's smug expression get to her. She was pretty sure the snotty judge doubted she had anyone close enough to meet the qualifications to help her.

"Well, Kenya?" Rebecca raised an eyebrow. "Do you have a significant other who can help you in this final round, like Ben does?"

Kenya carefully blanked her expression so they wouldn't notice she was internally seething. She'd broken up with her last boyfriend months ago for good reasons, but she'd be damned if she'd give Becky the satisfaction of knowing that. "I do."

Rebecca tilted her head in surprise. "Really. Who might that be?"

"There's only one person who's been with me all through my

cosplay journey," she said, her voice quavering as nerves stretched tight. "The one who believes in me the most. The one who helped me get here, who's cheered me on from the start. The one person who's encouraged me to push myself, to be more and do more. My best friend, Cameron Lassiter."

"Ah." Rebecca's expression reminded Kenya of the shark in that movie about the missing clown fish. "That's your friend, right? I hope that won't put you at a disadvantage, considering Ben is working with his spouse."

Does this heifer think I can't get a man? Kenya unzipped a smile. "Cam is my best friend and my partner. Trust and believe I'm not disadvantaged in the least."

"You go, girl!" someone in the audience shouted, causing the crowd to explode with laughter, then applause. Vindication swelled in her chest, and she gave them a genuine grin and wave before giving Rebecca the same smug smile she'd received earlier. *Take that, Becky.*

"There you have it, folks!" Mark boomed. "Two couples going head-to-head to create iconic cosplay duos. Which team will come out on top to claim $100,000 and a chance to work on a major movie? We'll have to wait and see. Tune in next week as our finalists return to their home turf and begin the build of their lives on *Cosplay or No Way!*"

Thrills shot through her like fireworks. There really wasn't anyone else she wanted with her in the final round. That was the truth. Maybe she'd split hairs on the whole partner thing, but they really were partners, given her tiny stake in his shop. Their friendship had lasted longer than a bunch of marriages. Surely it wouldn't be a problem to fake that their relationship was more than just friends.

Now all she had to do was convince Cam to be her cosplay partner—and her significant other.

CHAPTER TWO

This is so hard . . . and I'm really sorry that I have to do this."

Cam reached for the emergency jar of gummy worms. Finding it empty, he chewed his fingernail to the quick instead, waiting for the perky judge to decide who should be the last finalist. How the hell they had decided to put Kenya in the bottom two, he didn't know. He'd yelled a few choice words at the television, grateful that he'd had to work late at the fabrication shop instead of having his weekly dinner with Kenya's parents. Her Dora the Milaje Explorer cosplay was a damn sight better than the simplistic Cat in the Hat Woman cosplay the other contestant had done. If he could have, he would have helped Kenya fabricate those gauntlets, incorporating the light and adding a charging sound effect, but she'd done an awesome job with the time and materials she'd had.

"Kenya."

His heart stopped. He bit down on another fingernail. No fucking way . . .

"Welcome to the final round."

"Yes!"

Cam surged to his feet, punching the air with his fists as he watched Kenya console the other woman then beam her thanks to the judges. She was a champ through and through even though he was pretty sure she couldn't stand Bitchy Becky. He sure couldn't.

He packed up his latest fabrication during the commercial break so that it would be ready to ship first thing in the morning. Now that he knew Kenya had made it into the final round, his belly reminded him that they'd missed whatever Kenya's father had made for dinner. Sunday dinners were command appearances with any family members who were in town but with Kenya off in California, he'd taken to also joining Mr. and Mrs. Davenport during the Wednesday night airing of the show. He got two home-cooked meals a week, and they got reassurance that he was doing okay.

A pang of regret hit him. It would have been great to celebrate Kenya's advancement to the finals with her parents, but completing and delivering this part on time meant signing on a new client, bringing in another much-needed income source. The Davenports would understand. They wanted his business to be a success as much as he did.

He loved them as if they were his own parents and appreciated their concern more than he could ever put into words. They didn't have to accept a half-feral thirteen-year-old that Kenya had befriended during school lunch. They certainly didn't have to give him food and shelter and comfort while his father drowned his grief in beer and liquor. The Davenports had shown him what a loving, healthy family was like, what his had been like before his mom had died, all because Kenya had sat across from him one day in the cafeteria, pushed her lunchbox toward him, and started talking about comics. Then she did it again the next day, then the day after that, until he started enjoying her company more than the free meal. He was certain he wouldn't have survived to eighteen without them, especially Kenya.

"And we're back with our two *Cosplay or No Way* finalists, Ben and Kenya!"

Cam applauded with everyone else as the first finalist stood with Kenya on the stage. He wondered what they'd have to do for the final round. Something huge, definitely.

The host announced that they'd get to go home to complete their final designs. "All right!" It would be good to have Kenya home. Better than good. He'd missed her more than he would have thought possible. More than he should have.

"I'm sure you're wondering what your challenge is for this final round," the host said, reading everyone's minds. "For that, we'll turn to the judges. Leon?"

The male judge announced the theme of iconic duos. Cam nodded. Kenya could handle that, no problem, but they'd just completed mashup cosplays. Why would they do it again?

Anticipation gripped him as he leaned forward while the camera focused on the perky judge. She dropped the bomb that it had to be a pairs cosplay. Hmm. He and Kenya had done those before, so he knew she could do it. Were they supposed to make two costumes in the same amount of time? Sure, Kenya had created multiple costumes simultaneously before, because they changed cosplays during Dragon Con weekend, and he'd done his fair share too. Maybe he'd be able to help out. He'd have no problem making fabricated pieces for her, he just needed to check the shop's production schedule—

"Rebecca?"

The camera tightened on the third judge's snarky expression. Rebecca obviously relished being the mean judge on the show, but the way she spoke to Kenya made Cam want to punch things. She was going to take another dig at Kenya, he could feel it. He moved the shipping box out of arm's reach before turning his attention back to the TV.

"Not only do we want to see how you juggle cosplaying with your normal life, we want you to create two costumes: one for you, and one for your cosplaying partner."

Shit. Kenya did have to make two costumes, but what the hell was this cosplaying partner business?

Cam chewed on another fingernail as they went through the final round parameters. Damn, the guidelines were insane. Even with a partner's help, as little as it was, it was going to be difficult to create two contest-winning costumes. If anyone could do it, Kenya could, but—

"Four fucking weeks?" he shouted at the TV. "What the hell?"

It was time for the contestants to choose their cosplay partners. Ben, of course, picked his husband, but Cam didn't care about that. He watched Kenya. Surprise, uncertainty, and dismay rolled across her features, a stormfront of emotion that lowered his brows. What was there to be uncertain about? Her choice should have been easy and instant. Her choice should have been him.

"Well, Kenya?" Becky the Bitch crooned. "Do you have a significant other who can help you in this final round, like Ben does?"

Cam shoved to his feet, looking for the remote to shut off the TV. If Kenya did, it would be news to him. News he didn't want to hear. He needed to get some dinner, prep for tomorrow's workday, call the Davenports, and not think about Kenya announcing her mystery partner to the world on live television. Where the fuck was the remote?

"Cameron Lassiter."

He jerked to a stop, his finger hovering over the power button. Had he heard Kenya right?

Kenya's choice had apparently surprised the redheaded judge as well. "That's your friend, right? I hope that won't put you at a disadvantage, considering Ben is working with his spouse."

Cam's vision reddened, his grip on the remote so tight his hand shook. What the hell was that supposed to mean? He and Kenya were best friends. He had fabrication skills, and he cosplayed with her regularly. How was choosing him putting her at a disadvantage?

"Cam is my best friend and my partner. Trust and believe I'm not disadvantaged in the least."

Smug satisfaction swept through him. "That's my girl."

His phone rang as he locked up the shop. Michaela Davenport's smiling face lit up his screen. "Hi, Mrs. D."

She cut to the chase. "Were you watching?"

"Yes, ma'am." He headed for his SUV. "Kenya's in the final round! How awesome is that?"

"Davenports give their all, and Kenya's done that. We're proud of her. And you."

Cam started the engine so that he could go hands-free while he drove. "Me? I didn't do anything. Kenya's done this all on her own."

"She wouldn't have entered this competition if you hadn't encouraged her," Mrs. Davenport reminded him, an edge to her tone. "And there's the fact that my daughter just announced you as her significant other on live TV. Do you have something that you want to tell us, Cameron?"

The Davenports never called him anything other than his full name, even when he was a scruffy teen hanging in their living room, but today it made his palms sweaty. He'd long suspected that Mrs. D knew he harbored more than friendly feelings for Kenya, but she'd never asked, so he'd never confessed. He wouldn't confess now, either. "What? She didn't announce me as her significant other, just her design partner."

"Really? Did you hear the same thing I heard?"

No, he hadn't because he'd been too busy being angry at the thought of her picking someone else. "Uh . . ."

"I know you broke up with Jessa a couple of weeks before Kenya left, and you haven't been seeing anyone since. The show also showed some photos of you and Kenya in costumes together early on."

He was so, so glad that he wasn't facing her across the dining room table at that moment. He didn't have any gummy worms or fingernails left to bite. "That's because we always cosplay together," he answered, but he wondered about that too. Kenya had plenty of solo photos of her cosplays. Why share so many of them together?

"I won't put you on the spot, Cameron," Mrs. D said when the silence stretched a little too long. "I'm sure your phone is about to blow up soon anyway. My baby's coming home as a finalist! Is there enough room in your apartment to do the designing, or whatever y'all have to do for the competition?"

"If that's what she wants. Her stuff's there anyway. There's also space at the shop." Matter of fact, the shop would be better, especially if cameras were going to follow her around. He didn't want them in the apartment, which would clearly prove he and Kenya were nothing more than best friends and roommates.

"The shop would probably be best," Mrs. D said, as if she'd read his mind. "Unless you did some rearranging and redecorating at home before she left?"

"No, ma'am," he answered cautiously, wondering where she was going. "I'll set up some space for her at the shop and bring over some of her most important supplies from home. Knowing Kenya, she'll want to work as much as possible."

"Unless it's in an engineering field."

Cam clamped his mouth shut. Even though Kenya had made it

to the final round, the Davenports still weren't happy that Kenya was pursuing her cosplay instead of using her degree. They probably weren't happy that he'd encouraged her to enter and helped her with her audition video, but how could he not help her with something that made her so happy? Even if it put him in a tug-of-war between her and her parents.

Mrs. Davenport sighed. "The way you two are partners in crime . . . it would have surprised me if she'd picked someone else."

"Yeah." Guilt heated his ears. He had imagined it, or rather, dreaded it. He could still feel that jangly moment of uncertainty and it was taking longer than he'd thought for it to fade. "I swear I'll do everything I can to help her win."

"I know you will." She sighed again, but before he could wonder what the sigh meant, she continued. "You still owe us a dinner visit, so we'll see you Sunday. Hopefully Kenya will be home by then."

"I hope so, too. I'll still swing by on Friday to help Mr. D with the yard." He enjoyed puttering around the yard with Mr. D almost as much as he enjoyed stuffing his face. With his dad spending most of his non-work hours drinking his grief away, Cam had been in sore need of fatherly attention. Doing hard work like building a gazebo and subduing wild raspberry thickets under Mr. D's calm supervision had done more to ease his grief and anger than any family counselor ever could.

"He'll appreciate that. His back isn't what it used to be."

"I can still throw you over my shoulder!" Lincoln Davenport yelled in the background.

God. "I can't unhear that," Cam complained. "I'm going to go and let y'all do whatever y'all do."

They shared a laugh before Mrs. D sobered. "I can't thank you enough for everything you do for us, Cameron, especially with Junior stationed overseas."

"Helping out is the least I can do after everything you've done for me."

"But you don't have to, which is why we appreciate you even more. We love you, son."

He pulled into the parking lot of a burger joint, jammed on the brakes, then shifted to park. His eyes slid closed as he swallowed down the sudden lump in his throat. These sweet little declarations still startled him, even though he'd known the Davenports for half his life. He hoarded them like the treasures they were because he didn't dare assume that he'd get another one.

"Thank you, Mrs. D," he said after clearing his throat. "I'll see y'all Friday."

After disconnecting, he went through the drive-thru for dinner. He couldn't shake the feeling that not only did Mrs. D know how he felt about Kenya, she approved. Good. That meant it was time to put his plan into action.

He'd pretend to pretend he was her boyfriend. He'd help Kenya win the competition, and then he'd win her heart.

What have I done?"

Finally alone and back in her temporary room, Kenya flopped onto the bed, staring up at the ceiling. Victory and vindication slowly but steadily eroded into anxiety and agitation. She needed to talk to Cam immediately, but what should she say? She had to apologize for volunteering him to help her without checking with him first, that was obvious, then hope he wouldn't be angry with her.

He'd only been angry with her once before, when she'd tried to end their friendship because Cam was being bullied for being her friend. They'd been sixteen, but she'd never seen him rage that much before or since.

This . . . this was asking a lot. The biggest ask of her life. The payoff would set them both up for future success. Surely that was worth a little pain now? She would take on the brunt of the work so that there was as little impact on the shop as possible. They could make this work. They had to.

Her phone buzzed with an incoming text. HEY FUTURE CHAMP. LOOKING FORWARD TO HELPING YOU WIN.

Relief spread through her like butter on hot grits. Cam had her back just as she'd hoped. Still, she had to make sure he understood exactly what she'd gotten him into.

Grinning, buoyed anew, she quickly called him. He answered on the first ring, belting out "We Are the Champions" at the top of his lungs.

She covered her mouth in a futile effort to muffle her laughter. The enormity of being a finalist hit her again, squeezing her vocal cords. "Oh God, can you believe this? I made it!"

"Of course I believe it. I've watched every episode," he answered, laughter threading his words. "Your cosplay is better than anyone else's hands down. I knew you could do it."

"You did." He believed she could before she'd believed it herself. "You're the reason I was able to make it this far."

"Speaking of making it, you want to fill me in on this status change you hinted at tonight?"

"Ah." She cringed into the mattress. "So uhm, about that . . . it's complicated?"

"I guess it is, *partner.*"

Heat flushed up her neck to singe her ears. "I'm so sorry for doing this to you. I—I just panicked. I'll find some way to fix this."

"You're breaking up with your fake boyfriend already? It's only been an hour."

"Okay, maybe I'm still panicking." She sucked in a breath, trying for calm. "I know it's a lot, a lot more than either of us thought when we started this. I'm sure I can come up with someone else to help me now that I'm not standing on a stage with a camera in my face. You already have so much to do and I don't want to burden you or make trouble for the shop. I can put out a call to our friends. Someone might be willing—"

"KeKe."

When he said her nickname like that it always made her stop, as if her brain had tripped a circuit. "Yeah?"

"Did I say no?"

"Oh. Uhm, no, but—"

"But nothing. I'm going to help."

Relief and guilt whooshed out of her on a loud exhale. "I know I put you on the spot and I'm sorry."

"Why are you apologizing?" he asked, his voice like a well-loved corset, soft with a spine of steel. "You were the one put on the spot, and that Rebecca judge made it seem like you didn't have anyone in your corner at the same level as that other guy. I'm glad you chose me."

"Really?"

"Yeah, really. Do you know how pissed I would have been if you hadn't picked me to help you?"

"You were my first choice," she admitted, "but then she started that whole disadvantage-because-I-don't-have-a-spouse thing, I really wanted to prove her wrong."

"And we will," he promised. "I'm going to cosplay so well as your boyfriend that even you will think it's the real deal!"

Butterflies took flight in her belly but she ignored them, forcing herself to focus on the main objective instead of indulging in a side quest. "Okay. I promise you won't regret this. I'll do all the heavy lifting and leave quick and easy stuff to you so the shop doesn't suffer. I'll even do my usual work stuff when I'm done working on the costumes for the day. I'll—"

"You'll come up with a killer idea for the iconic duo thing and let me worry about the shop."

She wanted to argue, but what he said made sense. "Okay."

"Okay." His tone softened. "I'm sure you're ready to decompress from that rollercoaster of a show, so we can talk this out when you get home. Speaking of which, when are you coming home? Your fake boyfriend wants to pick you up from the airport."

She laughed, her guilt dissipating completely as he seemed to take everything in stride. "I'm kinda looking forward to that," she confessed. "I'll text you as soon as I know, but it will probably be Saturday, with shooting starting on Monday."

She paused, then continued. "You really are the best, Cam. I couldn't have done this without you."

"Hey," he protested. "We started this together and we'll end it the same way. Good night, future champ."

"Good night, future fake boyfriend." She disconnected, holding the phone against her chest. Okay, so that had gone the way she'd hoped, but one hurdle down still left a whole bunch to go.

Shaking off sleep, she opened a note app on her phone and began making notes. Come up with a killer idea. Create a project plan and hope the dependencies and deadline were doable. Make sure Cam only got the easy tasks to do. Make a decent work area in their living room that could fit the production crew. Do all of that and somehow make it seem as if she and Cam were more than friends and had been for months.

The last one was the most difficult task. How in the hell was she supposed to pretend to be Cam's girlfriend, doing all of the things— well, almost all of the things—that couples did and somehow return to being just friends when the competition ended?

How could she pretend to be Cam's girlfriend without revealing that a tiny, long-ignored part of her wanted to be his girlfriend for real?

This was about to be the cosplay of her life, and everything—her future, his future, the success of the shop—everything hung on her ability to pull this off without a hitch.

She was so screwed.

CHAPTER THREE

Butterflies danced in Kenya's belly as she took the escalator up into the main terminal at Hartsfield-Jackson Atlanta Airport, hyperaware of the location producer, Jane, and cameraman, Ian, following close behind. She'd hoped to have a couple of hours alone with Cam but Jane had stuck to her nearly every moment since their introduction the day before. Considering how deep in conversation Jane had been with Rebecca before they'd left, Kenya suspected that the producer would be investigating her relationship just as much as she'd be producing segments.

Choosing Cam was a no-brainer—she'd been completely honest when she'd declared there was no one else she'd rather cosplay with. He was her cosplay partner, enthusiastically supporting and encouraging her. The rest, though? Despite what he'd said, she wasn't sure he'd go along with that. Would he still be as enthusiastic when he realized exactly what she'd signed him up for?

He was her best friend, had been since the day they'd met in high school. He'd helped her in ways big and small over the course of their friendship, and she'd done the same. Asking him to pretend to be her significant other was stretching the bonds of friendship. One thing she hadn't considered until packing for the trip home was, what if he was seeing someone? He'd broken up with his girlfriend a couple of months before Kenya had left for Los Angeles, but he'd seemed relieved instead of upset. He'd told her he was ready to move on. Why wouldn't he? Guys who looked like Cam didn't stay single for long unless they wanted to.

Stepping off the escalator into the main terminal, she scanned the crowd for Cam in the area where he'd promised to meet her. A couple of Mylar balloons, one saying CONGRATS and the other in the shape of Dora the Explorer, caught her eye. "Cam!"

He pointed his phone toward her. "There's my champion. Welcome home!"

Nerves vanished as she ran toward him and the bouquet of flowers he held. He opened his arms with a big grin and she crashed into him, so happy she could burst.

Arms, flowers, balloons, and Cam's scent cocooned her. She closed her eyes, breathing him in. Given how her parents felt about her cosplay hobby, she hadn't expected them to show up at the airport, but it would have crushed her if Cam hadn't been waiting for her. All the pressure and stress of competing on the show melted away in the heat of his embrace. Joy and relief swelled inside her, so when they parted for a moment, she didn't even think.

She kissed him.

I'm kissing Cam!

She hadn't intended to, but with the producer and cameraman filming and observing every single action, it wasn't a bad play to make. Judging by Cam's stiffness, she'd probably pushed too far. Flustered, she quickly broke from him with a laugh.

"Hey, babe, I missed you." Okay, *that* might have been too far. She silently pleaded for Cam to play along.

He kept his arm tight around her waist, his hand splayed on the center of her back. "I missed you, too."

He seemed like he was about to say something else—what, she didn't know. She quickly put her thumb to his lip. "Sorry—I've got lipstick all over you."

"I don't mind," he said, giving her a wink that told her he understood her game. His smile crinkled the corners of his eyes, their brilliant blue enhanced by his vintage *ThunderCats* T-shirt. "I don't mind at all."

Then he kissed her back.

Oh. *Oh*. This wasn't like the kiss she'd given him. This wasn't even like the kisses they'd shared when they were practicing at fourteen. This was—wow, Cam sure knew how to kiss, and he smelled good, and his beard wasn't scratchy, and she could lean into him like this all day . . .

An indiscreet cough sounded behind them. *Crap*. She'd totally forgotten about the camera crew—and the fact that Cam was *not* her boyfriend. Heat burned her ears as she took the flowers and balloons from him, then turned around. "Uhm, Cam, this is Jane, one of the producers, and Ian, the camera guy. This is Cameron Lassiter, my partner."

Yes, she didn't stumble over the word and Cam didn't look at her like she'd lost her mind under the pressure of competition. Which was good because Jane stared at both of them as if she was about to perform a dissection. While the crew assigned to her seemed nice enough, Kenya knew they wanted to capture drama more than her skill with a glue gun. The deliberate misconstruing of the depth of her relationship with Cam sat like a cement block in her belly. She needed to get over it real quick. Besides, *partner* wasn't a lie. The word could mean a lot of things: partner in life, business, crime. She couldn't help it if someone misconstrued her intent, right?

"It's a pleasure to finally meet you," Jane said, sticking out a hand to Cam. "Kenya's told us a lot about you."

"I bet." He shoved his phone into his back pocket, then grabbed the handle of Kenya's carry-on. "We've got years of history."

"You two have been friends for a while," Jane continued, as they made their way to the baggage claim area.

Kenya tensed, clutching her bouquet closer. Jane was doing her job, but that casual tone wasn't fooling anyone. This was a competition, yet they were treating it like an investigation. She hoped Cam wouldn't take the bait.

"We've been friends forever," Cam confirmed. Then he turned to Kenya, his smile soft. "And now we're more."

She melted—no, not melted. That would be weird. But relaxed? Yeah, definitely relaxed. Cam was holding his own. She didn't have anything to worry about.

Except Jane pressing for more. "When did you two decide that you wanted to be more than friends?"

Cam's brow puckered as he glowered at the producer. "If Kenya's already told you so much about me, I'm sure she's already told you that, too. But it was right before she left to do the show. The timing sucked, I know. Maybe now we'll get to make up some of that lost time. In between making costumes of course."

Okay, this time she did melt. A little. Maybe a lot. One thing for sure, she owed Cam big-time for this. "Oh, I think we can definitely make some time."

Enthusiastic and a teeny bit suggestive was what she was going for. It must have worked because Cam gave her a wink before grabbing her hot-pink leopard print suitcase off the baggage carousel. "Just wait until we're away from the cameras, babe."

"That might be a moment," Jane said, her smile sharp. "We officially start production when the rest of the crew gets here Monday, but we need to finish filming Kenya's homecoming. We'll be filming you, too, since you're Kenya's significant other. Wherever she goes, that's where we'll be. In fact, I have some forms for you to sign—"

"Wherever she goes?" Cam interrupted, his brow creasing. "I hope that doesn't include the apartment."

Jane looked at Cam, then Kenya, then back to Cam. "Is there a problem with filming there?"

"Of course not," Kenya protested, hoping he would go along with her. The other contestant, Ben, would have a camera crew filming in his personal space too. It was part of the agreement they both had signed. If Cam balked now . . .

He looked at her. "Babe, I'm just trying to protect your downtime."

Anxiety bounced around in Kenya's gut again like a beach ball at a concert. Yes, she needed downtime, but she also needed to create two costumes. It wasn't like she could commandeer a table at Starbucks. "I thought I'd do most of my work there."

"Oh." He pursed his lips. "Before you decide, I have a surprise for you."

She needed a giant ginger ale to douse the nerves bubbling in her belly. "What sort of surprise?"

"It's at the shop," he responded, ignoring the camera and the curious looks from other travelers as he settled a hand on her shoulder. "Do you want to go there now or wait until after dinner?"

She juggled her flowers to reach up to cover his hand, appreciating the comforting gesture. Her breath caught as she ran a fingertip over his, realizing he'd chewed his nails to the quick. This was stressing him out, too. She shook her head. No, she didn't want to wait. Jane would want to film whatever the surprise was, and she wanted to be alone with Cam and out of camera view sooner rather than later. "Now, please."

He squeezed her shoulder once in understanding before turning to the producer. "I guess you want to see the surprise, too."

"Of course. It will be perfect footage for the show."

He reached into his pocket to retrieve his wallet. "This is the address to my shop," he said, handing the producer a business card. "Are you grabbing a rideshare or a rental?"

"Rental, unless you have room?"

"For four adults and all this baggage? Sure don't," Cam said, a pleasant smile wreathing his face but missing his eyes. "Y'all gonna need something bigger than the Jeep for all this."

Uh-oh. When Cam started that polite drawl, that meant he was just a hair shy of irritated. Besides, the Jeep was hers. He owned a huge SUV to transport some of his larger fabrications. Which meant he'd deliberately chosen to drive her Jeep to the airport.

A frown skittered quickly across Jane's face. "Then we'll need to put a camera in your car to get more reunion footage."

"No thanks, ma'am," Cam said, his drawl even more pronounced. "My shop's a short ride from here. It'll probably take you longer to get your rental than it will to get there. We'll be more than happy to wait for you out front."

Kenya could tell that wasn't welcome news for the producer, but there wasn't anything Jane could do about it because Cam hadn't signed any release forms yet. Even if he had, he wouldn't want cameras in his personal space. Not until they had a chance to talk everything out.

Jane took the card. "All right then. We'll meet you at your shop. You can read over and sign the release forms there."

"No problem."

Cam sighed in relief as the producer and the camera guy made their way to ground transportation for rental cars while he and Kenya went to short-term parking. "Well, that was something."

Kenya echoed his sigh. "You said it. I thought I was going to vomit onto the bag carousel!"

"That definitely would have been must-see TV, but you were fine," Cam reassured her. "You didn't seem nervous at all."

She laughed, her shoulders relaxing. "Like I always say, you gotta fake it 'til you make it. But I'm gonna need some Tums or something soon."

He nearly tripped over a crack in the concrete path. "You're not wearing a microphone or anything, are you?"

"What? No. Why?"

"I don't need the producer hearing about all the nasty things I'm going to do to you when I get you alone."

"Cam!"

The way her mouth and eyes widened in shock would have been funny if it didn't sting. Was the idea of them together in that way truly so shocking?

"I just want to make sure we're really alone," he said.

"Smart." Her smile lit up her whole face. "You're a natural at this."

As usual, she wore her favorite color, hot-pink capri pants and sneakers topped with a white T-shirt bearing the image of Garnet from *Steven Universe*. She looked good. Better than good. And she felt even better. When you deserved a Kenya hug, she hugged you with her whole body. He wanted more of those. And the kisses. Definitely more of those.

"Cam?"

Crap. "Sorry." He dug his keys out as they approached her Jeep. "Got lost in my head for a sec. What's up?"

She stopped, her smile dimming. "I just want to say thank you. Not just for the flowers and balloons. I know I ambushed you with the kiss and saying you're my boyfriend and stuff. I appreciate you playing along."

Playing along. Right. He had to remember that's all this was, cosplaying for the cameras. "You don't have to thank me."

"Yeah, I do. I could have given you a heads-up before the plane landed, but Jane and Ian see everything."

"Don't worry about it. Your mom actually figured it out the night the show aired."

"My mom?"

"Yeah." He stowed her bags in the cargo area while she put her balloons and flowers in the backseat. "I watch the show with your parents every week, but this week I had to work late finishing up a high-priority project. When you made the finals and announced me as your partner, she called and asked if there was something I forgot to tell her."

"Oh my God. What did you say?"

"As little as possible, but I expect we're going to get a lot of questions at dinner tomorrow night." He held out the keys. "Wanna drive?"

"No. I need to think. I can't believe they watched the show with you."

He held her door, then made his way to the driver's side. He understood Kenya's disbelief. The Davenports hadn't minded Kenya's fascination with gaming, anime, and cosplay during high school as long as she'd kept her grades up. Once they were in college, the few clashes she'd had with her parents had been over her hobbies, their hobbies. Their biggest argument had been when Kenya hadn't immediately sought a career in her degree field or entered a master's program after graduating with her bachelor's. It had led to her moving out and becoming his roommate.

"Mom and Dad," she finally said as they made their way to the interstate. "Were they happy that I made it to the finals?"

He reached over to gather her hand. "They're both proud of you."

Her fingers tightened around his. "Really?"

So much hope and trepidation in that one word stabbed at him. He owed her parents a lot, but he owed Kenya more. "They're proud of you no matter what happens."

"Really?" This time derision filled her tone. "Even though I lied on national television?"

It didn't have to be a lie if she didn't want it to be. Problem was, he didn't know how she'd take the suggestion, and after being rebuffed a few years ago he wasn't ready to face that disappointment again. Besides, they had a competition to win. There would be time to talk about their relationship afterward.

"We'll tell them the same thing we're telling everyone else," Cam said. "We decided to become more than friends right before you left. Our relationship is still new, which explains any awkward moments we could have."

"That makes sense. It would be hard to overwrite a decade of friendship with a couple of months of dating. Are you sure you're up for this?"

"Why wouldn't I be?"

She ran a finger over his ragged nails. "Seems like you're already under enough stress without me adding to it. Are you tired of gummy worms?"

Suppressing the urge to pull his hand back, he focused on the road before answering. "I've been trying to cut back on my two-pack-a-day habit. I ran out while watching the last show and that bitchy judge. Was it really as bad as it looked on TV? Because it sure as hell looked like she's out to get you."

"Yeah." She squeezed his hand again before releasing it. "It was that bad. There were a lot of exchanges with her that didn't air. Trying to make me doubt myself and my choices, trying to make me feel like I didn't belong."

Anger roiled inside him. "How the hell did you deal with that?"

Hard-edged laughter filled the interior. "I'm like, 'Bish, my parents couldn't make me give up my dream, so you definitely don't have a shot in hell.' She can make me mad, but she can't make me quit."

"That's my girl!" He high-fived her. It wasn't fair that she had to deal with her parents and a mean judge pressuring her, but she seemed to be handling it with her usual breezy confidence. At least the Davenports wanted the best for her.

"She was so damn smug sitting there waiting for me to say I don't have a partner, like how could someone like me have a significant other?"

She snorted her opinion on that. "I couldn't stand seeing that damn smirk on her face at my expense. What else could I do but claim that you're my boyfriend? Fuck!"

Startled, he jammed on the brakes. "What?"

She turned to him. "I forgot to ask—are you seeing someone new now? It's been almost four months since you broke up with Jessa."

"I haven't been with anyone since," he said as he took the exit for the East Atlanta neighborhood where his shop was located. "Like I said before you left, I'm waiting for the right woman."

"Waiting for the right woman while playing pretend with me."

"There are worse things than pretending to be your boyfriend, you know. Brussels sprouts, root canals . . ."

She snorted. "I seem to recall you wolfing down a helping of Brussels sprouts the last time we had them."

"They were wrapped in bacon," he reminded her. "Everything's better with bacon."

"If we can pull this off, you can have all the bacon you want," she promised. "I'll help you find Mrs. Right. I'm already planning to split the prize money with you."

"Whoa." He turned off the main road into an eclectic mixed-use neighborhood. "I didn't ask for a cut of the prize money."

"I know you didn't." She shifted in her seat to face him as he pulled the Jeep to a stop in front of his shop. "I'm going to split it with you anyway. You're my ride or die. You've been a part of this journey since day one. You encouraged me to audition, you helped me brainstorm, and you played referee between me and my parents. You've been having dinner with them every week and cheering me on. Then there's the fact that you're all-in on the boyfriend thing."

"Kenya . . ."

"I know I'm asking a lot, considering everything else you've done for me," she rushed on, her voice warbling. "If there was another way, I'd—"

"Hey." He turned to cup her cheeks. "You got me and I got you. That's how this works."

She stared up at him, dark eyes darker with worry. "We have to make it work, Cam. That producer's gonna keep picking at us. They—everybody on the show—don't believe that we're really a couple. That we *could* be a couple."

"Why?"

Her features soured. "Because you're you and I'm me."

He frowned as he sat back. He had to be misunderstanding her, right? "What's that supposed to mean?"

"We're total opposites." She spread a hand between them. "I'm a chubby Black chick and you're Thor's twin brother."

Blood scorched his ears. "So, because we look different, we can't be attracted to each other? Have they never heard of 'opposites attract'? Besides, we have a helluva lot in common. Those assholes have no idea!"

"I know." She patted his shoulder, the gentle touch soothing his rage. "*We* know."

He swallowed down his anger with an effort. Getting pissed when they hadn't officially begun filming yet wouldn't help Kenya at all. "For their information, you are a goddess and I'm Thor's sexier twin."

"Yes to both points." Delighted laughter made her chest move in ways he shouldn't be thinking about. "I'm all for us thumbing our noses at them and telling them to fuck off."

"Damn right." He smiled, the last of his anger receding. "We'll be so good at pretending even we will think we're dating."

"That leads me to one more favor I need to ask," she said, her features scrunched as if she thought he wouldn't like her request. "I promise it's the last one."

"What is it?"

"We need to sleep together."

CHAPTER FOUR

Oh, God, I didn't mean it like that!"

The afternoon sunlight slanting into the car highlighted the teasing glint in his eyes. "So you don't want to sleep together?"

"No! I mean yes. I mean, of course I'd sleep with you—who wouldn't want to sleep with sexy Thor?"

"Thank you for that glowing endorsement," he murmured, his lips curving in devilish amusement.

Embarrassment flushed her body as Kenya mentally kicked herself again before sighing. "What I meant was, sleep together without, you know, sleeping together. The show needs to film me wherever I'm working, and if I'm working at home, they'll need to be there too. That's why Jane asked about the apartment."

"Ah." His brows rose in understanding. "Which means we need to make it look like we're more than roommates."

"Exactly," she said, relieved that he understood. "I don't think they're going to go snooping or anything, but I won't be able to keep track of everyone if a full crew is there. I want to make sure they don't find anything that will make them question our relationship."

"Like all your things in one bedroom and all my things in another." That smile returned. "If you wanted to get in my drawers, KeKe, all you had to do was ask."

She swatted his shoulder with a laugh, ignoring the suggestiveness in his tone and the butterflies that sprang to life in her belly. "Since when do you wear drawers?"

"Good point. I might have a solution to the problem, but we might as well do some redecorating tonight or tomorrow before we go over to your parents' house for dinner. I know they'll be glad to see you."

"Okay." Kenya had to take his word for it. The arguments she'd had with her parents for pursuing cosplay and entering the reality competition had left scars in her psyche. Then there was the ultimatum that they'd given her before she left, an ultimatum she hadn't shared with Cam. If she didn't win the competition, they wanted her to quit trying to make a cosplay career happen and instead use the degree they'd paid for. She wasn't sure if their stance had changed now that she'd made it to the final round. One thing was for sure, she didn't want her reunion with her parents to be recorded for the show. "Let me text them to let them know I'm home and that I'll see them tomorrow."

Time to change the subject. "Would you mind taking some pics of me and with me after the crew leaves? I want to post a couple of updates on my social media, maybe do a couple of videos."

He gave a mock sigh. "First you want to sleep together and now you want me to be your Instagram boyfriend? The next thing you know, we'll be announcing our engagement on TikTok."

She laughed. "We'll have to make sure we livestream the ceremony. Maybe we can get married at Dragon Con."

"It's a date." He pushed her bangs from her eyes, his gaze sobering and intent. Her belly gave a nervous roll. Was he going to kiss her again, without cameras capturing it? Did she want him to?

"Dammit."

She blinked, quickly moving back in her seat. "What?"

"Looks like our alone time is over for now," Cam said, glancing in the rearview mirror. "They caught up to us."

Kenya looked in the side-view mirror. Sure enough, a large black van had pulled into the spot behind them. Ian hopped out of the passenger side, his camera pointed toward the façade of Cam's shop, Make It Worx.

Pride for Cam spread through her like warm sunshine. He'd worked his ass off in shop class during high school, honed his skill in college while dealing with his father's death, and had achieved a huge chunk of his dream. He and his staff fabricated a little bit of everything and he'd expanded his services by acquiring a couple of 3-D printers the year before. The first couple of years had been hard, but he'd hustled and she'd hustled with him, even buying a small stake in his shop to show her faith in him. Now business was not only steady, it was good.

Still, she knew that lean times could strike without warning. A major machine malfunction, an error on a major order, bad customer reviews—all of it could be catastrophic for the shop. Giving him half the prize money would be a good cushion for him and the business.

Cam came around the front of the Jeep to open her door. "You ready to see your surprise?"

His excited grin was infectious. She bounced on her toes as she stepped onto the sidewalk. "Can't wait."

Ignoring the producer and cameraman, Cam led her to the entry. It was just after five, but she couldn't see the other guys through the shop door. She reached for the handle, but Cam stopped her.

"Close your eyes, KeKe. Don't open them until I say."

"Aye aye, captain," she quipped, then dutifully closed her eyes. He moved behind her, then placed his hands on her shoulders to guide her where he wanted her.

That earlier flush returned, radiating through her body like a shot of liquor. Cam was always so warm, a human furnace. Some of her favorite moments with him were their movie nights when they cuddled up on the couch for a marathon. Even when they'd dated others, they had made time once a week to hang out. Sometimes she didn't even care what they queued up, she simply enjoyed chilling in silence with her best friend, forgetting about the outside world for a while.

They weren't going to have much time for that until the competition ended. She didn't have a lot of time to conceive, design, and develop two costumes. Maybe they'd be able to grab a couple of hours if she could come up with a killer concept and get ahead of schedule and he wasn't too busy with running the shop. Then she could get more hugs and maybe another kiss or two . . .

No, no, no. You can't think like that. Not about Cam, no matter how much sexier he was than a certain blond superhero.

"Okay, babe." Cam's beard brushed against her cheek as he pressed closer, making her shiver. "You ready?"

She blew out a breath, trying to gather her equilibrium. "Hell yeah!"

He loosened his grip on her shoulders. "Open your eyes."

She did. Surprise rocked her, stealing her breath. Cam had created a workstation just for her in a corner of the shop. With a delighted squeak, she ran forward, running her hands over everything like a greedy miser. A gleaming white standing craft table with hot-pink storage bins filled with bits and baubles, including an assortment of needles and thread, adhesives, scissors, sandpapers and

blocks of various coarseness, embellishments, and her favorite rotary tool. He'd brought her sewing machine and plus-size manne-
quin over from the apartment, and cubbies against the wall held a
few of her cosplay wigs, bolts of fabric, and assorted pieces of foam
and PVC. He'd even mounted some of their cosplay photos from
over the years. The whole setup had her itching to get to work.

"Oh my God. Cam!" She covered her mouth with her hands,
overcome.

"I wanted you to have plenty of space to work, and having you
here means it's easier for me to pitch in." Cam chewed on his
thumbnail. "Do you like it?"

"I love it!" She threw her arms around his neck. "And you.
You're too good to me."

His arms encircled her, a warm feeling that she never wanted to
get used to, so she could experience the bright newness of it each
time. "It's not a big thing," he protested. "We'd talked about making you a space here before you left."

"I know, but this . . ." She pressed her face against his chest.

"Hey." He tilted her chin up, then carefully brushed his thumbs
beneath her eyes. "If the future *Cosplay or No Way* champion doesn't
deserve this, who does?"

She leaned into him, awed all over again. Every time she felt
like she'd been backed into a corner with no way out, Cam was
there to lend a hand. Creating a workspace for her was perfect. She
could work here in the shop and the film crew could record her
without impeding Cam and his staff—or filming at their apartment. If for some reason she didn't win the competition, the plan
was to ignore her parents' edict and parlay her fifteen minutes of
fame into a small costume-design business, which she could do
right here. "Have I told you lately how brilliantly awesome you are?"

"Not in the last three minutes," he answered, giving her a

squeeze she didn't mind at all. Then he released her, and that she did mind a little. "I expect to be properly rewarded when we get home."

"Cam!" She flushed at the teasing, then belatedly realized he was playing it up for the camera. "We have company."

"Right. Back to business it is then." He leaned a hip against the craft table. "Any ideas for the iconic duo cosplay?"

"I've had a few." She studied him. "Aquaman and Mera probably wouldn't cut it, although it would be fun to paint those tattoos on you."

"I'd enjoy every moment of it, too. What about Triton and sexy Ursula from *The Little Mermaid*?"

She set her hands to her hips and tossed her bright pink bangs out of her eyes. "My Ursula would be too sexy for them to handle, dahling. We could have you do Captain Marvel and I could be a gender-bent Nicole Fury."

"I'd rather be Rose Quartz to your Garnet," he told her, pointing to her *Steven Universe* tee. "Or maybe Hawkman and Hawkgirl?"

"Ooh! Dammit, there's no way we could do two sets of wings in the time we have, but I really love that idea for a future project." She pointed back at his shirt. "Or we could do old school ThunderCats. But if we're going to do skivvies, how about you do Dr. Manhattan to my Sister Night?"

"No one's seeing my junk except for you." He rubbed a hand over his chest. "We need to level up, something that's really going to wow the judges and the audience."

"You're right. I want us to both showcase our skills. That's why this is so hard." She sighed. "I guess I need to sleep on it. I'm feeling a little jet-lagged."

"Good idea." He turned to the producer. "Are we almost done? I'm ready to get my girl home."

"I think that's enough footage for today." Jane signaled to Ian to stop filming, then reached into her large bag to extract a portfolio. "These release forms give us permission to film wherever Kenya decides to work, whether that's here, her place, or yours."

Cam took the proffered documents. "Well, her place and my place are the same place, so that makes it easier."

"You live together?"

The surprise in Jane's voice had Kenya and Cam pausing. "Why wouldn't we?" Cam asked, staring the producer down.

Jane blinked. "No reason. Kenya didn't mention it so I . . . Anyway, this works out well for us. Fewer locations to cover is always a good thing. Kenya already has a diary cam to record her daily wrap-up. It would be great if you could do one as well. It's not required, but I'm sure the fans would love to see you talking about your work with Kenya."

"I'll just chime in on hers then." Cam scanned the forms then signed and initialed where indicated. "Is there anything else we need to cover today? You said you'd start the actual production on Monday, right?"

"Just a couple of things." Jane covered a few logistical items for Monday, and Cam arranged to meet her and the rest of her production crew early so that they could get everything set up.

Kenya heaved a sigh of relief as Jane and Ian left, leaving her alone with Cam. They'd survived, and it wasn't as terrifyingly awful as it could have been. They had one day to get their stuff together, then the faking would be on for real as they began preparations for the championship round.

The enormity of it all finally hit her. "Oh God." She sucked in a hard breath, then another, fluttering her hands to prevent a freak-out.

"Hey." Cam caught her hands. "What is it?"

"I made it through." She stared up at him, torn between bouncing up and down or passing out. "We're in the championship round, Cam. We're in the championship round!"

"Hell, yeah we are! Shout it out!"

She screamed then, bouncing with the glee she'd been holding in since the announcement. Cam dug out his phone to record her then joined her in her happy dance, hollering with the same level of enthusiasm as they spun around the room singing.

"Whew." Kenya slumped into her drafting chair, exhausted but happy. "You have no idea how badly I needed that!"

"I sorta figured as much." He stopped recording, then placed his phone on the table before leaning against it, his grin loose and easy. "You've been holding that in for a minute."

"Is it that obvious?" She carefully wiped at her eyes, not wanting to look like a raccoon for their next set of selfies. "I couldn't release pressure like that during the competition. Couldn't show any sort of negative emotion or else I'd be labeled the angry Black chick. And I didn't want anyone to think I was getting uppity each time I made it through a round."

"This is a safe space. You can gloat all you want with me." He sobered. "Did you have a hard time? I know they can do all kinds of crap with editing, but there were some serious what-the-fuck moments on the show."

"They pushed everyone hard." There was so much that hadn't made it to air, but she didn't want to burden him by recounting all the little digs she'd experienced on the show, all the microaggressions, slights, and attempts to paint her as the mouthy, angry stereotype.

Seeming to understand, he stepped closer, his gaze sympathetic as he reached out to brush her bangs back from her eyes. "They seemed to push you harder. It couldn't have been easy, with that one contestant calling you mean for not helping her and that judge who's obviously out to get you. I don't know how you dealt with that."

"Not as well as I should have." She leaned into his touch. "I wanted to call you so many times. Not just to bitch about stuff, but to share all the good things, too. You were always the first one I thought of, every step of the way. You should have been there with me."

He wrapped his arms around her, resting his chin on her head. "I'm sorry. I'm here now."

"No, I meant competing with me." She gave him a squeeze. "You're more than just my support, you know. I really missed you out there."

"I'm glad to hear it," he murmured against her hair. "I really missed you, too."

His voice thickened, causing emotion to swell in her throat. She should have been here, helping him get over his breakup. She pulled away until he tightened his hold. "I'm sorry I wasn't here for you the last couple of months."

"Hey. You're there when it counts."

"Maybe, but we didn't get to go through our breakup recovery ritual."

He grimaced. "You know it wasn't a messy breakup. Besides, you're home now. Speaking of home, we should grab something to-go for dinner, or have something delivered. We've got a lot of stuff to do tonight, and a lot more to talk about, especially about your expectations."

She followed him to the front, stepping out so that he could set the alarm and lock up. "What do you mean, expectations?"

"Just how real of a fake boyfriend do you expect me to be?"

CHAPTER FIVE

I really missed you.

Cam replayed the moment in his mind, recalling the softness of Kenya's words, the way she'd felt pressed against him, the sincerity in her gaze when she'd looked at him. The quiet declaration had hit him hard, harder than he'd expected. He wanted to take every sensation, every word and emotion of that moment, and tuck it away in the part of him where he kept all his most precious memories.

He had to keep telling himself not to make too much of a big deal out of it. Hard to do when he'd missed her too. The knowledge that she thought it was because of his amicable breakup with Jessa sobered him. As did the momentary panic that had flared in her eyes when he'd asked her how convincing a boyfriend she wanted him to be.

"Tell me about the shop," Kenya said then, breaking into his thoughts. "How's business doing?"

Cam looked down at his plate of pad prik, hiding his grimace. He didn't want to talk about business, but he could tell that she wanted to put off answering his earlier question. So instead of pressing her on expectations, he talked about the safe territory of work. "Business is great. We've had some gawkers since you mentioned us on the show, but we've also gotten serious inquiries and orders too."

"Awesome!" Her smile was everything, prompting him to smile in return. Then she sobered. "Do you think Mack and Javier will buy that we're a couple?"

"I don't think you'll have to worry about that." He wasn't going to tell her that the guys thought they'd already hooked up, and that Mack flirted with her to get a rise out of him.

"Good. I was hoping that—"

Her phone buzzed. She glanced at it, then grimaced. He leaned closer. "Who is it?"

"Janelle. I texted her while you were washing your hands, letting her know I was home. I guess she finally read my message."

Her phone buzzed again, skittering along the tabletop. "Seems like she's really trying to get in touch with you. Are you going to text her back?"

"Later." She stabbed her fork into her pad Thai. "I should have waited until tomorrow, so we could have time tonight."

Her casual delivery shouldn't have made him light-headed, but it did. Then he mentally corrected himself. Of course she wanted time with him tonight. They needed to finalize plans before Monday, if not before having dinner with her parents. They needed to finalize things before she talked to Janelle, her other best friend.

"Kenya." He gestured at her phone as it signaled another incoming text. "I don't think you're going to be able to wait until tomorrow to talk to Janelle."

"I know. I just need to figure out what to say." She held up the phone. "Ten messages, all about our relationship."

"Then you definitely need to tell her something," he urged. "If you don't, she'll be over first thing in the morning. Knowing Janelle, she might head over here tonight."

"Oh God." Her eyes widened with an edge of panic. "What do I say?"

"Hey, you've got this." He reached across the table to grab her free hand. "Just tell her what you told me. The truth-ish."

"Which is?"

"You just got home and you want some time with me tonight."

"That's not truth-ish. I meant what I said. I just want to eat dinner and chill with you, maybe catch up on some Adult Swim."

The way his insides warmed had nothing to do with the spice in his food. "Good thing I've got two months of your favorite shows on the DVR." Watching anime had been their late-night Saturday tradition for years. He was glad she still wanted to do it. This would probably be the only downtime she'd have until the competition was over, and he wanted to make sure she got it. "Tell her that. Hopefully, that should put her off until tomorrow."

"Okay." She pulled her hand free of his hold to quickly tap a message out before setting the phone down. "There. Now, where were we?"

"Talking about business and the shop." He reached for her hand again. "Maybe it's time to change the subject back to what we talked about at the shop. Janelle's going to be real curious when she shows up tomorrow."

"I know." Kenya sighed. "She should have been a reporter instead of an engineer. Why did I think I could pull this off? She's going to take one look at me and she's going to know."

"She's not going to know anything you don't tell her, but she's a big part of why I wanted to know how convincing you want this to be."

"Obviously I'm not thinking clearly." She rubbed at her forehead. "I want to sell this as well as we can, which means we have to convince our nearest and dearest that this is real."

He frowned, not liking how down she suddenly sounded. "Do you think I can't be a convincing boyfriend?" he asked, getting up to head to the fridge. The way the conversation had turned seemed to call for beer.

"It's not that." She accepted the bottle he handed her with a smile of thanks before taking a swig. "I feel bad about tricking everyone, but I can't back down now without disappointing all the people rooting for me."

"And rooting for us as a team and a couple."

"Exactly." She blew at her bright pink bangs. "I don't know if they're planning to interview our friends, but I wouldn't put it past them. That's why our people have to believe we're a couple, at least until the show's over."

In his mind they were already a couple. He could play his part because he wouldn't be playing. He simply needed to make his move with more finesse than his clumsy attempt back in college, right after she'd broken up with her dick of an ex. She'd friend-zoned him so hard he still had road rash. This, this was like being given a second chance, and he intended to get it right.

He gathered their plates to take to the sink. "Our first hurdle will be tomorrow, when Janelle comes over."

"The second hurdle will be dinner with my parents." She packed up their leftover containers, then joined him in the kitchen. "So I guess that means it needs to be as real as a relationship can be, minus the emotions and the sex."

He focused on scraping the remnants of his dinner into the garbage disposal so he wouldn't say something colossal and stupid, like asking her for a chance at a real relationship. It could work. They could work. He believed that so strongly that the words crawled up his throat, demanding to spill out. Only the protective need to shield her from more stress kept his mouth shut.

"Cam, did you hear me?"

"I heard you, I just want to be clear about what you want."

"Oh yeah. That makes sense." She pursed her lips as she considered. "I think a little PDA while the cameras are rolling would be good."

"Okay. What about around our people, especially Janelle and your parents, or if we have friends over for game night?"

"Dammit. I guess if we're going to sell it, we need to sell it to everybody." She rubbed at her forehead again. "I know I'm putting a lot on you and that this is more than you bargained for. I'm sorry."

"Hey." He squeezed her shoulders. "You act like showing you affection is a hard job. It's not."

She snorted. "Tell that to my ex."

"Tell me where he is and I will." He had a few more things he wanted to say to her last ex and the one before that.

"He's in the rearview where he belongs." She tossed her hair. "So, you wouldn't mind giving me a few PDAs?"

"The question is, do you mind a few PDAs?" He moved behind her. "For example, if I come up behind you and massage your shoulders, that's no big deal, right?"

"Of course not. You've done that plenty of times."

"Right. Your best friend has rubbed your shoulders plenty of times. But your boyfriend would probably lean in like this, put his arms around your waist, then give you a squeeze."

She squeaked.

"KeKe." He laughed despite himself. "As cute as it is, that squeak is a dead giveaway."

"What am I supposed to do when you're squeezing me like the Pillsbury Doughboy?" She gave a little shimmy he tried hard to ignore. "Okay, let's try again."

He moved to her right side, draping his arm about her shoulders. "Whatcha got there?"

"Wha—oh, this is a beer. I'm hoping to use it for inspiration."

"Inspiration, huh?" He slipped behind her, dropping his hands to her hips. "I'm not good enough inspiration for you?"

Damn, that sounded more plaintive than he'd intended. If she noticed, she gave no sign. Instead, she leaned back against him. "Baby, you know you're my muse. I'm all about coming up with costumes to show off how hot you are."

"I appreciate that." He dropped his chin to her shoulder. "I appreciate you, too." He kissed her cheek.

Her appreciative sigh was like a hard-won trophy. "You're good at this."

"What can I say?" He stepped back from her, not wanting to push his luck and needing to put some space between them. "You inspire me, too."

"Okay." She sighed again, a deep, regrouping sound, before turning to smile at him. "I could get used to this. Not that I would want to, because I wouldn't want to take it for granted, being on the receiving end of your PDAs. I gotta say, though, I think I'm jealous of your exes."

The teasing words punched him in the gut, making him realize that this whole game was going to be difficult. Not the displays of affection, the hugging and the kissing. No, pretending to pretend was going to be the most difficult thing he'd ever had to do after dealing with his father's death. How in the hell was he supposed to spend the next few weeks pretending to be Kenya's doting boyfriend without getting too deep—or worse, getting his heart trampled?

Kenya mentally kicked herself. How stupid was it to mention Cam's ex? His expression clearly telegraphed that he wasn't as over Jessa as he'd claimed. Hoping to gloss over her goof, she said, "Since you made that amazing work space in the shop, I guess we don't really need to share a room now."

"It's totally your choice," he answered, his tone careful. "But that producer made it seem like it would be a big deal if you did any work off-camera."

"True."

"Knowing you, you'll have production scheduled down to the minute, and you'll need every one of them. You can't tell me there won't be some late-night tasks. I'd much rather you do those here than at the shop. Besides, we already signed forms giving them permission to film."

"I know, but—"

"But nothing. If you don't want to share a room, no problem. If you think we should, that's no problem either. What I don't want you to do is keep pinging all over the place when you need to save that energy for Monday. This is the easy part."

"You're right." Having a serious case of nerves now, in her safe space, was ridiculous. "I figured I'd move a few of my things into your room since you have the better view. Besides, my room is full of all our costume parts."

His shoulders relaxed. "Like I could forget. You can move in whatever you want. It won't take me long to shift a few things in the dresser and closet, or the bathroom for that matter."

She snorted. "You do not want all my hair-care stuff in your bathroom."

"Double sinks and cabinets, remember? There's plenty of room." He grinned. "Besides, you make that hot-pink satin cap so sexy."

Buoyed by his teasing, she flicked her bangs and struck a pose. "Baby, I make everything look sexy."

"Yes, you do. I'll go make space for you and change out the sheets. Let me know if you need help with anything."

"Okay." Kenya grabbed her suitcases and made her way to her room, the rest of her stress draining away. She was home, Cam was on board, and she'd done relatively okay with their first practice run of PDAs. With a little more practice, she'd be able to convince Janelle and her parents that she and Cam really were a couple.

Yes, she definitely needed more practice with Cam. It wasn't that she was uncomfortable with his displays of affection. No, it had more to do with how her body went all *hell-o* when he came up behind her. And that squeeze! She'd been surprised, but she'd also been—

Stop. Do not ride that train of thought about your best friend! He's just helping you out to win this competition and rub it in Rebecca's face for good measure. You're doing this to launch your career and drive more business to his shop. After the win, you'll have a quiet, amicable breakup and then be free to date other people. Date for real, with other people, not the fake thing you're doing now.

Okay. She drew in a steadying breath. This was happening, this was working, this was possible. She would pretend her ass off until she clutched that prize money in her happy little hands. If that meant kissing and hugging on Cam in front of their friends, family, and the production crew, well, that wouldn't be a hardship at all.

It actually would be the best thing about the whole scheme.

After emptying her suitcase and filling her laundry hamper, she gathered a few things and made her way to Cam's bedroom. Where she still had her full-sized bed from her parents' house, Cam had a king-sized bed with pillows stacked like a mountain range against the dark wood headboard. "How could I forget Mount Pillow-more?"

"Hey, a guy's gotta have some comforts, you know." He gave her an arch look as he smoothed down a fresh sheet then pulled the dark green comforter back into place. "Besides, I needed something to cuddle up with while you were gone."

She shouldn't have gone all squishy inside at his words, but she did. Even though he didn't mean them as she'd taken them. With Jessa out of the picture and her in Los Angeles, the apartment probably had been too quiet. She tried to keep her response light. "Well, I'm back now. If you need a cuddle, I'm your girl."

His expression blanked into something unreadable before he gestured to the bundle she held. "That all you planning on bringing in here?"

She snorted. "Have you met me? This is just underwear."

"Okay. The right side of the dresser is cleared out. I'll help you bring the rest in."

Soon enough, they had her essentials moved into his bedroom. Other than his prized T-shirt collection and business casual clothes, there hadn't been much in Cam's closet. She'd kept her clothing to a minimum too, preferring to spend what little disposable income she had on cosplay supplies.

Cam surveyed the room. "You should probably put some girl stuff on the dresser and your nightstand."

"I'll bring my small jewelry box in to put on the dresser, and my phone and charger will go on the nightstand."

"Okay. What's next?"

Kenya tugged at her shirt. "A shower. It's been a long travel day and I'm worn out."

"Of course." He gestured toward the bathroom. "After you."

She took a step back. "Ah, that's okay. You go ahead. We have two bathrooms, remember?"

She retreated to her own bathroom, her face burning. As close as they were, she and Cam still had boundaries, and one of those was bathroom use. That was sacrosanct space that neither one had ever invaded.

Yet it was all that she could think about as she pulled on her shower cap and stepped into the warm spray. Standing at the dual sinks, brushing teeth as they got ready for bed. Wrapping her hair in her satin cap, talking about the day as Cam took a shower. Accepting his invitation to scrub his back . . .

Whoo chile. She scrubbed with more force than necessary, trying to wash away the inconvenient guilty flush that was quickly becoming a frequent but uninvited guest. No matter how much pretending they'd have to do around other people, she couldn't think of Cam like that. Like sexy times. With her.

"Must be early-onset jet lag," she muttered to herself as she rinsed off. It was the only explanation she had for the detour that her thoughts had taken. Not to mention that her lady-parts were all "Hey, how you doing?" instead of "Stop that!"

Sighing, she shut off the water, then reached for her towel. Nah, she had to be honest. It was because she hadn't had Vitamin D in more than four months. Jerrod had been one of those good-on-paper guys. Educated, decent job, fine, committed to the cause and the community. The fact that he was also a cosplayer scored him serious bonus points. The sex had been toe-curling too.

But good sex could make you do all sorts of things that you normally wouldn't do, like ignore warning signs. How cold he was to her mixed group of friends, the tone and content of his social media postings. How his cosplays were always about sending a message. Jerrod soured from hot to Hotep in less than six months. The breakup had been horrible but necessary. She'd made it through thanks to Janelle and Cam.

She moisturized, pulled on panties and a sleep shirt, wrapped her hair, then finally made her way back to Cam's bedroom—correction, their bedroom. He was already in bed, a pile of pillows behind him, laptop on his lap and glasses on his nose. Freakin' adorkable.

He looked up with a smile. "There's my girl, satin cap and all."

"You know I have to sleep in style." She circled to her side of the bed, placing her phone in the charging cradle. "Whatcha doing?"

"Checking for orders and paying a couple of bills."

"So, doing my job, you mean."

"I've gotten pretty good at it too, but I'll be glad to hand it back to you after the competition ends." He pushed his glasses up on his nose. "Of course, when you win, you'll be moving on to bigger gigs."

She pulled back the covers, then climbed in, taking note of his white T-shirt and blue-and-green plaid boxers, his usual sleeping attire. "When we win, both of us and the shop will be moving on to bigger things and you'll be able to expand."

"As your mama always says, speak it, believe it, achieve it. Ready to clear the DVR?"

"Actually, I think I'm ready to pass out." She punctuated her words with a jaw-cracking yawn. "Do you mind if I crash?"

"Are you serious? Of course I don't mind. I'm glad you're taking the time to rest while you can. Tomorrow starts the marathon."

"Yeah." Breakfast with Janelle. Early dinner with her parents. Brainstorming. Then filming at Cam's shop while pretending they were lovers and trying to create a pair of kick-ass costumes. "Maybe I should have had another beer."

"I think we've got some of the hard stuff in the freezer," he said, setting his laptop on the nightstand. "I could make a couple of shots. A proper toast to the future *Cosplay or No Way* champion."

His certainty of her win spread through her like sunshine, bringing a smile to her lips. "I like the way you think, pretend boy-friend." She turned onto her side to face him. "I think I'm gonna stick with skipping the hard stuff until this is over, though. I need a clear head for everything that's coming up. We'll have plenty of time for toasts."

She yawned again. "Right now, right here . . . this is really all I need."

His gaze softened as he handed her an extra pillow, then scrunched down beside her, the scent of his soap filling her nose with the blissful fragrance of summer rain. "Same. I'm glad you're home."

"Me too." A sigh of contentment seeped from her as she clutched the pillow against her chest. This was home, her safe space. Every morning of the competition she'd awakened in the group house with a poor proxy of pillows instead of Cam's warmth, a mix of dread and stress churning inside her as she wondered who she'd have to defend herself from. There had been two other people of color, but the only other Black cosplayer had been sent home the first week. She'd had to dance a fine line between being competitive and being labeled as angry, and the stress had weighed on her. Some of the contestants and judges had tried to break her in subtle and overt ways, a murder by a thousand paper cuts.

Keeping Cam in her thoughts had been her lifeline throughout the competition. He was her greatest cheerleader and her defender, his belief in her as great as her belief in herself. She owed him more than she'd ever be able to repay. This quiet interlude with him was a gift she'd treasure, knowing there wouldn't be much time in the coming weeks for moments like this.

CHAPTER SIX

Cam's internal clock woke him up before his phone's alarm did. Sundays were usually his sleeping-in days except for the few times a year he joined the Davenports for church service. He'd have found an excuse for a rain check this morning due to the woman still sleeping beside him. He figured God would understand.

Kenya had turned sometime during the night, pressing her back against his chest. He'd obviously decided being the big spoon was a great idea because he'd jettisoned his pillow surrogate for the real thing, draping his arm around her waist and burying his nose into the nape of her neck. He could still smell traces of her favorite honey-vanilla lotion.

Every morning could be like this. He felt that in his bones. He and Kenya were already good together, they just needed that one final step—a step his body strenuously demanded.

Needing to put space between his morning wood and her delectable ass, he shifted his hips backward. It was going to be a common occurrence if they continued sleeping together. There wasn't much he could do about it except lay a row of pillows between them, something she'd surely question him about. Maybe they'd just ignore it and act as if morning erections didn't happen.

Just one more thing to pretend about. By the time the competition ended, he'd be able to apply for a SAG membership.

Resisting the urge to disturb Kenya's slumber by raising his hand to gnaw on his fingernails, he ground his teeth together instead. He could do this, no matter how difficult it was. This was an easy price to pay if it meant he'd win Kenya in the end. She was worth it. They were worth it.

She'd believed in him from the moment they'd met. Believed he'd make a good friend. Believed he was worthy of the attention his father had denied him, sharing her parents with him instead. Believed he could start his own business and make a go of it, believed enough to contribute sweat equity until he could give them both a salary. She'd believed in him until he was able to believe in himself. She still believed he could do anything he set his mind to. He believed it as well. They could be together, for real, if they both believed enough to take the chance.

Intending to let her sleep a while longer, he slowly pulled his arm from her waist. She shifted with a sleepy mumble, entwining her fingers with his before pulling their hands up between her breasts. He froze, every sense focused on their hands. Was she aware of what she'd done, or was she still asleep? What should he do? Stay still and pretend it wasn't a big deal when she did wake up?

Her phone rang before he could decide, shattering the silence. Kenya jerked awake, releasing his hand to reach for her phone. He took the opportunity to jam a pillow between her and his very disappointed dick. "Who's calling you this early?"

She rolled onto her back, holding up the phone. "It's Janelle. She wants to FaceTime."

Perfect. "Do it."

She glanced at him, surprised. "Are you serious? She'll see us in bed!"

"That's the point. Her seeing us together like this will do more to convince her than anything you would tell her later."

"Good point. Ready?" She answered the call when he nodded. "Girl, do you know what time it is?"

"What? You always get up early."

"Yeah, except when I fly home from California."

"Uhm-hmm." Janelle's disbelief rang loud and clear before her tone turned sly. "Is jet lag the only reason that you're still in bed?"

"Well, if you must know . . ." Kenya pushed back against him— or rather, the pillow between them, then tilted the phone so that he was in view. "No, it's not the jet lag."

"Oh." Janelle's eyes rounded. *"Oh."*

"Morning," Cam said with a sleepy mumble, pressing his cheek against Kenya's shoulder. No need to blast her with morning dragon-breath. "How you doing?"

"Obviously not as good as the two of you. Sorry for interrupting," she added in a tone that implied she was anything but. "Should I call back later?"

"I thought you were coming by?" Kenya asked.

"That was the plan, but you guys look like you need more time—"

"I've gotta get up and get some work done anyway," Cam interrupted, figuring it was as good a time as any to make his exit. "See ya later."

He rolled out of bed and headed to the bathroom, whistling as he went. He stopped, looked over his shoulder. "Don't forget to tell her how good I am in bed."

He ducked inside the bathroom just before a pillow collided with the doorframe.

Girl!"

Kenya flicked a glance at Janelle over the rim of her coffee cup. Her friend stared at her with all the barely contained energy of a puppy waiting for a treat. "Can a girl get a hit of caffeine before the interrogation starts? I barely had time to brush my teeth and throw on clothes!"

"I noticed." She reached over to give Kenya's cap a tug. "You're still wearing your cap. The same one I saw on you when you were in bed with Cameron this morning!"

Kenya took her time taking a sip, hoping it would cover her fluster. Yeah, the bed thing. With Cam. Half-awake, she hadn't thought when she'd grabbed his hand and snuggled it between her boobs. Hadn't thought about what his reaction would be, and certainly hadn't expected to feel his dick pressed against her. That had been weird, but not bad. It had been nice until she'd realized that he was probably still asleep and morning wood was a thing. And that parting shot of how good he was in bed had been more for Janelle than her. She had to remember that.

That didn't mean she couldn't have a little fun with it. "Like I said, I didn't have a lot of time to get ready. I slept like a log."

"What's the matter?" Janelle gave her a wide grin. "Too tired from your reunion last night?"

"Can you keep your voice down?" She tilted her head toward their bedroom. "Cam went back to sleep." She knew he hadn't, but she didn't want him to hear too much of the conversation. It was embarrassing enough already.

"Wore him out, huh?" Janelle asked, her expression completely unrepentant. She lifted her coffee in a toast. "That's my girl."

"I'm glad you approve." Kenya took another swig of her coffee, her mind racing. She and Cam hadn't had time to cobble an intimacy story together. It was one thing to fool the production crew. She didn't care about them. But her friends and family?

Cam was her best friend, but Janelle was her sister from a different mister. They'd met in college, the only two Black women in their engineering class out of five women total. All five of them had bonded together out of necessity, but she and Janelle had developed a friendship that lasted after graduation, mainly because they always kept it real with each other. Not being fully truthful with Janelle now didn't sit well with Kenya, but her friend's enthusiasm quickly obliterated her misgivings.

"You know I want all the juicy details."

"You know good and damn well that you're not getting any." Especially since there weren't any details to tell.

That wasn't entirely true. She could tell Janelle about the kisses at the airport and how they'd made her both wake up and fall into a dream. Or she could mention the PDA practice in the kitchen that she couldn't stop thinking about. Then there was this morning in bed, their entwined hands cupped between her breasts, his erection pressed against her ass, and how simple and perfect it was. But since he wasn't her actual boyfriend, it wasn't anywhere near simple.

She had to admit, he was pretty good at playing the part so far. That kiss at the airport, the teasing talk at the shop, the touching in their kitchen, being spooned by him this morning . . . She blew out a breath. Yeah, he was good. Real good. Good enough that, in the warmth of his bed in dawn's early light caught between sleep and awake, she'd almost let her imagination get the better of her, envisioning what it would be like to be in a relationship with Cam for real.

Stop. He's your best friend. You are not going to ruin a friendship by bringing sex into it. Besides, he offered you the chance once and you didn't take it. There's no way he'd want to try again. Don't ruin this.

But what if it doesn't ruin it? What if—

"Kenya?" Janelle snapped her fingers. "I don't know where you went, but I want to book a flight there too."

"Sorry." Heat singed her ears. "Just thinking."

"You don't have to apologize to me. Not about this. I'm just glad you're happy."

It wasn't a question, but Kenya answered it anyway, honest and true. "I am. You know how awesome Cam is. This is just another layer of awesomeness."

She sighed, then confessed, "His kisses are amazing. To tell the truth, everything is amazing with him."

"I bet. He's been wanting to hit that for a while. I'm glad you finally decided to take the plunge. Have you told your parents yet?"

Kenya took a larger swallow of her coffee to cover her shock at Janelle's words. Cam wanted to hook up with her? Morning wood aside, if he wanted her like that, he would have said something, right? Besides, his girlfriends were of a certain type, and that type definitely wasn't thicc and Black.

She focused on the question instead. "I sent them a text when I landed yesterday, but we're going over there today for dinner. Do you want to come?"

"After the last dinner devolved into them comparing our lives, then suggesting that I'm a role model and life coach for you? Thank you, next."

An apology crawled up Kenya's throat, one in a long line of apologies that had followed that uncomfortable dinner, so uncomfortable they'd left before her dad had served his famous Mississippi mud cake. The thing was, she understood why her parents had done it. Everything about Janelle was on point—her style, her career, her life plan. Janelle was who her parents wanted Kenya to be, if only she'd face reality.

"It's probably just as well," Kenya finally said, wishing she had some Irish for her coffee. "This will be the first time seeing them since I left to do the show."

"Do you think they'll be okay with this?" Janelle asked, waving a hand between them. "You and Cam, I mean."

"They love Cam. They want him to be happy." Kenya stared at her coffee cup, swallowing her bitterness. There had been a few moments early on when she had been jealous of the positive attention they'd shown Cam, but she'd long ago resigned herself to the role of problem child, trying to balance her dreams with their wishes. "They'll be more concerned about me and the competition, and what happens after."

Janelle grimaced. "Are they still ragging on you about that, even with you being in the final round?"

"I guess I'll find out." Kenya shrugged. It would have been an easier competition if her parents had her back. Then again, their disapproval had honed her determination into a vibranium core. She'd thrived and survived over everything the contestants and the judges had dished out because they were insignificant compared to what she'd grown up with.

"Wish me luck?"

Janelle smiled. "Of course. Not that you need it. You're in the finals and you've got Cam by your side. I'd say you're already lucky, happy, and hella talented."

"You're right." She perked up. "I am. Thanks for the pep talk."

"Anytime." Janelle grabbed her Dooney & Bourke satchel then

stood. "I know this last round is going to be insane, but if you have a free moment or need to vent, hit me up."

"Wait. Aren't you too busy with work and being booed up with Terrence?"

"We're not together anymore. Some of his political views aren't compatible with mine, and I don't have time for that."

"Oh no! I'm sorry I wasn't here for you."

"Don't be." Janelle waved a hand as she headed for the door. "He was all promise with little follow-through. Dev, on the other hand? Whew!"

"Hold up. Who the hell is Dev? You can't drop that tidbit and then just leave. I need details!"

A knowing grin bowed Janelle's plum-colored lips. Kenya still wasn't sure how she kept her lipstick on and unsmeared while drinking, but she was sure it was one of Janelle's superpowers. "I'll tell mine when you tell yours."

"Bitch."

"Yes, but I'm your favorite bitch."

"Of course you are." Kenya hugged her tight. "Thank you for everything."

"You're welcome." Janelle returned the hug. "That offer to vent is still open, but we'll definitely get together after you win. I want all the tea on the contestants and those judges."

"You'll need to take the night off from Dev," Kenya said, opening the door. "There's a lot of tea to serve."

"Maybe we can make it a double date if he continues to exceed expectations. We'll have a lot to celebrate after all. See ya."

"See ya." Kenya shut then locked the door then leaned against it with a sigh. Even though Kenya's creative side drove her more than her technical side, Janelle remained her friend, never once calling her flighty or thinking she was throwing away her life. She couldn't quite squelch the twinge of guilt over the deception, but seeing Janelle's genuine happiness made her wish she and Cam were really in a relationship.

"Did it go badly? I thought I heard y'all laughing."

Kenya opened her eyes at Cam's question. The concern in his expression had her stretching out a hand to him. He took it, drawing her into a hug. "It went better than I could have hoped," she said against his chest. "She's happy for us and wants a double date when the competition is over."

"Sounds good to me."

Before she could react to that, he backed up. "I guess I didn't rate a cup of coffee?"

"I made you some and brought it to you before she got here." She narrowed her eyes. "Used fresh water and sweetened it just the way you like it. Does my coffee not rate?"

"Babe, everything about you rates." He turned to the kitchen. "I need food. What about you?"

"I looked in the fridge. If you need food, we need groceries. It's too early for leftover Thai."

"I'm a guy. It's never too early for leftovers."

Kenya arched a brow. "Even if I promise you bacon?"

"Mmm, bacon." He rubbed his belly. "I'd do anything for bacon."

"Good. Let me do something with my hair, then we can head out."

"You stay here and brainstorm a concept," Cam said. "I can—"

"Not buy a vegetable if your life depended on it," she chided, smiling to take the sting out of her words. "Besides, I'm probably going to do a lot of stress cooking. I need to make sure I have enough ingredients to last the week."

His expression sobered. "Now I'm conflicted."

A frisson of alarm slid down her spine. Cam wouldn't back out on her. Not on something as important as this. "Are you getting cold feet?"

"Kenya." Suddenly he was in front of her, his hands warm and solid on her shoulders. "My job is to keep you from stressing out. But a man's gotta eat, and your stress cooking is some of the best eating I've had."

She smiled at him. "I did learn from my dad, whose cooking you also adore." She covered his hands with hers. "Stress cooking helps me think through issues, so maybe you can help me minimize my stress instead of stopping it completely."

"That I can do." He turned her toward the bedroom. "Go on and get ready. I'll do a quick inventory and start a list on my phone."

"Make sure you add a crapton of gummy worms to the list. I have a feeling I'm going to need them."

CHAPTER SEVEN

Three months ago

Y ou're doing what?"

Kenya hunched her shoulders reflexively, then deliberately squared them as she met her mother's disbelieving glare. "Going to Los Angeles. I've been picked to compete in a new cosplay reality show. It's called *Cosplay or No Way* and I'm leaving for California in a couple of wee—"

"Have you lost your mind?" Her mother rounded the kitchen counter. "I thought you were done with this foolishness!"

"Fooli—" Kenya bit off the word so hard her teeth clicked together. "Mama, this is a great opportunity for me. I get to compete against some of the best cosplay creators in the country, in front of judges who can make or break a career—"

"You have a career! Or you would if you would just stop playing dress-up and give that firm a tenth of the attention."

"I already have a job," she pointed out, trying to keep the defensiveness out of her tone.

"Working for Cameron," her mother pointed out. "Which you're apparently willing to quit to chase this dream."

Her ears burned. "I'm not quitting!" Dammit, she'd wanted to hold on to her temper a little longer. "I'm taking an extended vacation to do the show."

"I can't believe this." Her mother shook her head. "Lincoln, come talk to your daughter!"

"What does Cameron think of all this?" her father asked in a tone only slightly less angry than her mother's.

Kenya couldn't hide her frown. Her father's inflection made it seem as if Cam had some sort of authority over her. Sure, ostensibly he was her boss, but they were friends first. Thank goodness she hadn't let Cam come with her to deliver the news. She didn't like putting him between her and her parents, and she knew the clashes made him uncomfortable.

Still, she had to let them know where things stood, where Cam stood. "Cam supports me in this. He helped me film my audition video."

Her parents exchanged a look that made her instantly defensive. "What was that look for?"

They exchanged another look before her father spoke again. "That shop is Cam's dream."

"I know that." She and Cam always talked about their dreams. Those dreams had evolved since high school, but she knew and supported his dreams with the same fervor that he knew and supported hers.

"You must have some idea how difficult it can be to start and manage a business. All of Cameron's time and focus needs to be on making his company a success."

Her right eye began to twitch with a blossoming headache. "Are you trying to say that I'm preventing Cam from doing that?"

Her mother parted her lips to reply but her father raised a hand. "What I'm saying is don't destroy his dreams trying to realize your own."

Is that what they thought she was doing? How could they think that of her? "Cam and I talked about this. He's the one who heard about the competition and told me to apply, and when I got selected, we worked out a fix for my temporary absence. I'm going to hype him and the shop every chance I get. We hope that's going to translate into more business for him. And the further I go into the competition, the more advertising I get for my costuming business. I should have lots of commission requests waiting for me when I get back. That also helps Cam's business. I am helping him with his dream, just as he's helping me with mine."

"You'd help him much more by using your degree in a career that will actually make you more money and benefit you both."

Back to this old argument again. "Y'all have never understood how important this is to me."

"We understand that you focus on this hobby to the detriment of everything else," her mother retorted. "All this playing dress-up has done is cost you time and money that could have been spent on more important things, like your engineering career."

"This is the career I want! This is my big opportunity. I'll have the chance to showcase my ability to a national audience. I'll get to build my brand for the entire country to see. And if I win, I get $100,000 and a chance to work in the costuming department of a major studio film. I can't pass this up."

"What if you lose?" her father asked.

"I'm not going to lose."

"What if you do?" her mother pressed. "What are your contingency plans?"

"The same as they are now. Take temp and contract work to

supplement my income when Cam doesn't need me at the shop. That gives me money and time to work on my design business—"

"Cam doesn't need you at the shop," her mother cut in, in a tone that made it seem as if it should have been obvious. "He's been keeping you afloat. It's time to return the favor."

Kenya's ears burned. Her parents couldn't make up their minds whether her duties at the shop mattered or not, and she was tired of trying to convince them of that. "Fine. If I lose, I'll dust off my degree and 'get a real job' just like you want," she retorted, using finger quotes for emphasis. "If Cam wants it, I'll pay him back the salary he's paid me for the last year."

"You've finally said something we can all agree on," her father said. "I'll check with some of my friends, see if their firms are hiring. You get a job in your degree field, and we'll underwrite the cost of you going back to get your doctorate. It's not too late."

Dammit. None of that sounded palatable to Kenya, but they'd backed her into a corner. She did more at Cam's shop than answering phones, but her parents either didn't know or didn't care. The fact that they'd already had a plan in place if she failed proved they were just waiting for the perfect time to hold an intervention. Too bad she had no intention of losing. She'd already dreamed up ways to parlay her win into success for them both, so it was easy to look her parents in the eye and say, "Deal."

Present Day

"Are you all right?"

"I'm fine."

Cam side-eyed her. "You've got my hand in a death grip. You are not *fine*."

"Sorry." She released his hand. "I'm nervous and trying not to stress about it."

He stopped for a red light, then gathered her hand in a looser grip. "It's my job to reduce your stress, remember? I don't think this dinner will be as bad as you think."

"I'm trying to think positive, but you weren't there when I first told them about the show. Their reactions . . . they weren't happy."

No, he hadn't been there, but he'd come home to a three-course meal, so he'd known it hadn't gone well even though Kenya refused to talk about it. "I think they've softened their stance a bit," he said, hoping to reassure her. "Like I said, we've watched all the episodes together every week, and I think it's really opened their eyes to how hard you work to create the magic you do."

"Cam." The way she said his name, all soft and shiny-eyed, was a treasure. "I'm gonna hold that close to my heart so I have something to focus on in case things go sideways."

He squeezed her fingers. "Just focus on me. Everything will be all right."

"I believe you." She squeezed back. "Just in case, I wore my positivity panties."

Dammit. As if on command, his brain supplied an image of Kenya all dolled up like a pinup, with a pair of hot-pink lacy panties hugging her cheeks. Her smile promised everything, as did her "come here" gesture.

Her low laugh snapped his daydream. "You're imagining my positivity panties, aren't you?"

"How can I not? I have a healthy imagination."

Belatedly he realized that they'd passed his old house half a block back. "You deliberately distracted me, didn't you?" he asked, torn between gratitude and disappointment.

"You didn't seem focused on which way we were entering the

neighborhood, so I didn't want you to be blindsided by seeing your old house." She paused. "You still don't regret selling it?"

"It was a house I lived in with my dad. It was never our home." Home was the two-story split-level they'd lived in before his mom had died, the one his dad had become an alcoholic in because she had enlivened every square foot. Selling that house had been a survival tactic for his father; selling this house had been the same for Cam. And he had no intention of drinking himself to death over it either.

"By the way," Kenya said, her tone a purr, "my positivity panties are hot pink with black polka dots."

"Dammit. Kenya. Warn a guy before you say something like that!"

"Oh. Ah, sorry." She released his hand. "I guess I did go too far with that, didn't I?"

He silently cursed himself for making her retreat. "Go as far as you want. I can take it."

"I don't want you to be uncomfortable."

"I'm not uncomfortable," he confessed. "I kinda like your teasing."

"Really?"

"Yep." He wasn't about to explain that he took her teasing as flirting, as another sign of their relationship becoming something more, something real. He did not want to be one more thing for her to stress out about. Especially now. "Looks like we're here."

"Yeah." She blew out a harsh breath as he pulled into the driveway, killed the engine, then stared up at the house for so long he wondered what she was thinking. Then she tossed her bangs and straightened her shoulders, shifting her demeanor to what he could only describe as *on*. "Let's do this."

He came around to her side to help her out, giving her a reassuring smile and the catchphrase they always used before seeing her parents. "Avengers, assemble."

A teasing light glinted in her eyes as she gave him a devilish smile. "Avengers, assemble, dating mode activated."

He liked the sound of that. Even if it was only pretend, he'd do his part as if the fate of the universe hung in the balance.

He tangled his fingers with hers and headed for the front door, feeling as powerful as a certain Asgardian.

CHAPTER EIGHT

Kenya wasn't sure why she'd teased Cam about her positivity panties. Maybe she'd done it to help her slip into the role of girlfriend for the charade they needed to play with her parents. Maybe it was to give herself a little boost before seeing them for the first time since she'd left for the competition. Maybe—

Maybe you did it because you like teasing him that way.

Cam caught her as she tripped over a crack in the walkway. "You okay?"

"Yeah. Maybe I shouldn't have worn a tight skirt."

He gave her a slow glance, taking in her hot-pink pencil skirt, black V-neck blouse, and chunky black heels. "I think you look amazing. Especially now that I know what your underwear looks like."

Her surprised laugh soured into angry wasps buzzing in her stomach as Cam rang the doorbell. Anxiety, pride, and the desire for approval swarmed inside her, each fighting for dominance. She remembered all too well the fight she'd had with them before she'd left, the fight she'd had with them off and on for most of her adolescence. She squelched it all down and reached for the self-belief that had gotten her this far.

Things are different now. I've been on national television. I'm a finalist for an amazing prize, and I'm getting a ton of inquiries to make costumes for other cosplayers. Cam's by my side. I'm living my best life.

It was easy to spread on a smile as her father opened the door. "Hi, Dad."

"There's my baby girl." He reached out, drawing her into a hug. "We've missed you."

"I missed y'all too."

He released her, then turned to Cam. "Cameron."

Did her father's tone cool just a bit? Cam must have thought so because he stuck out his hand and said, "Hi, Mr. Davenport."

That seemed to nudge her father. He blinked, then pulled Cam into that quick hug-and-release thing that men tended to do, then stepped back to let them in. "You weren't this formal when you were here a few days ago."

"A few days ago you didn't know I was dating your daughter," Cam explained, his tone easy but cautious. "I wasn't sure if things would be different or not."

"Are they?"

Michaela Davenport glided into the foyer from the great room, looking every inch an African queen in her turquoise-print caftan and head wrap. In a few of her angsty-teenager moments Kenya had wondered if she'd been adopted or switched at birth, especially given that her parents and siblings were less creative and less round than her. But no—she'd definitely inherited her mother's stubbornness and sense of purpose, as well as her father's love of cooking.

"Hi, Mama." Kenya gave her mother a hug. Despite their argument over her joining the show, Kenya had missed her parents. "It's good to see you."

"Good to see you too, baby," her mother said, giving her an equally tight hug. "I'm sure Cameron's told you that we've been watching the show."

"He did." The fact still surprised her. "What do you think?" she asked, steeling herself for the answer.

Her mother held her at arm's length, assessing her. "The people on that show are trash. I'm proud of you for holding your own."

That startled a laugh out of her. "They thought I was a fluke, so of course I had to prove them wrong. Some of them had to be extra, though."

"I suppose if you can't rely on your talent, being extra is all that's left." A delicate snort conveyed her mother's opinion of that. "Thank God you resisted being labeled as the Angry Black Woman."

Kenya had no doubt that her mother had faced her share of unfair labeling as she forged a successful career while being un-apologetically Black and female in a field that didn't support either. The Davenports had ingrained the will to succeed despite the odds in all of their children, often using the phrase, "Our ancestors didn't suffer so you could be mediocre."

"They tried it," Kenya said, "but my mama taught me better than that."

"Speaking of things your mama taught you . . ." Michaela Davenport turned to Cam for a welcoming hug. "You've been holding out on us, Cameron. I recall specifically asking you about a relationship with Kenya after the show Wednesday night."

She did? Kenya blanked her expression as her mind raced. Cam hadn't told her about that, had he? Unsure how to respond to the question, she looked to Cam, acutely aware that her parents were also staring.

Cam took the perusal in stride, looping an arm about Kenya's shoulders. "It was hard keeping this from y'all," he finally said, contrition ringing in his tone. "But we'd decided that we would break the news to you together when Kenya came back."

She leaned against him, grateful for his quick-witted thinking. She owed him big. "I kept making it through each round and couldn't contact him, so we stayed with our original plan of waiting until I got back. I definitely did not mean to spring it on you via the show."

"Hmm."

Her mother loaded a nuclear warhead's worth of skepticism into that syllable, but Kenya ignored it. "What did you make today, Dad? It smells wonderful!"

"Come help me bring dishes to the table and you'll find out. This is a conversation that should be had over a good meal."

They fell into their usual routine, Cam helping his mother set the table while Kenya helped her father bring the food out. It was a mouthwatering spread of thick braised pork chops, glazed carrots, green beans with potatoes, and her mother's skillet cornbread.

"Oh, I have missed this!" Kenya exclaimed as she settled into the chair across from Cam. "I didn't get to eat anything like this in Los Angeles."

"I hope not," her father said with a laugh. "My baby girl's first Sunday dinner home in two months, I wanted to give you a proper welcome home meal. Now let's say grace then get to eating."

They held hands and bowed their heads as her father blessed their meal. After a soft chorus of "Amen," they passed around the food and the sweet tea until every plate and glass brimmed.

"Mmm," Kenya hummed as the first bite hit her tongue. "Everything we had in LA was catered, but nothing can beat home cooking!"

Her father frowned over his iced tea. "So, they not only took your devices so you couldn't contact Cameron or us, they didn't allow you time to leave the competition area and explore the city?"

"Not really. They wanted to keep us insulated and focused on the show and other contestants. The only time we went out was on supervised excursions that turned into mini-competitions that you saw on TV. Mostly we went from the house to the competition area and then back again."

Her mother matched her father's frown. "That doesn't sound like fun."

Kenya nearly swooned over her first bite of hot, buttery cornbread, but managed to pull herself together enough to answer. "I look at it as work. I have fun doing it, but it's still work. It's my job to take the resources and concept they give me and transform it into magic using my skills and creativity. That means I keep my head down and focus on my process."

"Some people clearly didn't appreciate that," Cam said, his brows crunching down. "I'm thinking of that one woman who stress-cried in particular."

"Amanda, you mean." She rolled her eyes. "I still don't know if she was faking all of that so that we'd help her, or if that's just how she deals with pressure. At the end of the day I had to make sure that I had my sh . . . stuff together. I didn't get into this to lose. I also wasn't there to make friends, even though I thought I was being nice, and professional with everyone. Whether they liked me or not, what they thought of me, that's on them."

"Some of them called you names behind your back. Conceited. Uppity. Mean."

Kenya dropped her head at the heat in her mother's words, knowing she'd experienced some of the same name-calling in her career. She and the other contestants had been prevented from viewing any of the shows, but they all were encouraged to make video diaries. She'd tried to keep hers focused on the work even when the producers continually asked her about the other contestants. Now she knew why.

"Limited people with limited vocabularies," her father declared, patting her hand as he smiled at her mother. "The correct words are *confident*, *competent*, and *crowned with God's grace*. Both of you. Don't let anyone try to steal your crown."

Her eyes watered. "Thanks, Dad."

"Good thing the people voting didn't agree with the haters," Cam said. "They saw everything your father said and then some. They saw talent they couldn't ignore. That's why you're in the finals."

His belief and pride in her gleamed in every word, his eyes, his smile. How could she not succeed with Cam beside her? No matter what happened, she would always remember how Cam had her back. Gratitude swelled inside her, radiating out in a smile. If there wasn't a table separating them, she'd give him a hug.

Cam's answering smile held the support of a coconspirator wrapped in the warmth of more. It was the more she found herself leaning for like a flower to the sun.

She laughed to cover her sudden discomfort over wanting to kiss him again. "Y'all are not going to make me cry at Sunday dinner! Pass me the tea."

Her mother passed the pitcher. "Cameron, I can understand why you were evasive when I questioned you on Wednesday, especially since you hadn't talked to Kenya yet. I need some clarification, though, so I hope you can help me."

Kenya's stomach knotted as Cam straightened in his chair and focused on her mother. "Of course, Mrs. D. What would you like to know?"

"Your girlfriend—I mean, your former girlfriend. What was her name? Jessa?"

Caution entered Cam's eyes. He set his fork down and curled his hand. "Yes, ma'am."

Kenya pretended to sit there and eat her food, unbothered by her mother's prosecutorial line of questioning. Her father's food, so delicious at the start, sat like a stone in her stomach. She'd known they'd get quizzed, she'd just hoped to delay it until dessert, when they could make a graceful exit.

"Jessa." Her mother nodded as if she'd forgotten the name. Kenya knew she hadn't. Michaela Davenport had an eidetic memory, one of many tools in the arsenal she used to be a success in her field. Having a mother who remembered everything you did or were supposed to do hadn't been fun growing up. It still wasn't.

"I thought y'all were doing well," her mother added. "What happened, and when did you break up?"

Kenya watched Cam rub his thumb over the tip of his forefinger, a subtle move, but one she knew telegraphed growing stress. Yet he kept his tone easy as he answered. "We broke up a little while before Kenya got the call that she'd been picked for the show."

"Oh, I'm sorry to hear that."

Kenya's fork clattered to her plate. There's no way she heard her mother right. She did not just hear sympathy in her mother's tone for Cam's ex, when she, his new girlfriend, was sitting right there.

"You don't have to be," Cam said before she could form a heated retort. "Jessa and I grew apart and started wanting different things. Breaking up was a mutual decision."

Then he flashed that thunder-god smile. "Besides, it cleared my way to Kenya."

Lincoln Davenport cleared his throat. "You're not using my daughter as a rebound, are you, Cameron?"

"Dad!" She glared at her father, shocked. "Why are y'all grilling Cam like this? You know him!"

"They're just protective of you, sweetheart," Cam explained. "So am I."

Kenya bristled. She didn't want Cam to feel protective of her. It was enough trying to live her life her way under the protective eye of her parents. She didn't know what she wanted Cam to feel for her, but protective sure as hell wasn't it.

Then she remembered that this wasn't real, this was a show for her parents. She gave him what she hoped was a convincing smile of adoration, then murmured, "Thanks, sweetie."

He stretched his hand across the table. She stared at the nails he'd tried to smooth out, but she knew he'd stress-bitten a couple of them. Cosplaying as her boyfriend wasn't easy on him, and this was only the first full day. She had to do whatever it took to make this easier for him.

She wrapped her fingers around his. Because she was attuned to him, she caught the minute relaxing of his shoulders before he smiled at her.

"To answer your question, Mr. D," he said, turning back to her father, "no. Kenya isn't a rebound for me. She's been my partner from the start, and I'm hers. We just needed to realize it so we can take it to the next level."

"Which we did." She focused on Cam so she wouldn't have to look at her parents as she embellished the truth. "We talked about the relationship and our expectations. We're going into this with our eyes wide open."

"Are you?" her mother asked, her voice soft but her gaze sharpened on Cam, demanding an answer.

Kenya gritted her teeth. Of course her mother didn't believe her. Michaela Davenport probably wouldn't have believed Kenya was a finalist if she hadn't been watching every week with Cam. Did her mother think she'd somehow tricked Cam into her scheme?

Cam squeezed her hand, drawing her attention. The smile he gave her telegraphed that he understood what the question had done to her. His smile loosened the tension in her jaw, allowing her to return his smile.

"Yes," Cam said, and it took her a moment to realize he was answering her mother's question. "What we would like to know is, are you okay with this? With us?"

Her father sat back. "You're asking for our blessing now, two months after the fact?"

That was enough. Cam had had her back throughout this dinner; it was time for her to return the favor. "We already explained why we waited to tell you. You know Cam well enough to know he wouldn't turn to me immediately after breaking up with Jessa. He's a better man than that. Right now, we're just hanging out, testing the waters, seeing where this thing goes. It may go nowhere or it may go somewhere pretty damn fantastic. We won't know until we try."

Whoa. She hadn't intended to do a full-on monologue. Cam's expression matched the surprise that rippled through her. She'd never defended a relationship to her parents, real or not, with her whole chest. It didn't matter much if her parents approved of her relationship with Cam or not, given that it wasn't real. But it still stung. Then again, it wouldn't be the first time she'd disappointed her parents. She didn't want Cam to endure the same.

Lincoln Davenport cleared his throat. "We just want you to be happy," he said into the thick silence. He patted their linked hands. "Both of you."

"Yes," her mother agreed. "That's the most important thing."

Kenya's stomach churned with unease. She didn't like thinking negatively about her parents, didn't like the automatic need to examine every word they spoke and the way those words were spoken in an attempt to uncover some hidden meaning. They were good parents, but it seemed as if they were more concerned with Cam's happiness than hers.

Guilt made her stomach roil again. They'd taken their guardianship of Cam seriously, ensuring his health, education, and future. But Cam didn't need that smothering concern anymore. He was an adult, and he could damn well make his own decisions, even those concerning their fake relationship.

"Then you have nothing to worry about, Mrs. D," Cam said, squeezing her hand. "I got my girl. I can't help but be happy."

He said it with such sincerity that even Kenya believed him for a moment. She definitely had to help him find a new girlfriend after the competition ended. Any woman with a lick of sense would be blessed to have him.

"Love you," she whispered, because it was true. Because he was going so far above and beyond for her. Somehow she would repay him for all of this.

"Y'all's happiness is important to us." Her mother sipped her tea, then leaned forward. "So does this mean that the show will be shooting in the apartment or the shop? I'm assuming that the point of bringing in significant others is to document how couples work together under the stress of competing and creating and being together?"

Kenya pulled her hand free of Cam's in surprise. Her mother really had watched the show. Sure, Cam had told her that, but on some level she hadn't believed it. She checked herself, vowing to do better by her mother.

"Actually, Cam built me this amazing work nook in the shop." Excitement bubbled. "He took me to see it yesterday. It's so beautiful. I can't wait to start work there tomorrow!"

"We'll be able to do the collaboration that the show requires and

I'll still be able to manage the shop," Cam added. "Shooting in the shop means we'll also be able to have private downtime away from the cameras."

Private downtime. Kenya tried not to blush as she recalled waking up with Cam spooning her. "I still have to make a video diary at the end of each day, but everything I need to do for the costumes will be done at the shop."

Concern crossed her mother's features. "This won't be too much of a strain on you and the shop, will it?"

"It shouldn't be," Cam cheerfully answered. He rubbed his fingers together. "I'm limited to twenty-five percent of the work on the costumes, and I'm sure Kenya will do her logistical magic to make sure any work I have to do with her doesn't infringe on the work I need to do for the shop. I also talked to my guys when they helped me set up Kenya's work space. They know I'm marking certain areas off-limits for proprietary reasons, so they're cool. I met the film crew yesterday when I picked Kenya up at the airport and they filmed us for a bit in the shop then, so I have an idea of how they operate. I'm going in early tomorrow so that the crew can set up cameras in the areas we want."

Wow. Cam had done a lot since she'd declared him her significant other on national television five whole days before. "My goal is to make this as easy for Cam and his crew as possible. The last thing I want to do is hurt him or his business."

She looked to her mother as she spoke, hoping her conviction showed on her face and in her words. She knew her parents were protective of Cam. She wanted them to know that she was too.

Her mother nodded, and the mood immediately lightened. They finished the meal—with a decadent Mississippi mud cake for dessert—with discussions of her older siblings, the paper her father was writing, and her mother's ever-evolving plan to retire or not.

Kenya fully relaxed into the vibe of food, family, and her best friend. Her parents had accepted their relationship and seemed supportive of what she and Cam were doing. The relief that knowledge gave her made her realize just how much she'd wanted their approval, how much it meant. They might never truly accept the life path she wanted to take but they'd support her, and she was thankful for it.

That sense of thankfulness lasted until Cam and her father went to the kitchen with the leftovers, leaving her at the table with her mother. She topped off her tea. "It looks like you have everything covered."

"I think so," she answered. "Well, everything except what we're cosplaying."

Her mother leaned closer. "I'm sure you'll come up with something great that will showcase your talents."

Kenya blinked. "Thanks, Mom. I've got a couple of ideas, I just need to narrow them down with Cam."

"I know you'll do your best." Michaela Davenport set her glass on the table with precise movements. "But what if it's not good enough?"

There it was. She should've been grateful that her mother had waited until they were alone. "I have a plan." It didn't involve dusting off her degree, either.

"Hmph. Do you have a plan to pay back Cameron's investment if you don't win? He rearranged his shop, adjusted his work schedule and projects to work on costumes. He's putting massive amounts of his time and money into your venture, neither of which he has an abundance of as a small business owner."

"I know that, Mom." She was well aware of the sacrifices Cam had made and was still making for her. It drove her need to win. If he'd take it, she would give him the prize money while she worked the paid internship into something they could both leverage. "I also remember the deal we made before I left, if that's what you're hinting at."

Her mother pursed her lips. "I'm just looking out for both of you."

"I know you are." She sighed. "You don't have to break out the pom-poms or anything, but it would be nice if you could pretend to be supportive of what we're doing, especially for this final round."

"Baby." Her mother gripped her hand. "I support you. Your father and I both do. We can't help worrying about you, though. That's what parents do. I worry that you're not reaching your full potential. I worry that you're not using your degree, and your field is passing you by. I worry that you're chasing a dream that can't possibly come true. I worry about what will happen once you realize that. I worry that you or Cameron or both of you will be irrevocably hurt if this doesn't go the way you hope it will."

Kenya bowed her head as emotion tumbled through her like a rough wave threatening to pull her under. She needed to process her mother's words, needed to respond to them. Needed to assure her mother, and herself, that she could handle this and the worry was for nothing. On an intellectual level, she understood where her mother was coming from. On an emotional level, though? She wanted to escape before she said something she'd regret.

"Hey, babe." Cam dropped a hand to her shoulder, giving it a squeeze. "We should get going. You've got a long day tomorrow and we have to get up early."

She gave him a grateful smile. "You're right. They'll want to film for hours, longer than a normal workday. I'll need all the beauty sleep I can get."

Her mother stood when she did. Cam stepped between them to kiss her mother's cheek. "Good night, Mrs. D."

She patted his cheek. "Good night, Cameron. You take care of yourself, all right?"

"Yes, ma'am."

Kenya took her turn, locking down her emotions and pretending everything was copacetic as she gave her mom a hug and a kiss, then her father. "We might be scarce for the next couple of weeks. They're not giving us a lot of time to conceive, design, and create two costumes."

"Of course, baby," her father said, sliding an arm around her mother's waist. "Use all that Black Girl Magic and kick some cosplaying ass."

"You know it. Good night."

Kenya didn't breathe normally again until they pulled out of her parents' driveway. "I'm so glad that's over!"

"It wasn't too terrible," Cam said. "I mean, it could have been worse."

"You're right. She could have called your ex and invited her to dinner."

"Yeah." He raked a hand through his hair. "That part was weird. I guess they just wanted to make sure we were serious about this. About us."

"Well, you convinced them with some A-list acting. I owe you big."

He grimaced. "You can pay me back by not talking about how much you owe me. Please."

That "please" kept her from pressing further. "All right. No more talk. I won't bring it up again."

"Okay." He paused a beat. "What were you and Mrs. D talking about? It looked intense."

She folded her arms. "If you can have something you don't want to talk about, I can have something I don't want to talk about."

"Petty, party of one, your table is ready." He continued before she could punch his shoulder. "It was that bad, huh?"

She closed her eyes, rubbing at her temples to ease a blossoming headache. "She thinks she wants better for me than I want for myself. Of all the reasons why I want to win, proving to her that this will lead to good things for us is a big one. I have to prove her wrong. I have to prove that achieving my dreams is what's best for me, and something I can make work for both of us."

"If anyone can do it, you're the one. After all, you do ten impossible things before coffee every morning."

She didn't think deciding what hair to wear with which outfit was considered impossible, but she'd take every bit of encouragement she could get. "Hey, do you think we could go by the shop for a little bit? I want to film a diary entry there. I should have done it yesterday, but my brain was on overload."

"No problem. That'll give me a chance to see how you do it in case I feel the need to jump in or make one of my own."

Kenya gathered her thoughts as Cam drove, her mother's admonitions foremost in her mind. Filming her video diary at the shop not only meant that she could show off her new work space, but she could also talk up how wonderful Cam was for making it happen. There were no guarantees that the show would use all of it, but they certainly couldn't use what she didn't record.

Afternoon sunlight filled the front of the shop, giving everything a golden orange glow. "Do you want the overhead lights on?" he asked as he deactivated the alarm.

"Nah, I brought my stand and light kit," she answered, digging into her tote. "I'll be ready in just a sec."

"You and your Bag of Everything," he said with a shake of his head. "How could I have forgotten about that?"

"Yeah, how could you?" she asked in mock anger, cocking her

head. "I've only had some version of it every day since high school. I guess it's a case of out of sight, out of mind."

He fiddled with a white pencil cup emblazoned with a hot-pink *K*, his expression as gruff as his tone. "Forgetting about a tote bag is one thing, forgetting you is impossible. I thought about you every day."

She hid a smile by fixing the light setting. They joked with each other all the time with a freedom based on more than ten years of friendship. This sort of teasing was new, but not unwelcome. "I thought about you every day too."

She pulled both task chairs together. "Why don't you sit with me on this one so we can introduce you to everyone? It's not much different from other videos we've done, so just relax and be yourself. Jane will edit the video for the show anyway."

"All right." He took a seat, fidgeting with his collar. Kenya squeezed his knee in support, then started to record.

"Hey, everyone, it's your girl Kenya. I'm so excited to be home for this final round because I'm back with my best friend, my partner, and my own personal superhero, Cameron Lassiter."

"Hey, guys." He lifted one hand in greeting, then draped his arm across her shoulders. "I'm glad to have my girl back home, and I'm looking forward to helping her win this thing."

"I thought I'd be showing you guys my home setup today, but Cam surprised me with a new work space at his shop, Make It Worx. Take a look at this!"

She carefully turned the phone to capture the area, adding a running commentary on the cubbies and supplies. "Isn't it amazing? He brought over everything from home and set it up for me. He's just the best. I'm so lucky!" She pressed a loud kiss on his cheek.

"The feeling's mutual, babe, you know that," he answered, giving her a squeeze and a peck at her temple.

Her cheeks hurt from smiling but containing her happiness and excitement was impossible. "Tomorrow is the official start of the final round and I can't wait to get started. Still finalizing ideas for an iconic duo we can cosplay, but we'll definitely have a choice locked and loaded tomorrow. For now, we're going to go home and get some rest while we can. See you next time, until then, take care."

She signed off with her usual perky side-smile, flexing her fingers into an American Sign Language *K*, then stopped the video. "See, not so bad, was it?"

"No. Remember, we've done a few for the shop? But you know me. I'd rather let the products do the talking. Anything else you need?"

"No, that's it." She packed her things back into her tote. "Definitely ready to go home now."

"Me too. I ate so much at dinner, I'm about to pop a button."

"Good thing I have a sewing kit in my Bag of Everything, huh?"

"Hey." He guided her toward the door. "Lesson learned. I will never besmirch the mighty Bag of Everything ever again."

"Better not." She savored the rest of the night for the break that it was. Monday would bring the chaos of their ridiculous production schedule and she was sure moments like this would be few. Whatever stress she had to endure would be worth it because Cam was worth it. She was worth it. Winning was worth it.

Anything less wasn't an option. Because failure meant the end of everything, and she couldn't let that happen.

CHAPTER NINE

Thank you again for coming in early so we could get set up," Jane the producer said. "I think we've got everything in place, and we've double-checked the camera angles to make sure we don't shoot the areas you want to keep secret."

Cam generally considered himself a decent guy, even pre-caffeine. But he'd left Kenya blissfully sleeping in their bed and losing that extra hour of curling up with her left him churlish. It took everything he had not to bristle at the passive-aggressive bullshit Jane had been pulling all morning. It was too early for it. "Not secret," he corrected her. "Proprietary. We make parts for a variety of clients and we pride ourselves on our confidentiality. Besides, you're here to film me and Kenya, not my crew, right?"

"Of course," Jane said, her brown ponytail bobbing sharply as she nodded. She reached into her gear bag. "That reminds me. I need to give you this."

Cam took the handheld camera with reluctance. "Why?"

"So that you can create a video diary."

Ugh. "Why?"

Jane lowered her brows in confusion. "We talked about this when you signed the release forms."

"We did, and I said I'd sit in when Kenya did hers. We filmed one yesterday."

He scraped his nails across his denim-clad thigh, trying to keep his voice pleasant. The producer gave him a weird vibe that made her difficult to trust. That didn't mean he should be rude when dealing with her. He wanted Kenya to win, and antagonizing the production crew wasn't going to help.

"Besides, my work will be limited, and this is about her journey as a cosplayer and costumer, right?"

Jane smiled, the edges sharp. "Up to the finals, it was about Kenya. Now it's about you. Both of you, as cosplayers and as a couple. Your video diaries will help us capture that."

"I suppose that makes sense." He could use the video diaries to talk up Kenya and her skills as well as talk about the project. Not too hard, considering. "Anything else?"

"Actually, yes." She gestured to her crew. "As I said, this final round is about you and Kenya as a couple who cosplay together. I want to do a quick interview with you. Introduce you to the audience so they can learn all about you and get your relationship with Kenya, with cosplaying."

It sounded innocent enough. "When do you want to do it?"

"We can start right now, before Kenya and your team get here," Jane suggested. "We can even shoot you in front of your shop sign at the counter. I'll ask you a few questions to get you started, and then just let you riff."

"Sounds easy enough." The Q&A in front of the logo would give the shop more exposure, and he'd get to tell everyone that Kenya was much more than what they believed she was.

"Okay," Jane said after the crew set up the shot. "Let's start with something simple. How did you meet Kenya?"

It was a simple question, but the answer needed a story. "I met Kenya in our freshman year of high school. I'd just transferred in, didn't know anyone. Didn't want to. But Kenya's hard to resist, you know?"

He smiled at the memories. "I was sitting by myself at lunch, reading an *X-Men* comic. I'd forgotten to bring lunch and I was grumpy, but she didn't care. She sat down next to me, split her lunch with me, then took out her own *X-Men* comic."

An embarrassed laugh escaped him. "I can admit now that I was a bit of a jerk. A girl reading a comic and not whatever they read on their phones? She schooled me real quick, though, and I'm not a slow learner. We've been friends ever since. And now we're more."

"When did you realize that you should be more than friends?"

Cam paused, unsure how to answer. That was a trickier question and it needed a careful answer, especially since he wasn't sure if the producer had already quizzed Kenya. "That's a good question," he finally said. "We've been extremely close from the start, and a bunch of our friends have wondered why it took as long as it did for us to get together."

He shrugged. "The timing before now wasn't right. We didn't want to ruin our friendship. One or both of us were seeing someone else. Then a couple of months ago, we were simultaneously single and I decided it was time to make a move."

"You were seeing someone else then," Jane said.

Of course they'd done their homework. "I was. And then I wasn't."

Jane nodded, too easily for Cam's comfort. Then she smiled. "Kenya and your former girlfriend . . . they're polar opposites."

What the hell? Cam had an idea of what the producer meant, but he wasn't going to give her the satisfaction of having him say.

He decided to play stupid and make her say the quiet part out loud. "No, they're both amazing in their own ways. Kenya, of course, is into cosplay and anime, and my ex is a gamer."

"So it's an 'opposites attract' type thing."

He didn't bother to smother his frown. "Kenya and I have a lot in common, so the 'opposites attract' thing is ridiculous to say. As far as a type is concerned, what type do you think I have? Because my type is someone who is kind, creative, generous, fun, and hot. Kenya is all of those things. She makes it easy to love her."

Say something else. I dare you. One more wrong word about Kenya and I'm kicking you out until she gets here.

Someone tapped on the window, causing Jane to jump with a squeak. Cam grinned as Mack gestured at the front door. He'd have to give the man a bonus. "Are we done here? My crew and I have to get to work."

Jane made a cutting motion, and her team fell back. "For now. We'll go grab breakfast and talk about today's schedule while we wait for Kenya to arrive."

"You can leave your equipment in the back room if you don't want to take it with you." Cam unlocked the front door, allowing Mack inside. "There are a couple of local places within walking distance if you want a sit-down meal, and a fast-food place a couple of blocks down."

"We'll leave it here, thanks." Jane and her crew headed to the back.

"Morning," Mack said as he entered, craning his neck to take everything in. "You shooting already?"

"Nah, I came in early so they could set up their stationary cameras. They're heading out to breakfast now."

Javier arrived just as the production crew came back to the floor. Cam quickly made introductions, then heaved a sigh of relief when they left. "Hey, guys, before we get started today, let me show you where the cameras are. They're also going to have two cameramen filming while Kenya is working on show stuff, but they'll make sure to focus on her area."

Javier tossed his backpack on his worktable. "Did you show her the new setup yet?" he asked, removing his motorcycle jacket.

"Saturday, after I picked her up from the airport," Cam answered, then broke into a grin. "She loves it! I can't thank you guys enough for helping me get everything set up."

Mack laughed. "It's for Kenya, of course we were going to help. Besides, we were on the clock."

Cam barked out a much-needed laugh, putting his interview with the producer out of his mind. "There may be a performance bonus when all this is over, just saying."

Both men looked at each other, then back at him in a way that hunched Cam's shoulders in self-defense. "What?"

The guys exchanged glances again, then Mack cleared his throat. "I was joking about being on the clock—you know we wanted to help with that. You're the boss and everything, but we know your pockets ain't deep like that."

Yeah, his pockets weren't deep. Business was good, but it could be better. He set aside a little each pay period into savings, but every spare penny went back into the business, and even that was not enough to afford to put someone else on the payroll. "I'm hoping Make It Worx will get some free publicity out of the next few weeks and it will be good for business. It certainly couldn't hurt." He hoped.

"So, you offering a bonus . . ." Mack paused. "I saw your face while that woman interviewed you. Is this filming thing going to be a bad thing?"

"I hope the hell not. I'm going to do everything I can to make this as pain-free as possible for you guys. For all of us."

"It's still a helluva lot better than having a bunch of strangers and their equipment all up in your apartment," Javier said, waggling his eyebrows. "Wouldn't want to mess up the new lovebird vibe, am I right?"

"Yeah, man, I can't believe y'all kept that on the down low like that!"

Cam shook his head. Thanks to their dinner with Kenya's parents the previous day, he was ready for this conversation. "We weren't going to tell anyone before we told Kenya's parents, and we wanted to be together when we did that."

"Do they know?"

"We officially told them yesterday over dinner," he answered, glossing over the fact that Kenya had announced their nonexistent relationship on national television.

Mack snorted. "How did that go?"

Cam spread his arms wide. "I'm still alive, aren't I?"

"I guess this explains why you ignored all those hotties trying to hit on you every time we went to the bar while Kenya was gone. All this time we thought you were moping over Jessa, despite you saying you were good."

"How could I mope over Jessa when I get to date Kenya?" He kept his tone light, but he was ready to change the subject even though he needed them to buy the story. "Besides, I told y'all that Jessa and I both decided it was time to move on. She's not moping either."

Javier elbowed him. "And you're free to be with your soul mate, right?"

"Hold up." Cam threw up both hands. "Kenya and I may be old friends but this part is all new. So cut it out with the soul mate stuff. We're nowhere near that kind of talk."

And they probably wouldn't be for a while. Kenya was still skittish about a pretend relationship despite all the affectionate gestures they'd both initiated while having dinner with her parents. Despite readily climbing into bed with him last night. Despite him waking up with her pressed wonderfully close to him, his hand once again clasped against her chest.

Yeah, he had hope. Mad hope. But he had to get them to actually dating before he could get them to soul mate territory.

"Hey, man," Mack said, snapping his fingers in Cam's face. "I would ask you what you were thinking about but it's probably X-rated. I don't want to get punched!"

"All right, smart-ass. It's time to get our collective asses in gear. We do have actual work to do. That film crew will be back soon enough, and Kenya will probably show up any minute. Today's gonna be weird for all of us. Let's just do what we do and give Kenya space to do what she does."

"Kenya's our girl," Javier said. "We're not gonna mess this up for her. I mean, she's your girl, but she's part of the team."

Mack stood next to him, his expression serious. "Ain't nobody gonna do her wrong."

"I know." Mack and Javier thought of Kenya as their little sister, and they were as protective of her as he was. They'd do right by her.

The interview with the producer flickered through his mind, dampening his mood again. He wasn't worried about the guys ruining things for Kenya. He was worried about himself.

Kenya sent a quick text to Cam. HEY. COFFEE?

It took less than a minute for him to reply. GOD YES. AND CARBS.

K. MACK N JAVIER THERE?

YEP. BRING XTRA SO THEY CAN STOP BITCHING.

OMW.

Kenya smiled as she pulled up the Nubian Coffee app and placed the usual order for the guys, with a little extra carby goodness thrown in. She didn't really think the guys were bitching—Javier and Mack were just as even-keeled as Cam—but they were probably feeling some sort of way about the film crew being there. Jane wasn't supposed to interact with them, but Kenya wouldn't be surprised if the producer didn't interview both guys to get their take on her relationship with Cam. After all, the show needed content to fill the time before they returned for the finale.

It was part of the reason why she'd wanted to come in with Cam so that she could be a buffer between the guys and the production crew. She'd been a bit bummed to wake up without Cam, but she knew he wanted the cameras set up a certain way to protect the guys and their products. Cam was a perfectionist when it came to the shop, but he had to be to keep the business going and customer orders coming in.

She wondered how Javier and Mack had taken the news of her involvement with Cam and how they'd react when they finally saw her. Was that why Cam said they were bitching? She hoped they didn't think she'd get any special treatment now. They were all friends as well as coworkers, but she considered them more like brothers. Would they treat her differently now that she was dating Cam?

Pretend-dating Cam. She had to keep that straight in her head. This was all just pretend to win a prize that could possibly benefit all of them. Hopefully, the guys would understand the deception when all was said and done.

She parked in her usual spot, then made her way around the corner to the café. She loved the Elmwood neighborhood east of Atlanta, balanced as it was between old school and gentrification. Some of the businesses and locals had been there for decades, like Nubian Coffee, a neighborhood hub serving Southern-style breakfast and coffee long before lattes were cool. Some had arrived in the last few years. Cam had been lucky to grab his storefront, a former auto repair shop, before gentrification jacked the prices into the stratosphere.

Glancing at her activity watch, she hiked her tote higher on her shoulder and pushed her way into the breakfast eatery. Nubian Coffee had the best caffeine on the block, but Mr. Nelson and Miss Catherine also served homemade biscuits and a country ham and red-eye gravy platter so good it would make her father jealous if she ever told him. As a reluctant nod to gentrification, Mr. Nelson also served New York–style bagels and coffees with French and Italian names with a commensurate markup.

"Hey, hey!" The man himself greeted her, a wide smile splitting his dark features. He was somewhere between fifty and ninety, but Kenya didn't know and Mr. Nelson wouldn't tell. "There she is, Ms. Rich and Famous TV Star!"

Kenya laughed as she gave him a fist bump. "More like Broke and Trying TV Finalist."

"You got to be more positive, young lady," he reprimanded her. "Me and Miss Catherine been watching. You are in the finals! The whole neighborhood's rooting for you!"

Her heart fluttered in a twist of panicked happiness. "Really?"

Mr. Nelson gave her a look that reminded her of her father. "We root for our own. Believe that."

"Yes, sir."

He handed over a loaded sack of food then started on the drinks. "So, are you home for a mini-break before you and Cameron head back to Los Angeles together?"

"Actually, no. We're filming in the shop. The production crew is already there, and we'll probably start the moment I walk in the door. I just came by to pick up some fuel."

"You made the right choice, then, because you know what they say about Nubian Coffee." He gestured to the mural above the wall menu.

"The darker the bean, the stronger the juice!"

"All right, Ms. Broke and Trying, that's everything." He placed the four coffees in a drink carrier. "And here's your total."

Kenya's mouth dropped as she saw the amount. "Mr. Nelson, that's half of what I usually pay. I can't let you do that!"

"You don't 'let' me do anything," he retorted. "Consider it payment for the product placement that's about to happen—and let those production crew people know we close at two."

"You know I will. Thank you, Mr. Nelson." She left a cash tip, tucked the food bag into her cavernous tote, then carefully lifted the drink carrier. With a final wave, she backed her way out the door.

She hummed a Beyoncé song as she made her way down the sidewalk to the shop. It wasn't quite eight a.m. yet, but the sun already peeked through the pines and oaks that dominated the neighborhood. She loved Elmwood and its split personality, its energy and calm, its trendiness and tradition, as if it wasn't sure what it wanted to be. Kinda like the way she felt sometimes.

Especially given that she and Cam had grown up in the suburbs in a cookie-cutter subdivision in a web of cookie-cutter streets leading to cookie-cutter shopping centers anchored by chain stores and restaurants. Here, almost all of the shops were one-offs owned by locals who proudly held on to their OG status and turned their noses up at the trendy establishments that began their sprawl just a few blocks down.

Cam had only had his shop for two years but he'd been making parts out of his garage in high school and college until his father had died. He'd sold the house and finished college while building things in the apartment, building a reputation through cons and other sales until it became too much to store equipment and parts and projects, even with Kenya being his first employee.

She was so proud of everything that Cam had accomplished despite his father's benign neglect and subsequent death just before the start of their sophomore year of college. Those events might have broken someone else, but not Cam. She wanted nothing but good things, better things, from here on out. Winning the competition would help her help him.

Which meant it was time to be on. Pausing outside the shop, she took a couple of cleansing breaths, pasted on a smile, then pulled open the door. "Hey, y'all! I got caffeine and carbs!"

CHAPTER TEN

"Kenya, welcome back!" Mack reached her first, waiting for her to set the drinks down on the sales counter before enveloping her in a beefy-armed hug. He stepped back from her to give her the once-over. "Damn, girl, that TV life sure does agree with you!"

"And that's why I brought you an extra hot link biscuit," she said with a laugh, digging into her tote for the breakfast goodies and sure that the cameras were already zooming in. "You know just what to say."

She'd taken extra care with her appearance that morning, donning her hot-pink lace-front bob and dramatic lashes. She'd contoured to within an inch of her life and painted her lips into the perfect fuchsia pout. Her outfit had been chosen with intent too: fuchsia high-tops, tropical-print capris, and a flared goldenrod-colored tunic that showed off her cleavage and hit her at her hips. She looked good and she knew it.

"Hey, man, you can't hug on her like that anymore," Javier cautioned as he joined them. "She's the boss's girl now."

Mack pulled a mock pout as he sniffed his latte. "You broke my heart. I thought we had a thing."

She laughed in relief as she extracted two wrapped biscuits from her tote. They had bought her and Cam's relationship and didn't seem to have an issue with it. "A breakfast delivery service thing, you mean?"

"You're the only one who gets my order right." He sighed dramatically. "I guess I'll have to eat my feelings."

"Man, you know you ain't never had a chance." Javier snorted as he squeezed her shoulders. "I'm glad you're back, *hermanita*. He was miserable without you."

An inelegant snort broke free before she could catch it. Not something she wanted documented for the cameras, but she had to clear up any potential misunderstanding, especially with Jane watching her like a hawk. Surely they hadn't misunderstood Cam?

"Who, Mack?" She tossed her head. "Don't tell me he never walked down to Nubian Coffee to get his own biscuits!"

Javier rolled his eyes. "No. I mean Cam."

"Oh." Kenya smiled. Cam must have really played up things with the guys if Javier thought he'd been miserable without her. "Speaking of my guy, where is he?"

"Right here."

She turned as she heard his voice close behind her, wonderfully close. His arm encircled her waist and he dropped a kiss to her lips. She thought it was supposed to be a quick one on the kiss-o-meter scale, more like a peck, but she was happily surprised when it was longer, when her eyes fluttered closed, and everything went sort of hazy.

She opened her eyes as he stepped back, feeling as if she'd just woken up, fuzzed and soft. "Hey."

His answering smile lit his eyes in a way she found mesmerizing. "Hey yourself."

Mack's wolf whistle snapped her out of her haze. "I, uhm, brought your favorites," she said, thrusting Cam's cup and his cinnamon roll at him. "You should have woke me up. I would have come in with you."

"I know, but you were sleeping so soundly when I got up that I decided not to." He smiled again, giving her that up-and-down glance that would have made her bristle with anyone but him. "Besides, this look was worth the wait."

"Why, thank you." She pirouetted. "I'll be sure to keep it up."

"Hey, Kenya?"

Jane's voice doused her good mood. Ah yes, a none-too-subtle reminder that every word and act was being recorded. She pasted on a smile and turned to Jane. "Good morning. Y'all ready to get started?"

Jane gave her an answering smile. "We got good footage of you greeting the other guys, but now we're ready to shoot you with your actual guy." She gestured behind them. "We've got cameras set up around your area. I understand Cameron has a lot of shop work to do and probably won't be helping much at this stage, so let's maximize your time together, okay?"

She didn't seem all that happy about the restriction, but it was important to Cam's business for his crew to be able to work unimpeded. Besides, if she had a problem with Cam only being available for twenty-five percent of the work, she needed to take it up with her bosses, not Kenya. "No worries there," she replied. "With this setup, I don't need to be anywhere else."

"Good. Do you know what you're planning to create for the finals?"

"I do." Inspiration had come as she'd put on her makeup.

"Does Cameron know yet?"

He stepped closer to Kenya. "I do not."

"Okay." Jane rubbed her hands. "Let's shoot you at your work space. Kenya, stand here, and, Cameron, if I could get you to stand there. Perfect! All right, just remember to act natural and pretend that we're not here. Start when you're ready."

"Okay."

Kenya dug into her tote. "Hey, Cam, let me run something by you."

"Of course, babe." He joined her. "What's up?"

"I've been thinking about what we can do for our iconic duos cosplay," she said, extracting her portfolio from her tote. "We really need to do something that showcases what we're good at: your fabrication magic and my design and art skills."

"Okay." He partially unwrapped his cinnamon roll then took a big bite. "What do you have in mind?"

She opened her portfolio. "Iron Man and Thanos."

"That's a good idea!" He sidled closer. "I'd like to see your take on Ironheart, but you know I'm allergic to most body paint. What's your fix for turning me purple?"

"Nothing." She flipped to the rough concept sketch she'd made then placed the pad on the worktable. "I'm going to be the purple one."

While getting ready, she'd made another list of famous duos from some of their favorite anime, games, and movies. While she thought they were iconic and had distinctive costumes it would be awesome to cosplay, she didn't think obscure character representations would hype up mainstream America enough to vote for them. She needed a pair of costumes that would need no explanation. What better than two of the main characters from one of the biggest blockbusters ever?

"I figured that we'd go with the Marvel Cinematic Universe versions, since that's what the majority of people will be familiar with," she explained, pointing at her sketch. "I chose to do Thanos in his golden armor. That ups the difficulty and technical levels because that's a lot of armor we have to make for both of us. Not to mention the Infinity Gauntlet and the Arc Reactor. I can wear platform boots to make myself a little bit taller than you and the armor will hide my boobs."

"That's a shame."

"Cam!" Heat burned her cheeks and her ears.

"What?" he teased. "I like your assets a lot. Like really a lot."

"I know, but . . ." She was certain the heat flushing through her would melt the glue holding down her edges. He'd promised that he would be so good at faking being her boyfriend that even they would believe it. He needed to start work on his Academy Award acceptance speech.

Needing a distraction, she reached for her coffee. "Maybe we should get back to the project."

"All right." He stepped closer, practically looking over her shoulder so that the cameraman had enough room to film them and the sketches she'd made. "You can use the 3-D printer to make the pieces for the armor and helmets for both costumes," he suggested. "That will save you a lot of time."

"It would, but that would be expensive, and you need the printer available for shop business."

"Good point. Does that mean you're going old school?"

"Yeah." Excitement had her bouncing on her toes. "I think molding the armor out of foam will give me a skill advantage. I did find a template for printing the components of the Arc Reactor, so we could run that one night after the shop closes for the day."

"Sounds good. I can start on that tonight."

"Not yet." She reached into the folder pocket and pulled out another sheet. "There are other dependencies that have to be completed before we can get to the Arc Reactor."

"You have a spreadsheet." He snorted. "Of course you have a spreadsheet. I bet the electronic copy has pivot tables and everything."

"It's almost like you know me." She pulled her tablet out of the same padfolio pocket, then called up the spreadsheet app. "It's the best way to track your tasks to make sure we stay under that twenty-five percent parameter. It's a hellacious timeline regardless."

Anxiety bubbled in her stomach. "We're basically having to do six months of work in four weeks. I had to chart out the major production steps and the corresponding dependencies so we can stay on track. For instance, today is about getting the patterns for each set of armor printed and traced onto poster board to make the templates. I've also got to buy supplies and trace the templates onto the foam sheets, which I'm sure I also need."

He whistled. "That's a lot."

"Yeah. At least I've already found the Pepakura files for the Mark LXXXV suit and the golden armor. I'll download them and send them to the print shop around the corner after I verify our measurements. I can pick them up on the way back from shopping."

"I love the way your brain works." He reached past her to pick up the printed spreadsheet. Her nerve endings danced at his nearness. "You aren't kidding about the hellacious timeline. I guess the ones in blue are my tasks?"

"Hmm." Was men's deodorant supposed to smell this good? She leaned closer. No wait—did he use her honey-vanilla body wash? Why did it smell so damn irresistible on him?

"KeKe?"

You smell good.

Silence.

"Babe." Cam's voice was barely a whisper. "You said the quiet part out loud."

Shit. Shock widened her eyes. She did not mean to say that. Did someone on the crew just laugh? There was no doubt that the mics had picked up her words, and the camera caught her reaction to being caught. Nothing to do but brazen it out. "Well, you do."

"For now," he laughed. "Based on this schedule, I have the feeling we're going to end every day covered in sweat."

"You will if you play your cards right," she quipped. Might as well continue what she'd begun.

"I'll be sure to take my vitamins every morning," he said, his tone grave but his eyes twinkling. "We may need to stock up on energy drinks, too. Are there other supplies we need to get today?"

She turned to survey her cubbies. "I have to verify our inventory to see what we need but I know we definitely need to get more EVA foam sheets and Bondo. It wouldn't hurt to get more glue sticks and a couple of guns either, and blades for the utility knives. It looks like I've got the cardstock to get the patterns for both suits traced and cut this morning. I also want to double-check your measurements in case I have to resize anything."

"All right." He nodded. "You want to go ahead and get the measuring out of the way? I need to do a couple of administrative things in the office before I jump into my next project."

"Uhm, okay." She shouldn't have mentioned it. It wouldn't have been a big deal to measure him at home, but here? With Javier and Mack and the production crew all watching?

"Okay, let's stop for a moment," Jane called out. She removed her headphones and approached them. "We need to block the shot for this next part. Are you planning to take Cameron's measurements here or someplace else?"

Kenya looked around the shop floor. Jane probably wanted two cameras at least, which meant the office wasn't useable. The idea of kneeling on the floor in the stock area or their little break room didn't thrill her. That just left her work area. "I think right here is the best bet. Cam, if you'll stand right here, I'll have enough room to get around you."

"Sure thing."

Her mind raced as she fumbled through the drawers holding sewing supplies. *You got this, girl. You've taken Cam's measurements before. It's no big deal.*

Yeah, but that was before you knew how good he smelled and before he became your boyfriend.

Pretend. Cosplaying it, remember?

I know. Cam knows. Nobody else knows that, though. So how are we gonna play this?

Like a boss.

"Here it is." She turned around, holding the measuring tape aloft. Taking note of his navy plaid Oxford, she asked, "Are you wearing a T-shirt under that?"

He rubbed a hand down his chest, smoothing the fabric down. "Yeah."

"All right, then." She gave him a wink. "Take it off. So I can get accurate measurements."

"Yes, ma'am." He grinned at her as he reached for the first button. "Do you want a little shimmy to go with it?"

God. She wouldn't be able to handle that. "We can save that for later, when we're alone."

No idea why her voice sounded all breathy or why her hands suddenly felt slick. Maybe Mr. Nelson had added an extra shot of espresso to her coffee. Or maybe watching Cam slowly unbutton his shirt made her brain misfire.

He removed his shirt, hanging it on the back of her task chair. "Okay, babe, assume the position."

Waggling his eyebrows at her, he widened his stance and spread his arms wide. "How's this?"

"Perfect." Kenya polished off her coffee, then stepped closer to Cam. This was not the time to not have Altoids in her bag of tricks, but if Cam didn't complain about her morning breath, he wouldn't say anything about caramel macchiato breath either.

"I'm going to do your neck first," she announced, mostly for the cameras but to also give Cam forewarning of her movements. She looped the tape over his head. His expression ricocheted from amused to sharp as her fingers brushed against the base of his throat so that she could hold the tape against his bare skin. Against his warm, honey-and-vanilla-scented skin. She needed to make a honey-and-vanilla pound cake to go with dinner tonight.

Clearing her throat to cover her discomfiture, she backed up to note his neck size on her tablet, then stepped in front of him again. "I'm going to measure your chest next, okay?"

He nodded, his gaze gliding over her like a physical touch that made her glad she'd worn one of her better bras with the extra padding. Then they were touching for real, her chest pressed against his as she passed the tape behind him. Sure, she could have had him hold the start of the tape so that she could walk around him or he could spin, but that wouldn't give her the payoff of hugging him. Measuring, not hugging, she reminded herself. Yeah, that was it.

Then Cam placed his hands on her shoulders.

She looked up. No amusement lit his eyes. Instead something much more intense darkened them as he gave her shoulders a light squeeze. Then his gaze dropped, and she knew from his soft inhale that he was staring at her cleavage, which she didn't mind one bit.

It almost made her forget that she was supposed to be measuring his chest, not caressing it.

Chagrined, she stepped back slightly to take note of the number and add it to the list.

Pull yourself together, girl. You can't be flipping out like this on the first day of shooting. Too much is riding on this.

With a calming breath, she quickly and efficiently measured his waist, his arms, then the center of his back from neck to waist. So far, so good. Now all she needed to do was his seams.

Cam was one step ahead of her, raising one eyebrow as he said, "For the record, I'm not taking off my pants."

"Damn right you're not," she retorted. "That's between you and me."

"I'll be more than happy to give you a better measurement when we get home," he said, pulling her chair closer before retrieving his shirt. "Your chair should lower a little more. It'll make getting my inseam easier."

Good point. Using the chair would be a lot more elegant than getting on her knees on the shop floor, never mind the optics of her kneeling in front of Cam, fake boyfriend or no. Settling into the ergonomic seat, she pulled the lever to lower the chair as far down as it would go. It put her in an awkward placement, but it was better than the alternative.

She placed the start of the measuring tape at his natural waist. "Hold this here, please."

He complied, his expression tight. Was that anger, worry, or discomfort? Yeah, probably the latter. She had to remember that despite how she reacted to him, it didn't mean the feeling was necessarily reciprocated. Cam had good acting chops, but this situation wasn't something Cam had asked for. Having her all up in his junk taking measurements in front of an audience had to be the height of *I'm so over this.*

Not wanting to torture him longer than necessary, Kenya took note of his outseam numbers, then took the tape from him. She dangled the start of the tape next to Cam's foot, making a mental note of where his jeans stopped. Then she pressed the tape against his inseam, following it up the inside of his shin, his thigh, then up to his crotch.

Just look at the tape, nothing else. Just look at the tape, nothing else.

He adjusted his shirt, the hem long enough to conceal his zipper. Disappointed yet relieved, Kenya noted the measurement. "Okay, torture session done."

He helped her to her feet, his features relaxing. "Does this mean that it's time to return the favor?"

Oh hell no. She tossed her hair and dredged up a saucy grin. "Baby, they couldn't handle you sizing me up on national TV. Besides, I've been making costumes all this time on the show. I know my measurements."

There was no way she could stand docile while Cam ran a measuring tape all over her body. Pretending to be unaffected for Cam's sake while also pretending to be affected for her own sake was more pretending than she could handle, especially on day one. Somehow she'd find a balancing act that would work for all of them.

Eyes on the prize. She had to keep that first and foremost. All of this was a means to an end, nothing more than that. All she had to do was stay in the friend zone.

CHAPTER ELEVEN

Staying in the friend zone was bullshit.

Cam flexed his hands as he shut down his laptop. He'd come into the office to take care of the administrative tasks that he absolutely hated to do. Kenya had offered to take those chores back but she needed every extra second she could get for the costumes.

Frustration crawled through him like oil sludge. Frustration at the amount of work she'd taken on. Frustration at the rules that prevented him from helping as much as he wanted. And yes, the frustration of sleeping next to her for the last few nights and not being able to act on the red-hot lava of need that threatened to burn him alive.

"Stop being so fucking dramatic," he muttered to himself, pushing up his glasses to rub at his eyes. He couldn't help it, though he tried. A little less than a full week in, and the fake-boyfriend thing was wearing him down. What was the word for someone who was a glutton for punishment? Punk? Yeah, but that wasn't quite right. Something involving whips and chains and leather. Masochist. Yeah, that was the word.

He was a fucking masochist.

How else could he explain why he'd willingly stood still, fighting a boner while Kenya ran her hands all over him? He'd rubbed his dick raw in the shower fantasizing how that scenario could have gone if they'd been at home and nearly naked. Gah, he'd felt guilty about that and had tried to rein in his feelings while still putting on the required show. Pretending to be Kenya's boyfriend while pretending to not want to be her boyfriend felt like going through increasingly difficult levels in a game that had started with a suicide run.

He wasn't about to stop, though. Every touch, every hug, every kiss, every press of her body against his was a treasure, even if it was all fool's gold. As pathetic as it sounded, these fake moments with Kenya were better than none. He'd do his part to get them through these next few weeks and once the competition was over, he'd roll the dice and tell her how he really felt. This time, he hoped, he'd get the win.

But he had to get her through the competition first. Kenya had finally let him help her with the armor pieces, allowing him to trace some of the patterns on the foam sheets and stage them so that she could cut them. Dozens and dozens of pieces she'd carefully cut with a utility knife, only pausing long enough to sharpen the blade or replace it entirely. It was painstaking work. Attention to detail was critical, and he understood why she had wanted to focus on getting the Iron Man armor to the primer stage before starting on the Thanos pieces.

His eyebrows bunched as he eyed his phone. Paying the bills and watching the shop's bank balance decrease had taken longer than he'd thought. Since Kenya hadn't come to check on him, he assumed she was still deep in foam and would put up a protest if he suggested they stop for the day.

He eyed the camera Jane had given him. He could give Kenya a little more time by recording a diary entry, then go record Kenya's part. Hopefully, that would be enough to convince her to stop for the day.

He turned the camera on, then thumped his elbows onto the desk so that he could hold the device at the proper angle. "Hey, everybody, this is Cam. It's half past late, and we're still at the shop. Last I checked, Kenya was about done with cutting all of the Iron Man armor pieces. We got them all labeled so there won't be any mix-ups, and tomorrow we'll probably start the heating and molding process."

He leaned forward. "She's being such a trooper with this project. Cutting all that foam and making sure the angles are perfect so the pieces will fit together is no joke, and even though I've seen her do this a bunch of times, I'm still a little—okay, maybe a lot—awed at the magic she creates. I'm worried about her being overworked to make these deadlines, and this twenty-five percent rule is very frustrating. But I know Kenya, and I know she gives her all to whatever she does. It's part of why I love her so much."

He looked down, a self-deprecating laugh escaping his chest. It was what he was supposed to say, what he was supposed to pretend to mean. But every word he spoke was the truth, the truth for an audience of one who thought his reality show was nothing more than a fantasy.

"Anyway, I'm going to go check on her to make sure she's not buried beneath an avalanche of foam parts. See you next time."

He shut the recorder off, gathered his stuff, then closed up the office to return to the floor. Kenya was where he'd expected her to be, bent over her worktable. She was either deeply engrossed in her work or asleep because she didn't utter a sound when he approached her. "Kenya?"

She jerked, whatever she held clattering to the surface. "Dammit!"

Cam leapt forward at Kenya's soft curse. She held her left hand with her right, a glue gun emitting a trail of melted glue onto the newspaper-covered table. Her pained expression told him all he needed to know.

"Here." He grabbed his still-cold water bottle and pressed it to her hand. Her pained gasp ripped at him. "I think we've got some burn cream in the first aid kit. Be right back."

He raced to the stockroom, grabbed the kit, then ran back. He found Kenya slumped in her chair, her left hand propped on a piece of foam, the right cradling her head. Her eyes were closed but he could clearly see the exhaustion etched into her features.

"KeKe."

She jerked, then turned to him with a smile as he sat back down. "I think it's better now."

"You don't have to pretend to be fine with me," he retorted, opening the first aid box and finding the tube of burn cream. Thank God Mack was a stickler for keeping the kit fully stocked. "I know better. Let me see."

She only put up a small resistance when he took the water bottle and cradled her hand, held it beneath the bright task light. "I'm sure it's not a big deal. Like a sunburn."

"Have you ever had a sunburn?"

"Uhm, no." She gestured at herself, then to him. "I've seen you with one. You don't act like it's a big deal."

"First, you don't get sunburn because your sunscreen is SPF three thousand and you don't stay outside long enough to get burned. Second, I'm a guy. We always act like pain is no big deal unless it gets us sympathy points with our woman. Third, sunburns can hurt." He examined the bright red splotch on her left index finger where the dark brown of the back of her hand gave way to the beigey-pink of her palm. "Does this hurt?"

She parted her lips and he glared at her, daring her to lie. She frowned, then sighed. "Fine. I can still feel it."

Not wanting to let go of her, he used his teeth to unscrew the tube of ointment, then managed to squeeze out a drop before carefully applying it to her skin. He knew he'd overreacted, but the need to protect her had been ingrained in him since they were teenagers. It didn't matter that she did a damn good job of protecting herself without his help. If he could help her, keep her from getting hurt, he'd do it.

"Your hands are ice cold!"

"I was holding your water bottle," she pointed out.

He examined the backs of her hands. "And they're dry. Why are they so dry? Where's your lotion?"

She tried to pull back, but he refused to ease his grip. "In my bag," she finally said. "I didn't want to get oil on the foam."

He gritted his teeth to hold on to his temper. "How did you burn yourself?"

"With a hot-glue gun."

"Kenya."

She huffed. "I guess distraction and hot glue don't mix. I should have gotten up and walked around a bit when I started feeling tired."

Anger flared up, but he sucked it back down. Building one costume in four weeks was hard enough, but two? The production schedule was brutal, almost impossible without pulling sixteen-hour workdays. They were still early in the process and already dealing with strain.

He knew better than to demand that she stop or even take a nap in the office. Her commitment to the project and the schedule wouldn't let her back down without a fight, and he didn't want to fight with her, no matter how exciting that would be for the cameras. He tried a less confrontational tactic. "Maybe we should stop for the day."

She immediately shook her head. "But we still have so much left to do."

"I know, but we've already put in fourteen hours today. We're both tired and past the point where an energy drink will help."

"I like how you're saying we, but you mean me." Her attempt at a smile failed to form. "Let me finish this and record a diary entry—"

"I already took care of that." He glanced at her work surface, then back at her. "And don't think I don't realize that you're working ahead. According to your spreadsheet, you aren't supposed to work on my boots for another two days."

She gave that half shrug she did when she felt guilty about something. "I wanted to get ahead of our timeline. What's wrong with that?"

"KeKe." He softened his tone. "Nothing's wrong with that. But if you're pushing yourself past exhaustion and hurt yourself, there's a chance of making mistakes that could turn into setbacks, right?"

His heart thumped hard as tears glimmered in her eyes. "I can't afford setbacks," she whispered. "I can't lo—"

She bit off the words, glancing in the direction of the stationary camera before turning back, blinking rapidly to banish the tears. Then she gave him a half-hearted smile before unplugging her glue gun. "I think you're right. I'll be able to function better after some rest."

She was pretending again, but he wouldn't call her on it. Not when she'd agreed to leave. "Okay."

He stood, then helped her to her feet. "It's not a defeat, sweetheart," he whispered as he pulled her close. "It's not even a setback. We'll go home and crash, then kick ass in the morning."

Her arms encircling his waist was almost as perfect as her head resting on his shoulder. "You're right. Let's go home."

Home and showered and in her jammies, fatigue shredded into worry. Her mind simply would not let her think about anything other than everything that needed to be done in the ever-decreasing amount of time they had to finish. Maybe all she needed was a quick nap, and then she'd head back to the shop.

Cam entered the bedroom, frowning when he saw her sitting on the edge of the bed. "I thought you'd be asleep by now."

She turned to him. "Do you think there's enough room in the office for a folding cot? Or maybe even the stockroom?"

"If you're suggesting that you should sleep in the shop, I'm not going to say no."

Her mouth dropped open. "You're not?"

"I'm going to say hell no." He sat on the bed beside her. "We're on track. If you count the work you started on the boots, then we're slightly ahead of schedule. That means it's way too early to be running yourself ragged. Why are you pushing yourself like this?"

She wanted to confide in him, she really did. But she didn't want to burden him, or worse yet, confide in him only to have him not understand. "I can't lose. There's too much riding on this for me to fail."

"You said that in the shop, to me. You know, the guy who's supposed to be your partner in this, which also means sharing the stress and the burden?"

"I know." Guilt hunched her shoulders. How could she explain things without making it seem like she was shutting him out? The last thing she wanted to do was hurt Cam, but keeping all this inside was killing her.

"KeKe." He laced her fingers with his. "Is this something you need to talk to Janelle about?"

She gasped. "How'd you guess?"

"Maybe I'm just a woke white guy."

Choking back a laugh, she elbowed him in the side, then leaned against him. "Maybe you're just a really good friend."

He stiffened, then draped an arm about her shoulders. "Yeah. Maybe I am. You've got two best friends. It's not hard to figure out that there's stuff you talk to her about that you wouldn't tell me."

"It works both ways." She raised her head. "There's also stuff I can talk to you about that I don't tell her. And don't think I haven't noticed that you've never talked to me about any of your girlfriends."

He shuddered. "That would be . . . no. What kind of guy do you think I am?"

"The best kind."

"Well, there's your first mistake." He laughed as he stood, a hard edge to it leaching out the humor. "Why don't you give Janelle a call? I'm gonna go watch TV for a while."

Kenya watched him leave, but each step he took increased her unease. Something was off. She couldn't shake the feeling that she'd hurt him, even though he was the one who'd suggested that she call Janelle. Truth was, there were things that she could talk to Janelle about, Black woman to Black woman, that she would understand without explanation.

Maybe Cam wouldn't understand, but he'd surely empathize. They had shared their hopes and dreams and fears with each other for more than a decade. There was no reason to doubt that she could tell him this fear, and the pressure and stress that came along with it, or that he'd react in any way other than being supportive.

She had to be honest with herself. Talking through this fear would be so much easier with Cam's arms wrapped around her.

Padding out to the living room, she found Cam lounging on their couch, aimlessly flipping channels. He paused when he saw her. "That was quick."

"I didn't call her." She nibbled on her fingernail, realized what she was doing, then dropped her hand. She didn't want him to think she was mocking his habit, but she couldn't shake her unease, her fear, or the pressure building inside her. She needed an outlet. "I wanted to talk to you."

He stared at her for a long moment. Just when she thought he was going to reject her, he patted the spot beside him. "Come here. I'll be your sounding board."

She sat down, too keyed up to settle back. Instead, she clasped her hands together between her knees. "Like you guessed, it's more than the stress of the timeline or building the costumes."

"Neither one of us want to lose, but you said you *can't* lose. What did you mean by that?"

So much, more than she wanted to say. The softness of his voice urged her to continue. "I haven't visited any of the message boards since the show started because I figured they'd be nasty, and I didn't want to see that negativity while I was competing. But . . . I've gotten some messages across my channels and I know I shouldn't have read them once I saw the first line of text but sometimes you can't help it. Some of them are so vile and hate-filled . . ."

Cam reached over to gather her hands in his, prying her fingers apart. She gasped as blood rushed back into the tips. "I try not to let them get to me, just delete and keep it moving, but sometimes it sinks down into your spirit, and it affects everything, making me doubt myself, what I'm doing. I've gotta prove the haters wrong and winning will be the biggest F-you to them."

She drew in a shaky breath. "To balance that out, I've gotten some DMs and e-mails from other plus-size and Black cosplayers. Messages of support and how they're rooting for me because I'm representing them. I represent the girls who were told they were too fat to play a certain character. I represent the Black people who've been told by white people that they can't play a fictional character in a fantasy world created by Japanese people. I represent everyone who's been labeled the Angry Black Woman because they're talented, confident, and adverse to bullshit. I've been fighting being cast in that role on the show ever since they partnered me up with Amanda, who cried whenever anyone, especially me, said something to her. It's the role the producers wanted to cast me into from day one. It's a lot of pressure, and somedays it's so h-hard trying to do everything and be everything and I just—"

Her voice cracked on the last word. Cam surged forward, and Kenya found herself lying against him, his arms wrapped tight around her. Even though it was what she needed, she still tried to pull away. "I'm okay."

"No, you're not, and that's okay." He cradled her head against his shoulder. "You deserve to take a break."

"I can't afford to take a break," she replied, aware of the brittleness in her voice. "There's so much riding on this, on me winning—us winning. Money and publicity for your shop. Proving to the people who are rooting for me that someone who looks like me can do this, can come out on top. I have to prove I can do this, no matter what it takes. I'll just keep stress-eating gummy worms."

"KeKe." He stroked her cheek. "There's only so much biting the heads off gummy candy can do. You don't want to be the Angry Black Woman, I get that. But you don't have to be the Strong Black Woman either. You need to take a break before this breaks you."

The sound that escaped her balanced on a knife's edge between tears and laughter. She patted his chest. "You really are woke."

"You invited me to the cookout when we were thirteen," he reminded her. "Your parents taught me how to play spades. I better be woke."

She did laugh then, some of the pressure seeping away. "You're amazing, you know that?"

"I'm trying to be the best that I can for you, Kenya," he said then, his voice hoarse. "I hope you know that."

"I know." She buried her head into the crook of his neck and placed her hand over his heart, inhaling his scent, feeling the pounding of his heart beneath her fingertips. Her eyes slid closed as stress and fear slipped away, allowing sleepiness to take their place. "But I hope you know that you already are. I promise, I'm doing everything I can to be the best for you too."

"The most important thing you can do right now is remember that you're not alone in this. Maybe I can't know all the pressure you're under, but I can share some of it if you'll let me."

She relaxed against him with a sigh. "Okay."

She heard the television switch channels, then the theme music for one of their favorite shows, *Anubis Rising*, began to play. "Two months of episodes to go through, but it's just background noise right now," he said, one hand stroking down her back, soothing her. "If you want to cry, then cry. If you want to rage, then rage. If you just want to stay like this and breathe, then do that. No matter what you want to do to let it out, it's okay. I got you."

CHAPTER TWELVE

I *got you.*

It was the last thing Kenya had heard before falling asleep, and the first thing she remembered upon waking. The simple phrase resonated within her, amplified by Cam's arms wrapped around her, the warmth of his body beneath hers.

Oh. She froze, suddenly wide awake. They had shifted during the night and she was now cradled between his thighs, her head on his rib cage. He had draped his mother's quilt, the only thing he still had of hers, over them sometime during the night, creating a cocoon of comfort. Since her phone alarm hadn't gone off, she knew it was still early. But nature called. There was no way for her to move off him without waking him or brushing against a very obvious part of his anatomy.

Part of her didn't want to move. And that part was very loudly telling her that deciding on no sex with her cosplay boyfriend was the stupidest idea she had ever come up with.

She thought she'd prepared for everything when she began the cosplay of her life. Had dotted all the I's and crossed every T. She'd accounted for every possible contingency except for one.

Cam was fucking hot.

On an intellectual level, she knew Cam was fine. She'd been his best friend for half their lives. She'd witnessed his evolution from sullen teen to happy hottie. Now, however, it wasn't her intellect taking notice. Now her body tingled whenever there was less than a foot of space between them, when he looked at her a certain way. Now she found herself staring at his hands, the flex of his biceps, the way his ass fit his jeans. She'd taken to wearing padded bras so no one could look at her chest and know the effect that Cam had on her.

She gave as good as she got when it came to flirting. Sharing a bed with Cam had added a depth of intimacy between them that undoubtedly enhanced their fake relationship. Sleeping together without sleeping together? That was a level of torture she hadn't prepared for.

Last night, the talisman of reminding herself that they were friends had lost its power. After an emotional night in which he'd soothed her fears, it felt as if things had shifted. Her brain said "friends," but the rest of her said "with benefits." Lying here like this with him, sharing a bed and kisses and touches, they were well beyond the definition of friends. Why couldn't they move to Friends 2.0?

The stress of the competition hadn't disappeared overnight. In fact, things were bound to get worse before they got better. What better way for them to relieve some stress than with a little horizontal tango? It would be an improvement over quick but fleeting self-satisfaction in the shower.

Only one thing kept her from suggesting it, and that was the thought that he wouldn't go for it. Then again, he didn't have a problem with all the other intimacies, and his dick—practically nestled between her breasts—seemed to think it was a good idea. What if he was game? What would happen after that? How would they be able to go back to just friends? What if involving sex ruined their friendship beyond repair?

What if it was so good, she wouldn't want to go back to just friends?

God, she was too muddled to think about stuff like this without coffee, and they really needed to get back to the shop. She had to figure out some way to slide off him without waking him and embarrassing them both.

She raised her head—and found him already awake and staring at her. Caught, there was only one thing to do: brazen her way out. Planting her hands on either side of him, she summoned a saucy smile and a thick Southern drawl. "Why, Cameron Lassiter, is that for me?"

His eyes were clear as he stared at her cleavage, then back to her face. "Yes."

God. He meant it.

Whatever reaction Cam expected Kenya to make, inflicting bodily injury definitely wasn't in the top three.

She blinked several times, as if her brain had shorted out in the middle of processing his answer. Then her eyes rounded and she scrambled off him with a squawk of surprise. Unfortunately, she tangled herself in his mother's quilt, elbowed him hard in the junk, then fell to the floor.

He jackknifed upright, cradling himself as he tried to breathe through the pain. "Damn, girl," he wheezed, "that's a sharp elbow."

"Oh, God, I'm so sorry!" She managed to untangle herself and clamber to her feet. "Are you okay?"

"I'll live," he gasped, carefully swinging his legs down. The pain eased. "I might even still be able to reproduce."

"Eep!" Her eyes rounded even more and she jerked back a step. "I—I-uhm, I think I'm going to get dressed and head into the shop. We've got so much to do and I want to get a head start on shaping the pieces I already beveled."

He tried to stand, but his body wasn't ready for that yet. "Kenya, we need to—"

She raised her hands, backing up another step. "We'll talk after work, okay? In fact, I'll just—I'll just meet you there." She made a mad dash—for her old bedroom.

Well, shit. Cam sat back on the couch, then slammed his fist against the cushion. Why the fuck didn't he keep his mouth shut? Or better yet, returned her teasing with teasing of his own instead of the blunt truth she clearly wasn't prepared for?

He'd awakened before she had to discover that she had scrunched down until her head rested on his abdomen, arms circling his waist, her breasts framing his dick. The visual had hit him hard and his body had reacted in the only way it could.

Now, it was more than wanting Kenya to be his. It was a bone-deep need for her, for moving them to the next logical step, for waking up every morning after this just like this but after a night of giving each other everything they wanted.

He pushed to his feet and hobbled his way to their bedroom. He'd thought Kenya was leaning toward deepening their relationship, but that overboard reaction left him stymied with doubts. Why would the thought of them being sexually intimate freak her out like that? Did she find the thought gross?

No, he couldn't believe that. Not with the way she snuggled up against him while sleeping, or initiated displays of affection. They were already friends with part-time benefits. The time had come for them to promote their relationship to full-time.

He just needed to convince her of that.

As expected, Kenya was already gone by the time he got dressed. He sent her a text before starting his engine. DID U STOP 4 COFFEE?

It took forever for her to reply, although it was probably only seconds. FORGOT, AND WE DON'T HAVE ANY IN THE SHOP. MACK AND JAVIER ARE GIVING ME PUPPY DOG LOOKS. I CAN'T RESIST THE PUPPY DOG LOOKS. HALP ME, OBI-WAN.

He released a heavy sigh of relief. If she was cracking jokes via text, that was a good sign, right? He'd take it as a good sign.

Then he frowned as a negative thought clobbered the positive one. Maybe she was going to pretend that the morning hadn't happened, in which case he'd have to let her know that wasn't an option. After making that admission, there was no going back. OMW.

Miss Catherine helmed the counter when he arrived at Nubian Coffee. "Morning, Miss Catherine."

"Morning yourself, Cameron," she replied, wiping her hands on a towel before pulling an order pad from her brightly patterned apron pocket. "You want your regular order?"

"Yes, ma'am."

She wrote the order down, ripped the slip off, then slid it through the pass-through before ringing the bell. Then she poured a cup of coffee and handed it to him. "Y'all still have that show in your shop?"

"Yes, ma'am." He inhaled deeply, taking the aroma into his lungs. Their coffee was so good on its own that he rarely doctored it, and today, adding cream and sugar to it would take too long. "They'll be there for a few more weeks."

"Well, our profit margin thanks you," she said, her laughter so boisterous her braids swung like a curtain. No one knew how old Miss Catherine was, and no one dared to ask. Not even her husband, Mr. Nelson, knew, or so he said. She proudly claimed neighborhood auntie status and almost all the locals, himself included, considered the couple to be the de facto leaders of the community. No wonder, with the restaurant being the hub of the neighborhood even though it closed shortly after lunch.

He stepped aside so that another customer could place their order, a coffee and pastry to go. Miss Catherine gave him a sharp look after the customer left. "Kenya is a wonderful girl."

Her tone had him straightening his spine. "She is."

"Good spirit on that girl," Miss Catherine said, then speared him with a look. "You've got a good spirit too."

"Thank you, Miss Catherine," he said, sure he was about to receive a warning not to hurt Kenya.

"Must have been something when she claimed you on national television."

He decided to go with the truth, as if lying to Miss Catherine was a thing that could be done. "Best moment of my life."

She nodded. "I like y'all together. I like how both of y'all have big dreams that complement each other. You make a great team."

"I think so too." He just had to convince Kenya of that.

The service bell chimed. "Order up!"

Miss Catherine bagged up his order and placed the drinks, including a fresh coffee for him, in a drink carrier. "We're rooting for y'all, but I'm sure Nelson already told y'all that. And I'm not just talking about the competition either."

Cam smiled, the conversation and the coffee improving his mood. "I appreciate that, ma'am. I'll take all the well wishes I can get."

"You got them." Miss Catherine held up a hand when he pulled out his wallet. "I'll just put it on your tab."

He blinked in surprise. "We have a tab?"

"You do now. I know y'all have a lot on your plate with doing your regular work and the work for the show. We can settle up when the show is over."

"Thank you," Cam said, his voice thick. "We appreciate y'all more than you know."

Miss Catherine smiled as they touched elbows. "We know. Now get out of here and go win that show!"

CHAPTER THIRTEEN

Nervous energy wrapped around Kenya as she waited for Cam to arrive. The text exchange was a good sign, right? If he was mad, he wouldn't have asked her if she'd had coffee. Hopefully, her enthusiastic response would let him know she was sorry at least until she could apologize in private.

Guilt pressed in on her. She shouldn't have run out on him the way she had, but what else could she do when confronted with that blunt, one-word response?

Disbelief popped into her crowded mind to join the party. Why had she asked him that question? She'd been teasing, hoping to show that she was over her emotional outburst from the night before, and that his morning wood didn't bother her. But he—then he—

Called her bluff and sent her running like there was a seventy-five-percent-off sale at the craft store.

"God." She held her head in her hands. Not only had she run, she'd elbowed him in the junk and fell on her ass in front of him. What could he possibly be thinking about her now?

You'd know if you'd stayed and talked like he'd wanted.

No, no, no. There was no way she could have remained after her clumsy dismount and talked—about what? About how he looked like a whole snack and sounded like he wanted to be her only menu option?

Her heart leapt, plummeted, leapt again. She reached for the glass jar stuffed full of gummy worms, extracted one, then savagely bit off a chunk. It wasn't that unbelievable, was it? Cam was into girls, she was into guys. They were two adults who'd been sharing a bed for nearly a week and cuddling and canoodling for the cameras. It was almost inevitable that after some first-rate Level One intimacy, they'd think about leveling up.

At least until Cam had received an elbow to the Infinity Stones.

A flush crept up her neck to singe her ears. What if he had been interested, but wasn't now? They'd gone through this before in college, when he'd made a move after she'd had a bad breakup. She'd refused then because she didn't want to be a pity fuck, although that wasn't the excuse she'd given him then. What if he thought she was rejecting him again? How was she supposed to move past that and get them to Level Two?

Her thoughts were interrupted by the sound of the dock doorbell. "Y'all expecting a delivery this early?" she asked Javier and Mack.

"No."

"Okay, I guess it's the production crew." Arriving earlier than usual.

Javier looked up from his project. "You want me to go let them in?"

"Nah, I've got it." She stood, then stretched. "Cam should be here in a bit with breakfast, so keep a lookout."

"Aye aye, co-captain."

Her tension rose as she headed to the back, wishing Cam had arrived before Jane and her crew. It wasn't that she disliked being the solo focus of filming, but it did cause unease to slither through her guts. Not that she feared for her safety, even if Mack and Javier weren't there. Yet her intuition told her that Jane didn't have her best interests at heart; her priority would always be about the show and creating content that would drive viewers to watch. That meant Kenya had to be on constant guard, exhausting her emotional energy even more.

"Morning," she said brightly as she let them in. "You guys are early."

"We finished our production meeting ahead of time and decided to come in since you were here," Jane answered. "Is Cameron here yet?"

"Not yet," she answered cheerfully, making sure the door was secured. "He's stopping for coffee, so he'll be here in a bit."

Jane gave her a sharp look as they made their way to the shop floor. "You two usually arrive together," she noted. "Is everything all right?"

They must have seen her sitting with her head in her hands this morning. Combine that with Cam's absence . . . "We're fine. If you remember, Cam and I didn't arrive together on the first day either. It's nothing unusual. He's still got a business to run, you know?"

"Of course," Jane replied, her tone soothing in a way that Kenya instantly distrusted. "I just wondered because I saw a bit of last night's and this morning's footage but didn't get a video diary. Are you still upset?"

"Cam told me that he'd recorded one," Kenya explained. "I hope that's okay. I was tired and frustrated, not upset, and accidentally burned myself with the glue gun. Cam rightfully pulled the plug on our day. I'm always going to worry about our timeline. One careless mistake, like damaging a part, could put our deadline in jeopardy. Cam knows I'd hate that more than anything, so he was right to suggest the stop. I needed the reset."

She pasted on a bright smile. "Now I need him to get here with the coffee so I can be clear-headed enough to finish heat-molding these parts!"

Jane seemed unaffected by her explanation as she surveyed Kenya's workstation. "Is your timeline in jeopardy already? We're just at the end of week one."

Talking about the schedule was safer territory than talking about Cam, so Kenya dove in. Besides, she loved talking about her craft. "A lot can happen in the next couple of weeks, but we're still on schedule. We've got all of the parts of the Iron Man armor cut out and prepped for molding, and we're now ready to begin gluing the pieces together and testing for fit. We're also doing some of the finer detail work. Next week is priming Cam's armor for painting and cutting out my armor pieces while Cam works on the Arc Reactor. We're really excited about how . . ."

Her voice faded as she caught sight of Cam at the front entrance. Her shoulders immediately relaxed, and she skipped over to the door to let him in. "Hey." She wanted to say more, but her throat tightened, choking off the words.

He tossed a glance behind her then pasted on a smile. "Hey, Cosplay Queen." He held up the Nubian Coffee bag. "I come bearing gifts of sweet treats and coffee."

Oh, right, they had an audience. "Ooh." She made grabby hands as she reached for the cup with her name on it, took a deep inhale. "Oh my God, I think I love you!"

His smile froze for a moment, then loosened. "Are you talking to me or the coffee?"

"Hmm." She took a tentative sip. "I'll love you after I finish this cup."

"Ah, I see how it is." Cam snorted. "Well, I guess I'll leave you two alone, Your Majesty, so I don't get another knee in the junk for my trouble."

"Cam!" She couldn't believe he went there. She jerked back in surprised hurt, then saw him wink, then subtly incline his head. Right. Just making a joke. He was doing a better job of minding the film crew than she was. They couldn't make anything of it if she didn't give them anything to work with.

Despite Cam's joke, she still wasn't sure if things were good between them or not. She continued their routine, hoping he'd understand that she wanted to talk later, away from the cameras. "We can settle up properly later, when we get home. I believe our minions are waiting for their breakfast."

Cam shot a look at Javier and Mack, who were way too interested in their little drama. "A kiss before I go, my Queen, if you can tear yourself away from the Chalice of Righteousness?"

Was that a challenge? She cocked an eyebrow, and he cocked one right back. Oh, that was most definitely a challenge. Did he forget who he was dealing with? They hadn't had a real lip-to-lip kiss since the airport. Instead, they'd exchanged quick pecks on the cheek or forehead for the camera's sake. If she went along with this, they'd have to make it look good. But what if it was too good? She made a show of setting her cup down, then dropped her lids to half-mast and channeled her inner Eartha Kitt as Catwoman. "Now that you mention it, my coffee could use a little more sugar."

"As you wish."

With a devilish smile worthy of any dread pirate, he set his things down then hooked one arm around her waist. She slid her hands up his well-defined biceps to his shoulders then his cheeks.

He gripped her waist in both hands, pulling her snug against him. For a long moment they stared at each other, nose to nose, chest to voluptuous chest, as if daring the other to make the first move.

The Davenports didn't raise any cowards. With a quick glance to see where the camera guys were, Kenya parted her lips the same time that Cam did. She met his kiss with her own and it was immediately evident that neither intended for it to be simple, or simply friendly. He intended his kiss to remind her of his blunt declaration that morning, and she intended hers to tell him, *Game on.*

This kiss, their kiss, delicious and daring, searing and sexy, catapulted Cam out of the friend zone. Out forever. This kiss kicked a Cardi B playlist into repeat in her head.

"Grab an office, you two!" Javier called.

They stopped but didn't break apart, still holding each other. Cam's ears and cheeks were red, but the look in his eyes told her he didn't flush out of embarrassment. A lot of her nude lipstick painted the rim of her coffee cup, but the rest of it now shaded Cam's lips.

"I'm gonna report you to HR," Mack joked, holding up his phone. "That went way over the allotted time limit."

How long were they kissing for? Long enough for her to forget that she had a competition to win. "I *am* HR," she retorted. Did her voice sound breathy? "It's time for all of us to get back to work."

Cam blinked at her. "I forgot what I was going to do today."

She couldn't remember what the hell she was doing before he'd arrived. She tried to recall which phase they were in on her spreadsheet, what order he'd slated for himself from the shop's work list. "Uhm, maybe printing the pieces for the Arc Reactor after finishing the Beaumont order?"

"Yeah. Right. Printing the reactor. Beaumont order." He didn't move.

"And I'm going to work on my boots before I go back to piecing your leg armor together." She didn't move either.

"You guys know you have to let go of each other to actually get work done, right?" Javier yelled. "Do that crap on your lunch break!"

This time Kenya did flush and forced herself to take a step back. Cam did too. With distance came a little bit of clarity, and they both erupted with laughter. "It's a good thing the printer's on the other side of the shop. I'm going to have a hard time focusing as it is!"

He snorted. "You expect me to have sympathy? I'm just going to have a hard time."

"Cam!" She swatted him with another laugh.

"I'm going, I'm going! Enjoy your coffee."

Only when he wandered off was she able to take a deep breath. She glanced at the camera, then made a show of fanning herself. *Hate on that, haters.*

Returning to her workstation, she bent her head to focus on turning the retro platform boots she'd scrounged from a vintage store into stompers worthy of the Mad Titan. The only thing they had going for them was that they were black platforms that stopped at the ankles. Everything else she'd have to create, including the shafts.

First, she covered each one with layers of duct tape that she could then cut off to make a pattern. She'd use the pattern to trace onto stretchy black fabric that she'd sew into a sleeve so that it would be easier to attach foam to. The rest would be covered by the shin guards. She didn't get very far before Jane came up to her. "Wow, that sure steamed our lenses up!"

Kenya refrained from giving her the stink eye, just barely. She smiled and shrugged instead. "I guess we did get a little carried away. It happens sometimes."

"I guess so, when the relationship is still new like yours." Jane released a light but conspiratorial laugh, then leaned in. "Seeing the way you two are together, it's hard to imagine that you've been best friends for so many years and never once crossed the line. How did you manage to remain just friends with a hottie like that?"

The hell? Kenya frowned and drew back before she could school her features. She wasn't friends with the producer, casual or otherwise. She certainly wasn't going to gush to her about Cam. "We've been friends since we were thirteen, and that friendship is important to both of us, and it's even more important now that we're more, because it enhances everything we are now. We love each other, but more than that, we respect and trust each other."

She picked up a pair of extremely large shears, then turned back to the boots, hoping Jane would get the hint. There was no way she was going to let the production team harsh her mellow and spoil that sweet, tingly moment she'd had with Cam.

Cam gathered the reactor parts and made his way back over to the workstation. The producer had finally left Kenya to her work, but he wondered what their conversation had entailed. Kenya hadn't looked happy, and that was unacceptable.

He wanted her to be happy. He wanted her. He wanted so many things he had to keep those wants buried down deep. He'd show her more when she considered him more than a friend.

"Looks like you're making good progress," he said as he joined her at the worktable. "Have you tried walking in those yet?"

"I know they fit," she answered, relaxing into a smile. She held up one of the boots, eyeing the thick sole critically. "I haven't tried walking around in them, though."

"You wanna give them a try now? I can help you."

"Sure."

She bent over to unlace her hot-pink Timbs while he knelt in front of her. He noted the casualness of her attire, dark jeans and a fuchsia V-neck T-shirt depicting a grumpy unicorn. He also noted the way the mythical animal's horn pointed right at her cleavage like a neon sign saying *look here*.

So, he looked. Looked and lusted and pretended like he wasn't doing either. If he tipped forward, he'd be nose-to-horn with that unicorn. He'd also be within knee-to-the-chin range, so instead he focused on helping her exchange her Timbs for the platform monster boots, rose to his feet, then offered her a hand up.

The boots gave her a three-inch height advantage. It also gave him a unicorn horn advantage, which he wasn't going to complain about. He stepped back from her, still holding her hand. "Let's see you strut your stuff, sweetcheeks."

She blew him a raspberry, then took a tentative step forward, followed by another. "I think I'm getting the hang of this. Let go of my hand now."

He did, then watched her prance around their work area like a newborn fawn. Her laughter rang out like a bell. "Look at me, doing my Thanos strut!"

"Good. Now let's see you sashay your way to the front counter."

She turned toward the front of the shop, catching sight of the courier who'd just entered. She was easy to spot with her bouquet of bright pink flowers and a large black gift box tied with a matching pink bow.

Kenya turned back to Cam, her mouth a rounded *O*. It pulled a smile from him as easily as a hot knife through butter. If little gestures rewarded him with big smiles, he'd shower them down on her every day. He nodded, urging her to go on.

Jane sidled up next to him, her cameraman behind her like a one-eyed shadow as Kenya strutted to the counter to accept the vase of pink flowers and the box of gummy snacks. "Looks like you know just what to do to get Kenya to forgive you."

Cam suppressed a groan and gritted his teeth. He wondered if the producer for the other contestant asked leading questions in an effort to dig up nonexistent dirt. "I don't need Kenya to forgive me for anything. This was just a way to boost her spirits and show my appreciation for all the hard work she's done to get this far."

"She did seem pretty stressed last night."

"You try building two separate costumes in the time frame we have. It's a helluva lot of stress for anyone. Luckily, we balance each other out. I'm calm when she's stressed, and she's calm when I'm stressed. It's part of why we work so well together."

A delighted squeal snagged his attention. The courier had gone, and Kenya had opened the black box. He knew what it contained: a collection of stress-relieving gummy snacks and others of her favorite treats. And a card.

Ignoring the producer beside him, he focused on Kenya as she opened the envelope, then pulled the card out. He lifted his thumb to his lips to chew on the nail, awaiting her response as she read the words he'd had written: *Sweet treats for the sweetest woman I know. Remember, you got this. And I got you.*

Her eyes blazed like stars as she looked at him as if he were the best thing in her entire world. At that moment he believed her. And if he hadn't already been in love with her, he would have fallen hard when she stumbled into his arms, pressed her cheek against his, and whispered, "I love you, Cam."

It didn't matter that she didn't say she was *in love* with him. He'd pretend that she did and enjoy the moment.

The moment didn't last long. A melodic chime had several of them reaching for their phones. Jane held hers aloft. "Kenya, I've got a request from the executive producer. He wants me to get footage of you and Cameron at home."

Cam and Kenya exchanged glances, then looked back at the producer. "What?" they asked in unison.

She glanced at her phone again, then gave them an earnest expression Cam didn't buy. "Ben and his husband are working at their house, so they also had some domestic scenes in their dailies that the EP feels will resonate with our audience. Since you and Cameron are also a couple, he thinks our viewers would like to see you two interacting in a domestic setting as well."

Kenya faced them. Although her expression was as placid as a still lake, he could see the worry in the slight tightening of her lips. He was worried as well, but this was why they'd shuffled things around last weekend. They were as prepared for home filming as they could possibly be.

"Think of it as an extended video diary," Jane suggested. "We'll only need me, Ian, and our sound tech inside. My AP will be in the production van."

"That's a good idea," Cam said, threading his arm around Kenya's waist. "You've got a lot of work to do, gluing the Iron Man armor together. If you're planning to work late, I would feel better if you do that at home."

"You have a point," she said, the flatness of her tone indicating that it wasn't a point she agreed with.

He gave her a reassuring smile. "I'll help you pack everything up and get it loaded. The sooner you get home, the sooner you can finish."

"Okay." She nodded in acceptance. "Will you be coming home too?"

"I wish I could, sweetheart, but I've got an emergency rush job to do before I can call it quits for the day. They agreed to a premium rush fee and everything. I'll try to be home for a late dinner."

"You'd better," she chided. "I spotted a couple of jars of my dad's homemade tomato sauce in the pantry earlier this week, so I'm going to make spaghetti."

"Now that's what I call motivation." He leaned closer. "You got this, just like every other challenge they've thrown at you. Be you and be awesome. I'll be home as soon as I can."

CHAPTER FOURTEEN

Anxiety performed a step show in her gut as Kenya led Jane and a small crew into the apartment. Anxiety and a good deal of protectiveness. This was her and Cam's safe space and they carefully curated who came over to hang out. Maybe she could get one of her friends to bless and smudge her place when filming was done.

"So, welcome to our humble abode," she exclaimed brightly, balancing the large but lightweight box of foam parts on her shoulder with one hand, and pulling her travel crafting bag with the other. She made her way through the main living area to the dining room. "This is where I usually work when I'm at home. Is this enough room for y'all to set up your stuff?"

"We'll make it work," Jane said, surveying the area. "Ian, let's put the light kit here. Emily, let's stage sound here and the monitor here. Kenya, if you'll sit at the far end, that will give us plenty of space to block the shot."

"All right." As long as she could focus on the project, she could handle this. She arranged the disparate pieces of the armor on the table along with her adhesive and safety equipment, including goggles and a respirator. "You might not want to get too close if I have to use the rotary tool," she explained, holding it up. "Using the rotary tool to bevel the edges is easy at the shop with a modified shop vac to capture the dust. If I have to use it here, I can't promise that there won't be some particulates flying."

"We've got our masks if we need them," Jane said, "and Ian will be able to zoom in from his position with no problem."

"All right. The powder room is just past the laundry room there. I'm going to work on my pasta sauce while y'all finish setting up. I'll also make some coffee in case someone wants some."

"Thanks. Coffee would be great."

She headed for the kitchen, dodging equipment cases as she went. After washing her hands and setting a full pot of Kona blend to brewing, she started on the meat sauce, sautéing pre-diced garlic and onions before adding ground Italian sausage and spices. Thank goodness they'd done grocery shopping last Sunday for ingredients for quick and easy meals, otherwise they'd be hitting whatever fast-food joint was still open by the time they left the shop.

Her mind whirled as she drained the sausage, then added in diced tomatoes, more spices, a healthy dose of red wine, and the jar of her father's homemade sauce. He could make a killing at a local farmers market if he wanted to, selling pasta sauces and salsa made from his own backyard garden. Instead, he preferred to have it as a hobby, puttering around the backyard on the weekends with Cam's help.

Sometimes Kenya thought her father had started the garden simply to give Cam another reason to be at their house on the weekend. Yard work had certainly helped him work off some of the resentment he'd felt toward his father. In time, he had come to enjoy working in the garden and harvesting the produce as much as her father did.

Even she had taken a break from her comics and costumes for a couple of hours just to spend time outside with her dad and Cam.

Spending time with Cam had been her favorite thing to do for years. It didn't matter what the activity was—working, watching anime, playing games, sleeping, or just sitting together in silence— if they were together, it was always quality time. Now they were going to take that quality time up a notch, and Kenya was pretty sure it was going to be her new favorite way to spend time with Cam.

"You're smiling," Jane observed. "Is this Cameron's favorite dish?"

Kenya blinked, so deep in her thoughts she hadn't noticed Jane and Ian step into the kitchen. Jane had said she wanted to shoot some domestic scenes, but Kenya didn't think she'd meant cooking. "It is," she answered, "especially when we have this sauce made from tomatoes and herbs from my father's garden. It's my way of thanking him for the flowers this afternoon."

The fuchsia flowers and gummy candy had been just the distraction she'd needed from her seesawing thoughts, but the note card he'd given her had been everything, softening something deep inside her. She was ready to act on the promise of that kiss.

Well, maybe not completely ready. She still needed to give Jane good footage and kick them out the door before she could do her pre-sex ritual: shower and shave, pamper and perfume with the honey-and-vanilla-infused shea butter products they both loved. Just to see his expression, she'd break out her hot-pink, black polka dot panties and matching bra.

"You guys are still in the brand-new stage of your relationship," Jane observed as she retrieved one of the mugs Kenya had staged along with cream and sweeteners on the counter next to the cofe feepot. "Hot and heavy."

"Well, we haven't seen each other in two months," Kenya re-

minded her, longingly staring at the dark brew. She needed a caffeine hit, but she never had food or drink during fabrication time.
A second of an accidental spill could ruin hours of a build or even
force a restart. No way could she afford to be that careless. "We
have to make up for lost time."

After placing the sauce on the back burner to simmer on low,
Kenya returned to her makeshift work area, taking her seat so that
the crew could test the sound and lighting. Jane wasn't finished with
her questions. "What made you decide to make the move from
friends to lovers?"

"The time was finally right," she answered, wondering if she
needed to touch up her makeup to combat shine. She'd had to do that
herself while filming in LA, because the powder they used reduced
her skin to a chalky vampire look. Inconvenient, since she'd never
cosplayed a vampire during the show. "We were both single and in a
place where we could move our relationship to the next level."

"When did you know you wanted to be more than friends?"

Kenya hesitated. She certainly wasn't about to share the elbow-
to-the-junk incident, or the not-quite-slow burn caused by sleeping
beside Cam every night. "I'm not really sure. We've been friends
and basically inseparable for years. Those years cemented our love
for each other. The being in love part? That was more subtle."

"Who made the first move?"

"Cam did." She laughed. "When he decides to go in, he's all in."

She picked up a piece of the right shin guard. "He's . . . I really
have a hard time coming up with different words to describe how
wonderful and amazing he is. I respect him for starting his business
and admire him for how hard he's worked to make it a success. He's
dedicated, focused, driven, but willing to step back when necessary.
Considerate, funny, and gorgeous, and he makes me feel like a
queen. He flips all the switches. All of mine, anyway."

She laughed again, this time in embarrassment for waxing poetic about Cam's virtues more personally than she'd intended. "Anyway, I should probably get to work. These parts aren't going to glue themselves together."

"All right." Jane studied her monitor. "Everything looks good here. Why don't you start by telling us what you're about to do?"

"Okay." She waited a moment to center herself, then began. "Now I'm going to start gluing the pieces of my foam armor together. For this, I use cement glue in a small applicator bottle."

She applied a line of adhesive to an edge she'd already beveled and smoothed at the shop, using a piece of scrap foam to spread the glue into an even layer on the edge. She repeated the process on the second piece. "With this adhesive, I wait until it's dry, which thankfully doesn't take that long, then press the edges together to form the seal. I'll do this four thousand seven hundred and fifty-eleven more times until I'm done."

It was an obvious exaggeration, but that was how it seemed. Ignoring the crew, she fell into focus, working around the table like a production line, taking her time to match the seams together as perfectly as she could. Once the foam parts were stuck together, they were stuck together and couldn't be separated without destroying the foam.

Because of the curves created by the beveling, a few of the seams tended to pop in places. Those she fixed by applying a bonding compound, similar to how car mechanics filled in dents. Once dry, she'd go back with her rotary tool to smooth the seams. The seams would be nearly invisible once she applied the Plasti Dip as primer, but that wasn't a step she had to worry about tonight. Priming would happen behind the shop with plenty of ventilation to be safe from the fumes.

She lifted her head as the apartment door opened, then Cam stepped inside. "Honey, I'm home!"

Kenya laughed, her stress instantly easing. "You're so silly," she said, grinning as she got up to meet him. "Did you finish that order?"

He met her halfway, pulling her in for a hug. "No, dammit." He sighed into her hair. "I still need to finish it, but I wasn't going to miss spaghetti night. I'll go back to the shop after dinner."

"Oh." It was already late. If enough work was left that he had to go back to the shop to finish fabricating the part, that easily meant a couple of hours at the minimum.

"How's the assembly going?"

"The legs are done, and so is the left arm. I still need to add the hook-and-loop fasteners to them after I finish the right arm. Then I'll start on the chest and back pieces." She probably should have started that first, but she'd wanted to wait until Cam came home so she could make sure the chest fit him properly.

Girl, you didn't need him while assembling the leg armor. Just admit you wanted the opportunity to touch him.

"Sounds like you have a long night ahead of you, too."

"Yeah." Which meant they wouldn't be leveling up tonight. "Well then, the least I can do is send you back with a full belly."

"But not too full." He stepped back, patting his stomach. "I don't want to go into a food coma while I'm working."

"All right. Why don't you go wash up while I finish making dinner?"

"Okay. I'll come back to help when I'm done."

She turned for the kitchen, then stopped when she caught sight of Jane, Emily, and Ian. They sure could be quiet when they wanted to. "Do you guys want to eat with us? There's enough spaghetti to go around. I'll make a salad too."

"Yes, please!" Emily piped up, but Jane shushed her before answering.

"Thank you for the offer, but I'll just order something for us."

"Well, if you're sure, I can give you some recs of places we like to order from if you want."

Cam joined them as she placed a pot of water on to boil. "Do we have any of that garlic toast?" he asked as he opened the freezer door.

"Yep. Should be in the drawer."

"Got it." He held it aloft. "Are we making enough for five?"

"No," Jane said.

"Yes," Kenya said, then turned to the producer. "You're our guests, and my parents would flip their collective lids if we let you eat takeout. Does anyone have some food restrictions? I should have asked earlier."

"Uhm . . . no."

Jane was clearly taken aback, causing Kenya to hide her smile. It was kind of fun to see the producer that way after several days of being on edge around her. Still, the manners her parents had taught her were deeply ingrained, and she didn't need to add to her list of perceived failures in their minds.

"We would be sitting down eating before your order gets here," she pointed out. "Besides, the sooner we finish, the sooner we can get back to work, and the sooner we can all finish and crash, right?"

Jane threw up her hands. "I surrender! Logic wins. Where did you say the guest bathroom is?"

Cam pointed it out while Kenya added pasta to the now-boiling water. Together they started on the salad, when Emily spoke up. "Thanks again for dinner. Is there another bathroom I can use?"

There were two, one in her room and one in Cam's. Since Jane hadn't returned and Emily was doing the bathroom shuffle, Kenya relented. "You can use the one in my old room, just down that hallway."

"Thanks!"

Cam eyed Ian. "You probably should have jumped the line."

"I'm used to it, so it's cool. I really appreciate you feeding us like this."

"Welcome to Southern hospitality," Cam said, then grinned. "Now you know another reason why I fell for my girl."

Kenya bumped him with a laugh. "You're already getting fed, mister. No need to butter me up more. Besides, there's no time to make a dessert."

"You'll just have to make it up to me later," he teased. "After all, between that green-colored pasta and the sauce, I'm pretty sure I'm over my daily requirement of vegetables."

"Smart-ass." She retrieved a grater and made it rain Parmesan into a bowl as he staged the bread, salad, pasta bowls, and utensils buffet style.

"Since the dining room table is covered in foam, we can all eat here," Cam suggested, pointing to the small kitchen table. "I think we'll all fit, as long as no one minds it being cozy."

They carried everything over to the table, sat down, said grace, then dug in. "Mmm." Cam closed his eyes on the first mouthful. "I was looking forward to this. You have the best vegetable-delivery system ever."

His compliments always made her smile, because she'd never had to question the motivation behind them. "I expect you to return the favor tomorrow with that chicken teriyaki thing you make."

"Ah, the first real meal I learned to make when I got tired of food that came in cans or cartons. Thank goodness I never fed you any of those earlier versions."

"I would have eaten it." Because it would have meant that he'd invited her over to his house. Those invites had been rare, but she'd understood. Cam's father would have never been nominated for Dad of the Year, and while he'd never been physically abusive, the emotional toll on Cam had hurt her heart. She was glad that she'd been able to share her parents with him, then and now.

Jane looked up from her salad. "If you guys normally eat in here, why didn't you convert your dining room into a work space, Kenya?"

Right. Never let your guard down, KeKe. Seeing Cam's frown, she quickly explained, "We like to have our friends over for dinner and old school board games a couple of times a week. It's usually more than four of us, and it would be a pain to have to pack everything up. That's why I work in my old bedroom."

"I saw some of your costumes," Emily piped up. "Your work is awesome."

"Thank you," she managed to say, concealing her unease at the thought of Emily examining her stuff. She was sure Jane would demand all the details when they left.

Or she wouldn't wait and would go right to the source. "So you guys aren't sharing?"

"Ma'am," said Cam, "maybe I'm too Southern, but that's a really rude question for a guest to ask in a host's home. I thought y'all were here to work, not do an exposé."

"It's just part of rounding out Kenya's contestant profile," Jane explained, her expression innocent. "It's my job to ask the questions and get the answers."

"I wonder if Ben's profile is going to be as thorough as Kenya's is," Cam said then, an obvious edge to his tone. "I'd really be interested in knowing that."

Kenya dropped a hand to Cam's thigh. It was as tight as his jaw, letting her know he was moments from kicking the crew out, which meant she'd have to stop work for the night. The idea of falling behind so early in the build made the spot between her shoulder blades itch.

"My bad for not giving you guys a tour, but the contract only specified filming in the area I'm working in," Kenya reminded Jane. "I figured that meant that private areas would remain private and off-limits. But if it helps, I didn't move all of my stuff into Cam's bedroom and bath because I have a lot of stuff, and there's no need to overwhelm the space when I can walk down the hall. I'm sure Emily can testify that my toothbrush wasn't on the counter in my old bathroom, right, Emily?"

The brunette squeaked. "It's not."

Kenya poured extra sugar into her smile. "Hope that helps."

Cam turned to Kenya before Jane could respond. "What's your plan for Saturday? I forgot to look at your production schedule before coming home."

"I have Saturdays set as half days for now and Sundays off for our usual church and dinner with my parents, but I may have to take that day too if I get behind. What's up?"

"What if we go out to Game and Flame instead? We could take a break from costume building and hang out, play some games, and you can catch up with everybody."

She'd been so focused on the competition that she didn't know what day of the week it was. They usually had a standing hangout with their expanded group of friends at Game and Flame, a bar and grill that catered to gamers and game fans of all types.

"I still want to do the half day, but it would be great to see everyone again."

"Awesome. I'll set everything up then."

They finished the meal, the conversation moving away from the personal to the generic. Emily volunteered to help with cleanup and Kenya let her, ready to start the second phase of filming so the production crew could leave. Then she'd Febreze the place like rain.

Cam grabbed her hand. "If y'all will excuse us, I want to say good-bye to my girl in private."

They went to their bedroom. Cam shut the door, paused, then led her into the walk-in closet, shutting the door behind him. "That was straight-up bullshit."

"Yes, it was, but we handled it."

"You handled it. I was ready to literally toss people and equipment out the door."

"But you didn't." She pulled his hands down, entwining their fingers so he wouldn't stress-chew his nails. "I count that as a win."

He stared down at her, anger held in check. "I don't want to leave you alone with them."

"That part you're making, it's important, isn't it?"

"Yes." His fingers curled against hers. "Yes, dammit."

"Then you need to go back and finish it. I'll be okay."

Reluctance pulled at his features, urging her to soothe him. "I will be okay," she repeated. "I think we one-two punched the wind out of their sails. I'm going to get to a good stopping point and send them on their way. I think they're limited to how many hours they can work each day anyway."

"Okay." A minute amount of tension left his shoulders. "I'll be home as soon as I can but call me if you need me."

"Nope. I'm going to let you focus on your work, and you're going to let me focus on mine." She released him, then stepped back. This wasn't the way she'd wanted the night to go for either of them, but she'd play the hand she had been dealt.

"Like you always say, do what you have to do to do what you want to do." He blew out a breath, then plastered on a smile. "We can do this."

Yes, they could. It was the only thing they could do.

CHAPTER FIFTEEN

Girl, look at you all glowing and grinning!" Janelle exclaimed as she sat down next to Kenya. "I know a happy and sexually satisfied woman when I see one."

"That's because you stared at yourself in the mirror," she retorted. Thanks to filming, nearly working around the clock on costumes, and an emergency order that the shop couldn't refuse, she and Cam hadn't had time to talk about the sexual tension rising between them, much less act on it. In fact, the few bits of sexual satisfaction she'd achieved had been half-hearted and one-handed.

She wiggled her eyebrows, ready to be distracted by someone else's love life. "Bringing your man to game night? Y'all must be serious!"

Janelle waved a perfectly manicured hand. "It's too early. I don't have serious relationship slated in my long-range plans for another two years."

Kenya followed her friend's gaze to see Janelle's boyfriend, Dev, and Cam competing against their friends Rachel and Sam in a hot new game called Legendsfall. The latter duo seemed to be winning. No surprise there, since Sam was on her way to becoming a professional gamer.

Yet Janelle wasn't watching the gameplay, and the expression she wore spoke volumes of poetry. "Life happens, and it has a way of fucking with our long-range plans," Kenya pointed out. "I'm going to guess that love does that, too."

Janelle exhaled, but she didn't deny it. Her eyes widened as if she'd just had a major revelation. "He wants me to go with him when he goes back to New Delhi to visit his family."

"Girl, what?"

Everyone turned at Kenya's shout. Both Cam and Dev wore matching expressions of concern. In unison, Kenya and Janelle waved them off with matching smiles of reassurance, and they turned their attention back to the game.

Kenya turned back to Janelle, dropping her volume to a whisper. "Girl. What?"

"Yeah." Shock layered the happiness in her expression. "Not only would it be our first real vacation together, but he wants me to meet his family. His entire family."

"*Girl*. What?" Shock pressed Kenya into the back of the love seat. She sat upright, then reached for her drink to take a healthy sip, and asked the question that needed to be asked. "Do they know?"

"Yeah. When we became Instagram official, he sent them pictures and my profile info, so I'm sure they mined the heck out of it. His parents . . . they want to FaceTime with us this weekend."

"Ohmygod." Kenya bounced in her seat, then grabbed Janelle in a hug. "I'm so happy for you!"

"Thanks?"

The uncertainty in that one word made Kenya put her enthusiasm on pause. Of all the words one could use to describe Janelle, *uncertain* never made the list. "Do you not want to meet them?"

"I think I do." Janelle sighed. "Once I recovered from the thought of having to trash my long-term plans, I liked the idea of re-forming them to include Dev. He's smart, warm, funny, kind, sexy, considerate, gorgeous, proactive, and . . . he ticks off almost all the boxes on my potential-partner checklist. He made it easy to fall for him."

The fact that Janelle had already readjusted her life plan for the man proved just how serious their relationship was. "Okay, so what's with all of this hesitation? This isn't like you at all. Is it because it seems like things are moving too fast?"

"That's the thing. It doesn't feel fast." Janelle turned on the love seat, hiking up her knee. "It feels like I, like I recognize him or something. The connection's that deep."

Whoa. "Something tells me there's a 'but' coming up."

Janelle nodded. "I haven't told my parents about him yet."

"Oh. *Oh.*" Kenya sat back, letting the information wash over her. "Do you think they'll have a problem with him?"

"I don't know. He's not Black, but we're the same shade of brown. He's not Christian, but we both have faith. We both value family, and that's important to my family. Mom might be okay. Dad will be the wild card because no one's good enough for his baby girl. My brothers will give him a hard time just because they're jerks. Once they know about him, they'll insist on meeting him on a Sunday, preferably before a Sunday service. For all I know, his family might have issues with me for the same reasons."

She pushed one finger against her wrinkled brow, then sighed again. "I didn't account for this. I didn't expect this to become serious, but afterglow makes you say stupid things."

"What stupid things?" Kenya didn't shout it, but the shock level was the same. "Stupid things like the L-word stupid?"

"Yeah," Janelle answered with a weak laugh. "Took us both by surprise, but then we looked at each other and said it again. And again, it just felt right."

She laughed again, a softer sound. "My carefully planned life is all upended because he wanted to ask me follow-up questions from a panel I participated in at a tech conference. The Q&A became drinks at the bar, then dinner. After the conference we kept in touch through messages and late-night chats. Once I realized I had more fun talking to him than I did being with my ex, I became happily single."

She shook her head. "I should have realized then, but I was completely clueless. When he told me he had a job offer with a firm here in Atlanta, I was thrilled for him and for us and I actually flew to California to help him celebrate and oh my God, I don't know who I am anymore."

"Sounds like you're a woman in love."

"I'll take your word for it, especially now that you're finally with your true love."

An automatic denial perched on Kenya's lips, ready to take flight, but she caged it in time. For all her reassurances to Janelle, her only real-life point of reference for being in love was her parents' forty-plus-year marriage. They'd had a few arguments over the years but they still flirted outrageously with each other and even went on dates, dressing up and stepping out.

For herself, she'd never been "in" love. Cam was her best friend, and she loved him dearly. She had no doubts he felt the same. That made it easy to pretend to be more with him, pretend so well that all their friends gathered tonight had congratulated them on "finally" becoming a couple.

Technically speaking, they *were* a couple, but they were a friends-with-benefits couple. A Friends 2.0 couple. At least, they would be once they did the do.

Maybe it was a sign that they shouldn't try turning their fake relationship into the real thing. Yes, it would make it easier to deal with Jane and her crew, but it would also complicate things at a time when she didn't need any more complications. There would be time for all that after the competition ended.

That didn't mean she couldn't live vicariously through her bestie. "Well, if you're going to take my word for it, I'll say that you look deliriously happy. I'm guessing that the reason for that is Dev."

"You're right. I am, and he is." Janelle's gaze was as soft and starry-eyed as any joyful anime character.

Her joy made Kenya smile. "I think your parents love you and want you to be happy. Let them see him through your eyes. If he makes you as happy as you seem, I think they'll have no problem with your relationship."

"I'm gonna name it and claim it." Janelle made a grabbing motion with her hand. "I should have told them about Dev a while ago."

"I just want to know one thing."

"What's that?"

Kenya wiggled her eyebrows. "Are you going to have two weddings like Nick and Priyanka?"

Janelle choked on her drink. "Girl, we're not anywhere near that, even if we've said the L-word. Seriously, there are so many things we haven't talked about, including who should move in with who. We can't even begin to plan stuff like that until we meet each other's families."

Janelle's parents, like Kenya's own, had a certain vision that they wanted for their daughter. Unlike Kenya's, Janelle's dreams dovetailed with theirs. Kenya was willing to bet neither side would have issues with their child's choice of a partner. Janelle was good people, and Dev seemed to be as well. "I don't think you have anything to worry about. Your parents love and trust you."

There must have been an edge to her tone because Janelle threw her a quizzical look. "Are you having issues with your parents?"

Kenya snorted over the rim of her drink. "When am I not having issues with my parents?"

Janelle rolled her eyes. "True, but it's been a week since you told them about you and Cam. Do they have a problem with your relationship? Or with Cam?"

"No, they love Cam. Sometimes I think they love him more than me." She laughed to coat the bitterness of her words. "If anything, they're worried that I'm putting too much on his shoulders, considering he's helping me with the contest and running the shop."

"They still aren't happy about the competition, even with you being a finalist?" Janelle asked, incredulous.

"They aren't unhappy. They just wish I wasn't in it, or that it was over so I can focus on a real career." She added finger quotes when she said the word *real*.

Janelle twirled the tiny straw in the remnants of her drink, her expression concerned and considering. "So what are you planning to do when this is over?"

"When we win, we'll put the money into the shop, and I'll be able to take on commissions, maybe even full-time. The publicity from the show helps with that, but the prize money will help even more."

"But . . . what if the competition doesn't go the way you want?"

The question cut, even though it was a perfectly natural one to ask. "Et tu, Brute?"

"What?"

Kenya sighed. She didn't like to think too much about the ultimatum her parents had given her, didn't like to invite any negative energy around the thought of losing, but she needed to talk to someone about it. "I made a deal with my parents. If . . . the competition doesn't go the way I hope, I have to quit working at the shop, get a job that utilizes my degree, and pursue my master's, which they'll fund."

"Are you serious?"

Janelle's shout drew everyone's attention again. Cam looked at Kenya, and whatever he saw in her expression was enough for him to hand off his controller and climb to his feet.

God. She leaned closer to Janelle to hurriedly whisper, "Cam doesn't know, and he doesn't need to know because we're not going to lose."

She plastered on a smile as he came over to them. "Hey, baby. Tired of Sam kicking your ass?"

"If I'm losing to anyone up in here, it better be to the one about to get paid to play." He turned to Janelle. "Dev's good too. I hope y'all are going to come back. We need a rematch."

"Thanks. As long as our schedules let us, we'll be here. This was a lot of fun." She stood. "Now if you'll excuse me, I have to go kiss him and make him feel better."

Cam nodded, then took the spot she vacated. "Everything all right? It looked like y'all were having a serious conversation over here."

Kenya laced his fingers with hers. "Janelle just filled me in on the dramatic turn her life has taken."

"Good drama or bad drama?"

She leaned against him, because it was hard to be so close to him and not touch. "Good drama. L-word drama. Meet-the-parents drama."

"Girl, what?"

He erupted with laughter when she jabbed him with her elbow. "Sorry, not sorry, but I couldn't resist. Which seems to be a common thing when you're involved."

She pressed closer to whisper in his ear. "That's because I'm simply irresistible."

"Ain't that the truth." He rested his temple against hers. "Your stress level better today?"

"I should be asking you that, don't you think? Thank you for getting everyone together for game night. I really needed this mental break. I missed you, I missed us, and I missed hanging out with our friends. So thank you for giving me this."

He cupped her cheek with his free hand. "Anytime, sweetheart. Anytime."

The background faded as she focused on his mouth. How close it was. How kissable it was.

"Hey, guys."

Kenya sat back as a voice intruded on their moment. Her eyes widened in surprise as she caught sight of Jessa, Cam's ex, standing in front of them, a couple of her friends flanking her. And Jane and cameraman Ian standing behind them.

Girl. What the fuck?

CHAPTER SIXTEEN

Since that bad-timing rejection from Kenya in college, Cam had stepped back, making preparations while waiting for a better time to approach her again. He had the Davenports to partially thank for that. While his father had been the king of drunken and benign neglect, he had left behind minimal debt and a decent amount of savings. Cam had launched his business and worked his ass off to stabilize his client base and his finances, so that he could get to a moment in which he could make a serious play for Kenya's heart. Working with the elder Davenports' financial advisor, he felt that he was finally on solid enough ground where he could begin to think about his personal future.

He wasn't a fan of spreadsheets and Gantt charts when it came to ordering his life, but he did have a four-step plan when it came to winning Kenya's heart. Step one: getting her to view him as boyfriend material. He'd started the process for that by parting ways with Jessa, never expecting that Kenya would volunteer him as her pretend boyfriend. Step two: getting her used to the idea of them being a couple. Practicing coupledom so their friends and family would accept them certainly helped. Step three: getting naked. Step four: saying the L-word. Step five: unlocking the Happily Ever After achievement.

While the first two steps had happened faster than he'd anticipated, he couldn't be happier about the results. Kenya's parents had accepted them as a couple, with understandable reservation. Their friends had accepted them with a chorus of "About damn time!" All he needed was for Kenya to accept that they were more than friends. As for step three . . .

Kenya had gotten over her surprise at his declaration. He'd gotten over the elbow to the junk. Neither one of them had gotten over the hot-as-hell kiss on the shop floor. And he was more than reasonably sure that she was interested in moving to Friends 2.0.

Then came the late-night film fests at the apartment, a surprising but financially welcome last-minute order at the shop. Both of them had pulled long hours and while he'd hoped that he could join Kenya for some of the filming at the apartment, most of the time she was already done and asleep by the time he got home and he was too exhausted to do more than shower and fall into bed beside her. No talk, no agreement to move to the next level.

It was a reality check more than a setback. He knew how to be patient. Step three was inevitable, and Kenya was worth the blue balls. Now, with his workload eased and the filming returning to the shop, it was time. Arranging this Saturday game night with their friends was a great way to celebrate and destress and would serve as a prelude to step three.

Which meant that getting to step four was a critical, delicate step. He knew it couldn't be rushed, couldn't be pushed, couldn't be assumed. Things could go sideways at any moment. The plan teetered at a precarious juncture and he needed to move carefully to keep it all from falling apart. What he did not plan for was his ex-girlfriend and a couple of her friends showing up game night. Or Jane and the cameraman to find them.

He shot to his feet, instinctively putting himself between Kenya and Jessa. "Hi, Jessa. We weren't expecting you." He looked at the producer. "You either. I thought y'all were off today."

"Kenya and I talked earlier about getting some more B-roll shots, and while discussing next week's schedule, she mentioned your game night," Jane explained. "Once the owner gave us permission, we came to get some candid shots."

How fortunate. "I hope you brought release forms then."

"Sure did," Jane said sweetly. "Of course, anyone who doesn't want to be on camera doesn't have to sign, we'll just blur you or do creative editing."

Before he could say anything else, Kenya nudged him to the side so that she could stand. "Hi, Jessa." Her tone was pleasant, friendly even, and gave no indication of what she thought of Jessa's unexpected appearance. "How are you doing?"

"I'm doing good. Great even." She flashed a smile. "I heard you were back in town and that a game night meet-up was happening, so I decided to drop by. I wanted to congratulate you for making it to the finals on that cosplay show . . . which, I guess, you're filming part of now?"

"Thank you, and yes, apparently so."

"I guess I should also congratulate both of you on your new relationship status," Jessa continued, glancing between them before settling her gaze on him. "The timing worked out perfectly."

Cam frowned. Was she trying to start something? He could see their friends behind her, all facing them, their expression ranging from avid curiosity to worry. Janelle was on her feet, ready to charge in if necessary. God, he hoped it wouldn't be necessary. Jessa wouldn't stand a chance if she started something.

"You and I broke up before Kenya and I started seeing each other," he reminded her.

"Like I said, perfect timing." She darted another glance at Kenya before looking at him again. "Or convenient. It's so . . . out of the norm for you."

"Is that really what you're saying, Jessa?" Kenya asked, her tone soft. "Because it seems like you want to say something else. Feel free to get it off your chest if it will make you feel better."

Shit. That quiet tone spelled trouble. Maybe Jessa didn't know it, but he did. He pressed his shoulder against Kenya's and when she glanced at him, he gave her a smile in what he hoped she took as support and agreement.

Jessa sighed, then turned to Cam, her expression sad and urgent. "Can I talk to you for a moment?"

"Sure." He didn't move.

"Alone?"

That would be asking for trouble. He was not about to jeopardize his plan to win Kenya or give her any reason to doubt him by having a private post-breakup conversation with Jessa. Cam slid his arm around Kenya's waist. "Whatever you want to say to me, you can say in front of Kenya."

Jessa tried again. "It's a little embarrassing."

"If it's a woman thing, you might feel better with Kenya here. We don't have any secrets."

Her expression soured. Clearly she didn't like that idea. "I think I may have left something at your place. I'd like to come get it."

Seriously? Cam knew there was nothing of hers at the apartment, embarrassing or not. He'd done a tag-and-bag of the few things she'd had when he knew they were over and had handed everything off to her as soon as he could. He was about to tell her so, when Kenya spoke up.

"If you tell us what you think you left, we can look for it tonight and you can come get it tomorrow after we get back from church and lunch with my parents. Honestly, though, I haven't seen anything of yours in our bedroom, closet, or bathroom. Anywhere in our apartment, really."

Damn. He had to fight to keep his expression neutral. Admiration and awe bloomed inside him with every word Kenya spoke. Sweetness and light dripped from each word, but each was an arrow expertly hitting its target.

He'd also caught the emphasis she'd placed on the word *our*. It felt as if she was staking a claim to him, and that made him want to pump his fist in excitement. Maybe they were further along the path to step three than he'd hoped.

"Never mind," Jessa said, disappointment threading her words. "It's been used anyway." She turned to go.

"Why don't you stay for a while, Jessa?" Kenya asked. "I mean, it *is* game night. If you're here to play games, I'm sure we can get a couple of folks to hand over their controllers."

Flawless victory.

"No, thanks," the other woman said, not bothering to disguise her disappointment. "I actually have somewhere else to be in a bit. Take care of yourself, Cam. Congrats again, Kenya. I hope you get everything you deserve." She spun on her heel and left, taking her silent friends with her.

Cam blew out a harsh breath as he turned back to Kenya. "Unbelievable."

She cocked her head, a slight gesture toward Jane and Ian. "Her or me?"

Damn the producer and the camera. He dragged his forefinger across the ragged edge of his thumbnail. "Me, actually. When I got on the group chat to let everyone know we were coming out for game night tonight, I had no idea Jessa would show up."

She shrugged, outwardly unbothered. "Game night is a regular thing for our group, and Jessa was part of that for a while. I'm not surprised she showed up. A bunch of people did."

She very deliberately didn't look toward Jane and her cameraman. Relief shoved worry off his shoulders. Jessa hadn't shown up to any game night since they'd broken up. Her appearance now that Kenya had returned could have made everything go sideways and he was so damn glad it hadn't.

That relief didn't mean he wanted to hang around, though. "Are you ready to go?"

"No." She laced her fingers with his, then squeezed, hard. "This is probably going to be the last game night we'll get to attend until the competition is over, and I want to enjoy it. Maybe you and I should challenge Janelle and Dev for the next round. What do you think?"

He thought she was trying to put on a good face for the cameras. The least he could do was play his part. He had no idea what Jessa's sudden appearance meant, but leaving so soon would make everyone think they were angry with Jessa at the minimum or irritated with each other at the most. More than anything, he wanted to prove to Kenya that she was his focus now.

"Guys versus girls or couple versus couple?"

She grinned. "Janelle and I are about to kick y'all's asses into next week!"

He grinned back. "Game on."

So, she faked it. That wasn't new. Why she faked it, yes, that was new, and rather uncomfortable.

She wasn't unbothered. Not by a long shot. Still, she had to pretend to be while they were out in public. Everyone, from casual observers to their closest friends, needed to buy that they were not only a couple, but also deeply and happily into each other and completely unconcerned about exes with unspoken agendas.

It had been fun hanging with their friends, marking their first "official" outing with fun, food, and photos that got plastered all over social media. Yet that interaction with Jessa nagged at her all the way home. It could have been innocent, but she didn't think so. Jessa had clearly wanted to talk to Cam alone, sparking Kenya's brain to speculate on various scenarios of increasing telenovela-like drama—everything from a communicable disease to a surprise pregnancy.

Her mind continued to race despite her efforts to squelch it. She tried to console herself with the knowledge that whatever Jessa had up her sleeve, Cam wanted no part of it. She appreciated that. She'd also thought it was cute when he'd stood between her and Jessa—for a couple of seconds, at least. She didn't need protection, even from an ex with an agenda. Still, she needed to talk to Cam about it, if only so she could concoct workable contingency plans.

"Was it just me or was that thing with Jessa and her backup group weird?" she asked as they entered the apartment.

"It's not just you." Cam hung his keys on the rack by the door. "It was weird, especially since the others just stood there and didn't say anything. Jane and her crew showing up like that was piss-poor timing, too."

Kenya had a sneaking suspicion that it wasn't bad luck but rather precision planning on Jane's part. It wouldn't have taken much to

trawl back through Cam's social media to find pictures of him and
Jessa looking happy together. At least she knew there weren't any of
them smooching—because of course she'd looked—but Cam had
never posed for photos like that.

"Thank you for understanding why we needed to stay." She
headed to the kitchen, trying to decide between green tea or something stronger. "I didn't want anyone, especially Jane and her crew,
to think that we were upset about Jessa showing up. Leaving soon
after her would give people, especially the production crew, the
wrong impression."

"That brain of yours continues to amaze me," he said, following
her into the kitchen. "It's like that saying, women play chess while
men play checkers."

It wasn't a game to her, though. It was about emotional survival,
about not letting things hurt her. She had to project an image of
being unbothered because there was always someone looking for a
weakness to exploit. Like Rebecca. Like Jane. Maybe even like Jessa.

Maybe it was a sign. She and Cam hadn't had much of a chance
to talk about the Infinity Stones Incident or that very real kiss at the
shop. Hadn't had a chance to see if they were just caught up in the
fantasy of cosplaying a couple or if there was something beyond
friendship brewing between them. And then Jessa showing up, giving everyone a chance to compare and contrast them?

She hadn't felt self-conscious about her size since high school.
She loved her curves, loved dressing them up and showing them off.
Standing there with Cam and Jessa, however, it was hard not to feel
anything but awkward and unsure.

Doubts assailed her. She almost would have thought she'd
imagined the growing chemistry between her and Cam if it weren't
for the flowers at her workstation. He was deep in shop work and
she was up to her eyeballs in foam armor. Even the teasing PDAs

had subsided. Maybe they couldn't pull this off. Maybe they wouldn't be able to fake it until the end of the competition. Maybe he didn't want her that way. Maybe it was better to remain best friends instead of reaching for something more.

No, better not to dive headfirst into the pool, only to find it wasn't that deep.

"Are you okay?"

She pulled herself back to their conversation with effort. "You have no idea what Jessa wanted to talk to you about? Because that whole 'left something embarrassing at the apartment' thing was just a ruse to get you alone."

"No. I don't have a clue what she wants to talk to me about. We've been over for months!"

She opened the refrigerator door, hesitated, then reached for two ciders before asking the fridge, "Any chance she could be pregnant?"

"What?"

She risked a glance at him. Shock blew out his eyes and paled his skin, as if a possible pregnancy wasn't in the realm of reality. Unfortunately, they lived in the real world and they had to consider every possible angle so they could figure out how to deal.

Closing the fridge, she turned to offer one of the ciders to him. "Is it possible?"

He blinked, then shook his head like a dog shedding water. "No. She was on birth control and I always wore protection when we were together. I think I would have noticed a broken condom, and considering the last time we actually had sex, she'd be showing by now if she was . . . was . . ."

His knuckles whitened as he gripped the bottle's neck. "I'm really uncomfortable having this conversation with you."

Who wanted to have a conversation with their new "girlfriend" about a possible pregnancy with their old girlfriend? What new girlfriend wanted to hear it? "I'm uncomfortable with it too, but we need to figure out what she's up to. She wanted to talk to you for a reason, something she thinks is important."

"You don't think this is done?"

Kenya popped the top on her bottle, took a fortifying swallow. "Not even close. She came out to game night specifically because she knew you'd be there—that we'd be there. That's why she brought backup. For whatever reason, she didn't go through with whatever she had planned, but she obviously planned something."

"Like what?" he wondered, frustration straining his expression.

"Like wanting to make another play for you." Kenya turned to face him. "Maybe your mutual decision wasn't as mutual as you thought."

"I thought things were pretty clear on my end."

"What about her end? It seems like it's not as cut and dried for her."

"Is that my fault?" he demanded, spreading his arms wide.

"Hold up." She held up her hands, palms out, trying to keep her temper in check as she checked him. "Did the words 'it's your fault' fall out of my mouth? Don't jump on me when I'm trying to help."

"No. You're right, I'm sorry." He lifted his hand, paused, then shoved his fingers through his hair. "I'm just . . . This is a lot."

"Yeah." She could feel her anxiety ramping up in reaction to his. She didn't like unknowns, and Jessa's appearance created a big unknown. Maybe she was overreacting, but something told her she wasn't. They didn't need any roadblocks or distractions during these final weeks of the competition—they needed a united front and a plan of action.

Taking his hand, she led him to the couch. It seemed forever ago that they had lain there, all snuggled up with him comforting her after her meltdown at the shop. Now, she had a chance to return the favor.

Placing her cider on the coffee table, she held out both hands to him. "Come here. Let's talk. Judgement-free zone."

He set his bottle next to hers, then joined her on the couch. "I don't know what's going on with Jessa. I swear it was a clean break."

"What guys consider clean and what women consider clean are two different things," she reminded him gently. "The breakup might have hit her harder than you thought."

"She didn't cry, or yell, or throw things. She just said, 'I think you should leave now,' so I left."

"There's a large chunk of the story missing, and I'm sorry I wasn't here when it happened so we could have gone through our breakup routine." Then again, maybe it was time to retire the cheesy movies and vodka-infused ice cream floats. "How did you break up? More important than that, why did you break up?"

CHAPTER SEVENTEEN

He didn't want to tell her. If he did, Kenya would blame herself, and it wasn't her fault at all. She'd simply been the inspiration. He'd been ready to put his plan into motion as soon as she'd received word that she'd been accepted for the cosplay competition, hoping that her time away would give their relationship the reset it needed to transition from friends to lovers. Then Jessa had made her move and he'd had no choice.

He picked at his nails. He wouldn't tell Kenya everything, but he could tell her most of it. "Jessa wanted to take our relationship to the next level. She wanted us to move in together."

"Really? Wow."

"Yeah. Surprised me too." He shifted on the couch. "I told her I couldn't do that."

"Why not?"

Jessa had asked the same question. He gave the same answer. "Because of you."

"Oh." Kenya leaned back in surprise, then realization. "Oh. She wanted both of you to kick your roommates to the curb and move in together, just the two of you."

He nodded. "I wasn't going to do that. Not with you going out to LA. Besides, we still have a few months on our lease."

"Cam." He heard the weight in her voice as she said his name, felt the chill in her fingers as she clasped his hand. "I . . . appreciate you considering me and my situation, but you can't let me hold you back, especially when we're talking about your future. We're adults now. It's okay to stop looking out for me."

His fingers flexed against hers involuntarily, a manifestation of his instinctive need to hold on to her for now, forever. He took a deep breath to smooth out the rhythm of his wildly racing heart, but his words came out in bursts anyway.

"What was I supposed to do, Kenya? Drop that on you as you were packing? Have that weighing on your mind when you needed to focus on winning the competition? No, I wasn't going to do that to you. Besides, I didn't want to move in with her."

"You didn't?"

"No."

"Why?"

"Because she wanted more than moving in together, and I didn't."

Her gaze lay heavy on him as she pondered all the things that could mean. Then she straightened her shoulders as if bracing herself. "So, do you want to get back with her?"

Panic flared in his chest again. "We're a team now."

Her soft laugh hurt to hear. "That doesn't answer the question."

He gathered her hands in his. He would have dropped to one knee if he had confidence that she wouldn't run out the door. Or worse, laugh it off. Instead, he gathered their joined hands and answered her. "I will never. Ever. Get back with her. I don't love her. She knows that. So we ended things."

"And now you're pretending to be my boyfriend, but she doesn't know it's just pretend." Kenya sat back, her mouth an *O* of surprise. "Oh, so that's what it is."

Whatever conclusion she'd jumped to, she'd left him behind. "That's what *what* is?"

"I don't know for sure, so it's just a gut feeling on my part. It's possible that Jessa wants to get back with you. Or it's possible that she has a problem with you being with me, even if we're just pretending for the show."

His first instinctive reaction was to laugh in denial, but as much as she reveled in her creativity, Kenya could also throw a switch into logical mode and create a workable hypothesis complete with supporting evidence. "What makes you think that?"

She turned to face him again, her expression determined. "Has she called or texted you since y'all broke up?"

"We texted the day after we broke up so that I could arrange to drop off the few things she'd left over here," he answered. "Nothing since then. I should have deleted her number."

She winced. "Harsh. So much for amicable."

He felt compelled to defend his description of the breakup. "I figured any relationship that ends without shouting, tears, or cursing is amicable," he said, rubbing the back of his neck. "I guess I was mistaken."

"It might have been a delayed reaction, a hope that you might change your mind. I suppose when you dropped off her stuff, she realized it was really over." Her lips twisted into a smile. "So she went radio silent on you until I declared you were my boyfriend on national television and came home."

He opened his mouth, then slowly closed it. "But why, though?

I hadn't heard from her since you were gone, which made it seem like she'd come to accept that it was over between us. So why come around now when it's clear that I've moved on?"

"Well . . ." Kenya bit her bottom lip. "Like I said, she might have a problem with me being with you. I didn't have any problems with her while you guys were dating, but given the stuff she said tonight . . . it's possible that she thinks I'm using you for the sake of the competition. That could be why she wanted to talk to you alone tonight."

Cam didn't want to believe it, but Kenya's observations made a sort of twisted sense. "If that's what she thinks, she's thinking wrong," he retorted. "You're not using me!"

Kenya gave him a small smile. "Aren't I, in a small way?" she said, her voice so soft he could hardly hear her. "She probably thinks I'm holding something over you. In her mind, that's the only reason why you'd dump her for me."

The tightness in his chest ratcheted up another notch. "That's bullshit!"

She polished off the remnants of her cider. "I'm hoping Jessa believes that we're real, because we don't need her coming to the shop making a scene. Jane and her crew will eat that up."

Shit. A knot of dread formed in his gut. A showdown at the shop was the last thing they needed. "Well, if she doesn't believe in us, she's the only one. Maybe I should do a preemptive strike and talk to her first."

Kenya grabbed his wrist with a brisk shake of her head. "No, that will only make her more suspicious. We should keep on doing what we're doing."

He tried to lighten the mood. "Can't we do more?"

Bitterness laced her laugh. "I don't know. What I do know is I need to wash this night right out of my hair. You don't have to wait up."

She patted his knee and made a beeline for her bathroom, leaving him with his cider and his dread to keep him company. Maybe Jessa wasn't the only one who couldn't believe in them as a couple. Maybe Kenya felt that way too.

He stood. It was finally time to have that conversation. If Kenya had any doubts about what he wanted from her, he'd just have to show her, show her in a way that left no room for doubt.

By the time Kenya had showered and pulled on a nightie and a cute pair of pink-striped boy shorts, she'd more or less pulled herself together, at least enough to pretend that she was all right. Stepping into Cam's bedroom, she could hear the shower going and retreated to the living room instead, appreciating the opportunity to have a few more moments to make some decisions.

She was prepared to pretend that that morning on the couch had never happened. She was also prepared to rationalize away the kiss and its effects by using the explanation that they had both been playing it up for the cameras. They both needed to focus on business, not pleasure.

So why was she sitting on the couch, torn between relief and disappointment?

Because that kiss had rocked her, rocked her so much that she was still thinking about it days later. So different from the cheek kisses they exchanged for the cameras, so different from even that welcome home kiss at the airport. That kiss staked new territory and boldly promised to deliver. She wanted another one. Several more, in fact.

She wanted Cam.

Standing in the middle of Game and Flame, facing Jessa, possessiveness had settled on her shoulders like a mantle of righteousness. She'd wanted to claim her territory, to show Jessa and the world that Cam belonged to her now, and she wasn't giving him up. Except he wasn't hers. Not in that way. And now, after that little face-off at the bar and pondering Jessa's motives, Kenya had to wonder if Cam's interest in her had faded back to just-friends territory.

Too keyed up, she called up YouTube on the TV and loaded a video from one of her favorite plus-size yoga instructors. She'd taken up the practice during college as a means to center her mind and stretch her body. It had surprised her how well she'd taken to it, especially considering the looks she'd garnered at her first couple of in-person classes. She'd persevered, and finally found a body-positive one to join instead of one where they gave her advice "out of concern for your health."

Shaking her head, she cleared her thoughts, planted her feet, and began a few breathing exercises to clear her mind and center her body. She didn't intend to do a full routine, just enough to clear her mind and her stress until she could sleep.

Mountain pose. Did the man really take showers this long? Flowing into tree pose. Surely he didn't think things were copacetic, right? Then into standing forward fold. Did he not want this? Sliding into downward dog. Was she going to have to confront him? Maybe even seduce him?

"You doing yoga?"

She blew out a breath as she hurriedly backed up into a standing fold, then straightened. Cam stood just outside the short hallway leading to his bedroom, hair damp and slicked back, navy boxers low on his hips. Not the boxer briefs, unfortunately, but he still looked like a snack and a half.

"KeKe?"

He'd asked something, and she scrambled to remember. "I'm done. I was trying to clear my head a little."

"Did it work?"

"No." She couldn't stop staring. Sure, she'd seen Cam topless before, after a run or doing yard work with her dad. But that was when she saw him with friend vision. Looking at him now, she wasn't thinking friendly thoughts at all.

I've been sleeping next to this man every night since I got back. I wake up nose-to-chest with him. Hell, I even woke up on top of him! What would it be like to wake up like that again, but not after a night of being comforted after freaking out? Waking up like that again, but after a night of making out, blissing out, wilding out?

"There's something I've been meaning to ask you."

The seriousness of his tone caused her to jerk her gaze away from his chest and to his eyes. A light gleamed there, something that made her feel tight all over. "Yeah?"

He tilted his head. "The other day . . . was it a joke?"

Which day did he mean? "I made a joke?"

He snorted, obviously not buying her attempt to play dumb. "That's what I'm trying to figure out. Was it a joke? You asking if my dick was for you?"

"Uh . . ." She stared down at her nightgown, glad she'd chosen one that kept her girls high and happy. Her cheeks burned with the memory of his erection pressed against her belly. All that hardness against her pudgy softness, and her insides had gone liquid. When she'd met his sleep-softened gaze, she'd blurted the question out, half teasing, but half hoping he'd say yes.

And he had.

Fuck it. She raised her chin. "I was teasing, but I wasn't joking."

"Good."

Good? Did that mean he was glad? She needed to make sure. "Were you joking when you said yes?"

"No."

That one word, so soft, put all her senses on high alert. "Oh."

He moved toward her slowly, his bare feet silent on the carpet. "I wasn't joking that first morning I woke up with you pressed against me with my hand trapped between your breasts. I wasn't joking when you broke out your measuring tape in the shop and I had to snatch on a wrinkled shirt so I wouldn't embarrass myself on national television. I wasn't joking about that kiss, or the flowers and candy. I definitely wasn't joking each time I jerked off in the shower over the past week."

The intensity of his words punched out every doubt and second thought in her mind. "I'm glad I'm not the only one taking longer showers to relieve some pressure."

A grunt worthy of any caveman escaped him. The atmosphere in the room changed, and her nipples tightened as they had when he'd kissed her. She couldn't help it, any more than she could help her mouth watering at the thought of having the best dessert ever.

"Kenya."

His voice, rough and deep, chopped through her chaotic thoughts. "I want to point something out."

She jerked her gaze away from his chest and back to his storm-filled gaze. "What?"

He settled his hands on his hips. "It's not morning anymore."

"What's that supposed to mea . . . glurgh." Her gaze dropped from his eyes to his chest to his hands fisted low on his hips, above the waistband of his boxers. To the imprint of his erection pressing against the loose fabric.

"Ergh."

Her brain short-circuited.

CHAPTER EIGHTEEN

Kenya's openmouthed expression shot a bright bolt of lust through his body, igniting a flame of need. It was instantly doused by her words.

"I, uhm, I think I made a mistake."

His body and his heart deflated. "What do you mean, you made a mistake?"

"Yeah." She looked down then back up at him. "It was a mistake thinking we could pretend to be lovers and do all the things that lovers do, except for one."

She shook her head. "No, not a mistake, a miscalculation. I thought I could pretend to be your girlfriend. Do all the girlfriend stuff and pretend that I didn't want the rest. Pretend like sharing the bed with you wasn't affecting me. Pretend like I wasn't having a reaction to you, like masturbating in the shower every day had no correlation to waking up cuddled against you, feeling your dick pressed against my ass and wondering what if."

"Kenya." Her name scraped like sandpaper across his tongue.

He wanted to yank her against him and kiss her stupid before dragging her to their bedroom, but more than that, he wanted her to say that she wanted him. He needed her to say it. So he waited and wanted and wrestled his hands into fists to keep from chewing his thumbnail to the quick.

She continued, blissfully unaware of his dilemma. "I can't pretend anymore. I don't want to pretend anymore."

He licked his lips. "What do you want, then?"

She stepped closer, then closer still, until the press of her breasts against his chest shredded at his control. "What do I want now?" Her hand flat over his heart scalded him. "Now I want to ride you like a pogo stick."

Snap! His will broke like a dam, his hands dropping open so that he could grip her hips and kiss her into oblivion. He kissed her with days, weeks, years of pent-up wanting, and when she met him kiss for kiss, her hands sliding down to grip his butt, his blood burned.

When the need for air overwhelmed the need to kiss, they broke apart, staring at each other, their breaths loud. Cam found enough air to speak. "Are we done talking?"

"Yeah." Her chest heaved as she leaned against him. "I'm ready for action."

Nerves descended on Kenya as she faced Cam at the foot of their bed. "I'm nervous," she confessed, just to get it out and over with. "I can't believe I'm nervous."

"You think I'm not?" He placed a hand over his heart. "After building up to this, the thought of it going sideways . . ."

The fact that he was nervous too settled her. "It won't go sideways. And if it does, we'll keep trying until we get it right."

She sobered. "I'm just—I guess I'm worried that this might hurt our friendship."

Something flickered in his eyes. "We're not going to ruin us. We'll still be friends in the morning. We'll just be a little more. For real."

The idea of *more* sent a frisson of something skittering down her back. She wasn't sure if she wanted to make grabby hands or make a Kool-Aid Man silhouette through the front door. "Like what?"

"Friends with benefits. Friends 2.0. Ride or die."

Okay, that she could handle. "Like Jay and Bey without the singing ability?"

He had the nerve to look insulted. "I'll have you know I'm the best rapper in my shower."

"Oh really?" She sashayed toward him, rolling her hips. "Maybe I should start using that shower, too."

"Please do." His gaze rose from her hips to her breasts to her eyes. "I still said what I said."

A snort-laugh escaped her. She enjoyed this sexy, teasing side of him. It emboldened her. "Feeling a little cocky, are you?" she purred as she slowly slid a hand down his chest to his waistband, giving him plenty of time to move or object. He didn't, so she continued down until she cupped him. "Correction, you're feeling a lot cocky."

His hips jerked forward as a grimace stretched his lips. "See, this is why I had to jerk off in the shower."

His hands settled low on her hips, his fingers digging into her ass. "I wanna do whatever you wanna do, and I want to take my time doing it."

His words left her breathless. "Are we going to have a rap battle as foreplay?"

"I'd prefer it if we had foreplay as foreplay," he answered, his voice dropping into a low, husky timbre that stroked over her nerves the same way she wanted his fingers to stroke her nipples. "Besides, there's a much better way to find out which one of us has the better mouth-game."

"Challenge accepted." She licked her lips, then reached for him. "Come here."

"No. I get to go first."

Her gut clenched on a rush of need. Knowing how he kissed . . . "I thought you wanted to do whatever I want to do?"

"I do, but I also don't want this to be over in five minutes. Besides, I'm really feeling the need to kiss you again. You okay with that?"

"Hell yeah." She leaned in to kiss him. He met her halfway, and sparks danced along her senses. Who knew the sequel to Hot Kiss was just as good, if not better, than the original?

She'd never get tired of this thrum of heat and want and pleasure. The breathy sigh he elicited when his hands slid up her sides to cup her breasts. His stuttered breath as she grabbed his ass, then plucked at his waistband. "Too many clothes."

"Right." He did that finger-skating thing again, only this time, he did it with the hem of her nightie, inching it up until it bunched around her waist. She took over from there, grabbing the clingy fabric before yanking it over her head and tossing it away.

"KeKe." The soft reverence in his tone melted her. His gaze grazed her body, stopped at the hot-pink boy-shorts, then back again. "Damn. I'm going to have so much fun seeing the panties of the day every day."

She knew her body shape, knew how to accentuate it to its best advantage. She did a slow turn, making sure he saw all that she had to offer, all the swerve in her curves. His hands hovered as if he didn't know where to put them. "I wanna touch," he breathed. "Can I touch?"

"As long as I can too."

He closed in on her. "Touch whatever you want, however you want."

They kissed again, kisses enhanced by touching, hands charting territory for the first time. Touching Cam as a lover was a completely different experience from touching him as a friend. As a friend, she touched him in comfort and camaraderie. Now she touched him to excite and incite. Now she touched him as he touched her—part familiar, part wonder, mostly hunger.

Caught up in each other, they fell onto the bed, kissing, touching, pressing close. She thrilled at the feel of his body against hers, separated by a few layers of cloth. Too many layers. "You're still wearing your boxers."

"On purpose," he answered against her neck. "This way, I can still think."

"Maybe I don't want you to think," she said, rubbing her leg against his. "Maybe thinking time is over. Do you still have some condoms?"

"Bought some the day you elbowed me in the junk." Nimble fingers cupped her breasts, teased the tips. "For a new start."

That touched her for some reason, melting her even more. Not as much as his mouth against her throat, on her nipples. Certainly not as much as when he kissed her panties off. And when he put his mouth on her, she had to admit his challenge was way better than a rap battle. So much better her thighs almost cracked his head like a walnut as she came.

She returned to her senses when Cam moved back up beside her in all his brother-of-Thor glory. "Can we move on to the riding-like-a-pogo-stick stage now?"

"God, yes." He grabbed a condom from his nightstand. Anticipation gripped her as she gripped him, stroking him to full readiness as he unsteadily rolled the condom on.

The time for talking was over. She straddled him, kissed him, then sunk down on him. His fingertips dug into her hips, helping as she rocked out the sweetest beat that sent her flying again. Feverishly flipping for the finale, she locked her legs around Cam's waist as the tempo took off, a racing rhythm that rocketed them over the edge.

A while later, when Cam got up to dispose of the condom, Kenya ninja-rolled off the bed, grabbed her crumpled nightie, then headed to her old bathroom for a postcoital cleanup. When she was done, she looked in the mirror to see what a person who'd had sex with their best friend looked like. Given the grin on her face, that person looked pretty damn satisfied.

She'd had sex with her best friend. With Cam. And she wanted to do it again.

Her grin remained in place as she made her way back to the bedroom. It was dark except for the night-light shining from the bathroom and the glow of Cam's phone screen—enough light to see that he chewed on his thumbnail.

That wasn't good. She hesitated a second, her grin faltering. Was it something about the shop? A text from Jessa? Were things going to be awkward between them now? She asked a feeler question. "Bad news?"

"Nope." He put the phone down as she climbed into bed. "Just waiting for you."

"Ah." She turned on her side to face him. "Did you think I wasn't coming back?"

"I wasn't sure." And uncertainty led to anxiety and nail biting or snapping the head off gummy worms. "But you're here now."

"I'm not about to miss my post-sex cuddle," she declared. "Also, I'm not ready to walk around naked with you yet."

He chuffed out a laugh and scooted down in the bed, drew her closer. "What about half-naked and wearing your hair bag?"

"Boy, if you call my satin cap a hair bag one more time . . ." She pressed her nose against his chest, then hugged him. "So, no regrets, right?"

"None over here." He rested his cheek on her head. "What about you?"

"Only one. I should have taken you up on your offer in college."

He froze, then gave a rueful laugh. "You were right to turn me down, coming off an ugly breakup like that. I had lousy timing. You clearly weren't ready for another relationship."

Yet he had never repeated the offer, even though there were other times when they had been simultaneously single. Kenya wanted to ask why but decided against it. That was the past, so why focus on it when the here and now was so damn good? "Well, I'm definitely ready for more of this Friends 2.0 relationship."

He was silent for so long, she thought he'd fallen asleep. Then he released a long, slow breath. "I was just thinking about this thing with Jessa," he finally said. "I don't want her to cause trouble for you."

She did not want to talk about his ex while she was still coming down from an endorphin high. "Let's not think about her anymore, especially not tonight. If something happens, I'll handle it."

He pulled her closer, his hand warm against her back. "I just don't want any problems for the rest of the competition. I look at your timeline every day. Every minute is critical, especially starting next week."

"I know how important this is, Cam," she said softly. "Whatever's on Jessa's mind isn't going to stop me. And I sure as hell don't plan to give Jane any ammunition. We'll deal with your ex when there's something to deal with."

"Okay. Are you tired?"

Tired of talking, but she didn't say that. "Not as much as I thought I would be," she admitted. "Why?"

He slid a hand down her belly to her happy place. "Because I don't want her to be the last thing on your mind before you go to sleep."

He made good on his word, so good that she almost forgot her own name as she lay with him in a hazy afterglow. She liked that he was a postcoital cuddler. She liked that he preferred to be the big spoon. She really liked the way that his hand splayed over her belly with a touch that was both possessive and soothing. More than anything, she liked Cam on a deeper level, a level that made her heart happy, a level she wanted to explore more.

She should have known the bliss wouldn't last long.

CHAPTER NINETEEN

We should have just 3-D printed the suits."

Kenya was inclined to agree as she stared down at the work-table. There was a hellified amount of foam pieces that they needed to paint, and that was just the Iron Man build. "We should have just ordered parts online, but we have that seventy-five-percent-handmade-by-us parameter we have to stick to."

Her bangs fluttered with the breath she blew out. "I'm beginning to regret picking these two for our iconic duo. Maybe I was overly ambitious."

"What? Are you having doubts that you can do what's normally a six-month build for one suit in four weeks?" Cam bumped her shoulder. "Since when have you let the word "impossible" stop you?"

She appreciated the cheerleading but couldn't shake the feeling of impending doom. "There's always a first time."

"Good thing this time ain't that time." He settled his hands on her waist, something she discovered he liked to do, and she liked him doing. "We can do this. Divide and conquer, like we always do."

She leaned into him, grateful for his confidence. This was part of why they worked so well together. When one was down, the other stepped in to build up. "I reviewed our timeline this morning. If we were doing one set of armor, I'd feel better about our chances. But two? With the time we have left?"

He pulled her in. "Well, if you're that worried about it, I have a suggestion."

"I'm listening."

"Instead of doing full-on battle-armor Thanos, how about doing a gender-bent version instead?"

"Uhm . . ." She didn't want to shoot him down, especially not with the cameras rolling. They'd already spent hours cutting foam for the Thanos fabrication, and he wanted to chuck it?

Her skepticism must have shown because he smiled and squeezed her hips. "Hear me out, babe. When you think of Iron Man, you think of his armor and his Arc Reactor. But what do you think of when you think of Thanos?"

"The color purple, that chin, and the Infinity Gauntlet."

"Exactly. So, I suggest ditching the battle armor. By doing a gender-bent Thanos, you can get creative in the way you interpret the character, especially since we're going to be judged on creativity, too."

He dug his phone out of his back pocket, then called up an image search of the purple Titan. "See? You can use fabric to create the top and add molded pieces to it. You could probably even do a corset if you want."

She snorted. "Sounds like you want me to do the corset."

"Babe, you're hot as you are, but you in a corset? Smoking."

"Thank you." Laughter bubbled up when he waggled his eyebrows. His happiness shone like a beacon, putting everyone in a good mood. The thought that she was partially responsible for that buoyed her spirits. "Okay."

"Okay?" His excitement animated his entire face, brightened his eyes, appled his cheeks, curved his kissable lips. "For real?"

"Of course, for real. You're making a lot of sense. I'll have you know that your talent for being sensible is one of your most attractive qualities."

He frowned. "You find my sensibleness my most attractive quality?"

"I said one of. The list is long but our time is not. We'll divide and conquer like you said. You get first dibs on the section you want to do."

"I'll take the chest and back," he decided. "That way I can also test the fit of the Arc Reactor."

"All right, then. I'll work on your bottom half." She slapped her forehead. "Of the armor. The bottom half of the armor."

He grinned. "I'll just say, 'Insert suggestive comment here,' and let your vivid imagination handle the rest."

"I'm vividly imagining a couple of things right now," she retorted, narrowing her eyes at him.

"I hope one of them is new concept art for your cosplay."

She sucked her teeth. "You know what? You're lucky you're so sexy."

"I know exactly how lucky I am," he replied, his tone and expression soft. Then he blinked, and that smile returned. "Speaking of luck, here's hoping that all the chest and back pieces fit together on the first try. Good luck on the design."

That was the cue to get to work and not stand there staring at each other longingly as if they were crushes in a teen movie. Things sort of felt that way, though, all of the happy, bright potential so sparkling and new. Cam would say things like that, almost throwaway lines, yet butterflies would take flight in her chest. Butterflies that made her eagerly anticipate going home with him each night.

Gah! She shook herself. It wasn't the time to think about Cam and what he made her feel or how many times he made her feel it. She had to focus on assembling Cam's lower body armor, then figure out how to redeem her Thanos cosplay so that she could use as much of their current supplies as possible, *without* extending their already precarious timeline. *Lord, this timeline. How I'll come up with—*

"Hey." Cam touched her arm, snagging her attention and halting her spiraling thoughts. "Why don't you go ahead and work out the plan for the new costume? You won't be able to focus on anything else until you design and plot it out on the timeline."

Some of the anxiety faded. "You know me so well. Okay, let me think about it and sketch out a couple of possibilities and update the timeline. Once I have that, I'll get to work on your suit. Just call me if you need me, okay?"

"Deal."

Kenya returned to her worktable. Jane and one of the cameramen approached as she sat down. "Before you get started, I'd like to get some commentary. You can still gather your supplies if you'd like. Sound good?"

"Sure." She was going to have to explain it at some point anyway.

"Okay. Brian, you got the shot?" The cameraman gave a thumbs-up.

"All right." Jane turned back to Kenya. "I heard you talking to your partner about your costume. Is your project in trouble?"

Kenya blanked her face, then lacquered on a smile. "Attempting two sets of armor in the time we have was always an ambitious plan," she said as she retrieved her sketch pad, several colored pencils, and her tablet. "Doing both would have pushed us to our limits with the very real possibility that we wouldn't finish in time. So, to keep the contest parameters top of mind, we're going to let our

Iron Man armor build showcase our technical skills and attention to detail while the revised Thanos will show off our creativity."

"Are you worried that tossing your previous design will put pressure on your timeline? You're basically starting over."

The concern in Jane's voice sounded so real, but Kenya knew the point was to drive up the drama and underscore the stakes. She didn't want to appear as anything other than calm, cool, and collected, but they'd explained to all of the contestants the need to give the audience things to root for. Since the public would vote in this final round as well, she had to be a bit more engaging.

She gave Jane a helpless smile. "This is a lot harder than I thought it would be, and the stress is on a whole other level. There's so much riding on this for me, for us, and I want it to go as smoothly as possible."

That was a multilevel truth. She needed the win for major credibility in the cosplay world, invites to cons, monetizing her social media, and relaunching her business. The cash prize would be a great investment in the shop. Cam ran the business lean and mean and kept to a tight budget, but with any small business, one bad event could topple it all. That money would be a great cushion for him, and she intended to win it.

She fiddled with her pencil.

"We're working our asses off to deliver great cosplays. We don't need any distractions or setbacks."

As soon as the words left her mouth, she realized that she'd probably just jinxed herself. Or at least inspired Jane to come up with some mayhem and foolishness to create more drama. Before she could recant and end on a positive note, Jane asked a question. "So what are you about to do now?"

Kenya picked up her tablet. "First, I'm going to search for other images of Thanos, both from the comics and the movies, to see what other gear he has that can serve as inspiration for the new costume. I'll sketch a couple of ideas out until I have something I like, then start a supplies list. I'm hoping we can source everything we need from things we already have. I already know I'm keeping the boots I started and the gauntlet, so we're in a good space to handle the change and fit it into our production timeline."

She explained more as she looked through the image search and began a rough sketch until Jane called for a cut. "Thank you, Kenya. We'll get a few close-ups as you sketch then step back so you can really get to work."

"Great." Relieved, she slipped in her earbuds and bent back to her task. While she mostly ignored the cameras when she focused on work, especially detail work, she always felt off balance when she had to talk to them. Talking to people about cosplay? She could do that for hours, brainstorming, sharing, comparing, bouncing with excitement. Talking to the camera about cosplay? She felt monotonous, uninspired, dull. She hoped like hell she didn't come off that way.

It worried her, and she tried not to let it. She already had to fight hard against being labeled unlikeable. There were worse descriptions out there and if she wanted to self-flagellate, all she had to do was visit the show's forums. She'd done just that early in the competition. Once was enough. She hoped Cam had followed her advice and stayed out of them.

Sitting back, she surveyed her sketch for the reimagined Thanos. Going with the movie version made switching the design easier. She had the boots and a pair of pants that would be easy to embellish. The helmet she would keep since they'd already cut foam for it, and they were slated to assemble her helmet the following day. All she needed to do was find the right fabric for the top, sew it, and appropriate some of the foam to frame the collar and other embellishments. After that, she had to test the body paint and decide on makeup and whether or not she should add a purple wig to complete the gender-bent Mad Titan.

Feeling better about the change and scheduling impact, she got up to retrieve the pieces to the armor legs. Cam stood at the front counter, talking to a couple of female customers. While Make It Worx primarily took job requests and quotes through the company website, having a few walk-ins wasn't surprising. She'd figured that the shop would get even more after the first at-home episode aired. She hadn't figured that Jane would have one of the camera guys filming the interaction. Shooting shop business wasn't a part of the agreement.

Pulling off her earbuds, she turned to search for Jane. "Why is your camera guy filming a customer intake? I thought we agreed that shop business is off-limits."

"Cameron gave us permission to film him there," Jane answered with an I-thought-you-knew look. "We were filming him working on his helmet as he talked about the process, the shop, and cosplaying with you. One of the other guys said someone was at the counter asking for him, so we asked to tag along to get voiceover footage."

It sounded perfectly reasonable. So reasonable that any objection Kenya may have had would be viewed as unreasonable. Then again, Cam would have waved the cameraman away if he didn't want them filming. Besides, it was fucking exhausting being continuously suspicious and searching for ulterior motives.

"Oh, okay then." She returned to her chair to heat up her hot-glue gun and really get to work. Walk-ins were a good sign. She spent a couple of hours each day before and after their build time to review and respond to quote requests from the Make It Worx website, arrange virtual consultations, and slot projects that Cam had approved based on each guy's workload. Mack and Javier already had new projects in their respective queues. Business was good. Hopefully, it would stay that way.

Giggles interrupted her thoughts as she laid down a thin string of glue along the edge of an embellishment for her boots. She glanced at the counter. The two women, a redhead and a blonde, laughed at whatever Cam showed them on his tablet—presumably, the digital flipboard of some of their projects. While Make It Worx had created some whimsical designs, including one for a gala at the Atlanta Botanical Garden, nothing in their portfolio solicited that sort of reaction.

Kenya carefully fit the two pieces of craft foam together, trying to focus on the project instead of her irritation. She'd told herself that when the competition was over, she'd help Cam find "the one." It was the least that she could do after having him pretend to be her boyfriend. That didn't mean she wanted potential partners taking it upon themselves to audition at the shop, especially while she and Cam were allegedly a couple. Especially while she was sitting right freakin' there.

She uncapped the jar of gummy worms and retrieved two, biting the head off one with a satisfying bite and pull. Sure, she and Cam had started out as a fake relationship for the sake of the competition, but nothing was fake about their super happy fun times. Nothing fake about how his kisses revved her engines. Nothing fake about how she wanted to cut a bitch with a rusty utility knife.

Well, not really. She wasn't a violent person, but she had a healthy imagination fed by the definitely-not-fake possessiveness that welled inside her.

And oh my God, was the blonde twisting a curl of hair like a high schooler while the redhead practically had her boobs resting on the counter?

Jane moved close. "They seem to be more focused on flirting than placing an order."

She agreed with Jane, but she'd snatch off her lace front before she admitted it. "Cam can handle them."

"I'm sure he can," Jane agreed, her tone reasonable but concerned, "but doesn't it bother you, the way they're looking at your boyfriend?"

Fixing her face to neutral, Kenya tossed a glance to the counter again. If not for said obstacle, the redhead would have tried to press her chest against Cam by now. He was being his usual warm yet professional self, but she noticed he stood as far back from them as he could while still showing them the portfolio. "It's not fair to objectify someone else, but Cam *is* fine. Women and men look at him like that. I have no problem with looking."

"What if it's more than looking?"

Knowing Jane was trying to get a rise out of her, Kenya stole another look at the counter. The blonde reached out to touch Cam's forearm, but he backed away again. Why weren't these alleged customers maintaining professional boundaries?

They probably weren't customers. Not with all that tittering and giggling going on. On top of that, it was the completely wrong approach with Cam. He appreciated women who laughed with their whole chest, lived with their whole spirit, loved with their whole heart. Women who were real. Women who played games, but not the mental ones.

That didn't stop a flare of something surprisingly close to jealousy spurting up in her chest. Aside from the inane flirting, the two were close to the type Cam had dated before. Despite the way they were acting, if one of them had a geek streak, they might have stood a chance.

The thought soured her stomach, reminding her again of her silent pledge. Her initial plan was for them to end their "relationship" with a mutual breakup, and then she'd try to help Cam find a girlfriend. But she didn't want that. She didn't want the end of the competition to be the end of their relationship. She didn't want Cam to be free. She didn't want to be free, either.

She blinked at the realization. Cam was her friend, yes, but he was also her partner, her lover. Using that word to describe him caused butterflies to dance in her belly like a victory celebration, as if her body was thanking her mind for finally catching on and catching up.

"Cam will reach his limit soon enough," she said, confident in her man. "At the end of the day, he's going home with me."

Cam's patience had reached its limit. It was obvious that the pair had no intentions of becoming customers. They didn't ask the right questions or give the right answers. All they seemed to want to do was flirt, and he had neither the time or the inclination for it, especially now that he was with Kenya. And even if he wasn't, he sure as hell wouldn't flirt with other women in front of her. Mr. Davenport had taught him better than that.

He cut his gaze to Kenya, wondering what she made of their customers. He'd caught her looking a couple of times, her poker face securely in place. Which meant that Jane had probably already attempted to drum up some drama. Jane obviously hadn't learned enough about Kenya. His girl wasn't the one to ramp up drama or start a fight. He knew from her last breakup that if a guy disrespected her with another woman, she would walk rather than cause a scene. Mrs. Davenport had taught her better than that.

Still, he wouldn't have minded a little green-eyed envy. Not that he was insecure or anything, but it would have been reassuring if Kenya displayed just a tiny bit of possessiveness. It was a stupid thought, and he had no intention of playing stupid games. Not when the prize he wanted most was within his grasp.

It was time to put a stop to this game, time for them to face the boss level. "Hey, sweetie?"

Kenya looked up from her work. "Hey, babe, what's up?"

He heard one of the women mutter "Sweetie?" in disbelief. "Would you mind coming over? These ladies have some questions that I can't answer."

Her smile spread as she gave him a nod of understanding. "Be there in a sec."

The women changed their flirty tune when Kenya rose. "That's all right," the more aggressive one said. "You don't need to call her over."

"It's not a problem. Kenya is the expert you're looking for."

Kenya joined him behind the counter. She wore jeans that hugged every curve and a hot-pink button-down with a cute little white top beneath it that drew his gaze like a neon sign. She surprised him by looping an arm around his waist. "How can I help?"

The redhead frowned as she looked at Cam. "I thought you were the boss."

"I am." He mirrored Kenya's gesture. "So's she. In fact, she's the expert in what you want."

Kenya's soft laugh was felt more than heard, and he realized his words had a double meaning. "What do you ladies want?"

Her tone was pleasant and professional, but Cam knew a challenge when he heard one. "They're interested in having some work done." What kind of work, he didn't know—they giggled too much for him to get a direct answer.

"Wonderful. What exactly were you looking to have fabricated?"

The blonde did a hair toss. "We were just discussing that with Cameron."

"I understand that. However, I handle intake for the shop and anything costume related."

"That's why I called her over. Kenya's good at what she does. Very good."

"Thank you," Kenya said with a giggle.

A giggle? Oh, she was enjoying herself. He leaned into her, then turned back to the now-scowling women.

"But we'd like *your* expertise."

"For what type of project?" Kenya asked, ignoring the woman's pout. "Everyone on staff has a particular skill set, so it's important that I get enough details about your project so that we can route it to the best person for the job."

"We want sexy angel costumes," the redhead said. "One angel, one devil."

She could have at least mentioned *Good Omens*. "That's Kenya's area of expertise. She's the lead on all cosplay requests. As a matter of fact, we're in the finals right now of a cosplay competition."

"But we want wings!" the blonde exclaimed. "And we want them to look real. Isn't that more of what you do?"

Cam tightened his grip on Kenya, irritated with them ignoring her. But she was undaunted. "The type of wing will depend on many different factors," she explained. "What do you envision? Cherub-style wings, or full-sized wings? Do you want real feathers for the angel and leathery wings for the devil? How soon do you want them? Also, what have you budgeted for them?"

"I want full-sized ones that can open when I want them to," the redhead declared. "That requires more than a glue gun, doesn't it?"

His tolerance meter hit full. The two would-be customers had taken up time they didn't have to spare for costumes he was sure were over their budget. Time to end this.

Kenya spoke before he could. "It's definitely a collaborative project. Generally speaking, I would do an initial consultation and provide renderings for you to approve. I provide an invoice listing materials and labor, then you pay a deposit and we slate your work for production. Unfortunately, because of our current workload and the amount of labor required, we do not have availability to take on a new cosplay order at this time."

"What if we wanted to move to the front of the line?" the redhead asked. "How much would that be?"

"Not including a rush fee, the deposit would be $3,000."

"Are you serious?" She turned to Cam. "Is she serious?"

"For a custom build of two pairs of fully articulated wings? Yes," Cam answered, then decided to go for full shock value. "That's not even fifty percent of the final cost. As Kenya said, there would be an additional fee if you wanted it sooner than the six to eight months something like that would usually take."

"Six to eight months?"

"Here at Make it Worx, we pride ourselves on delivering a high-quality product," Kenya explained. "Quality takes time. We do our best to accommodate current and future customers; however, we have a tight production schedule that we must adhere to, projects that have been promised, deposits that have been made. It would be a disservice to both of us if we weren't candid about what you could expect."

Cam watched in equal parts admiration and amusement as she snagged a brochure then rounded the counter. "If you'd like to take some time to review, we understand. This brochure has our contact information and a link to our gallery and customer testimonials.

Feel free to review it at your leisure. If you decide that the parameters we have will work for you, we'd love to have your business."

She herded the pair to the door before they knew what hit them. "Of course we're also more than happy to discuss more budget-friendly options and recommend other vendors who may be more suitable to your needs. We'd prefer that you use our contact form through the website, but we also can be contacted through our social media. Have a great day, and thank you for visiting Make It Worx."

Cam waited until the door closed before breaking into a slow clap. "That was epic."

She grinned at him. "Just providing great customer service with a dose of reality."

He joined her on the other side of the counter. "I don't think they'll be back."

"You never know," she said, ever the diplomat. "They might try again with something more basic. If so, I'll be happy to consult with them."

"That knowledge flex was damned sexy," he told her, sliding a hand down her arm because it was increasingly impossible to be so close without touching. "So was the way you claimed your territory."

"You're not my terri— Oh," she broke off, flustered. "What I meant to say was . . ."

She sobered then reached out to stroke his hair. "I got you, boo."

A simple statement paired with a simple gesture, yet he felt both down deep in his soul. Maybe, just maybe, he was closer to winning the competition and the girl than he'd thought.

chapter twenty

The next few days passed in a repetitious parade of people coming in, trying to snag Cam's attention, then failing miserably. It went from amusing to irritating with a quickness, fraying Kenya's temper and her concentration. The only upside was that a few of the drop-ins actually wanted to become customers. Too bad the gawkers and opportunists were working her last nerve.

Thank goodness for Cam's calming influence. His cheery demeanor blunted the edge of her frustration and stress so that she was better able to manage the pressure of their looming deadline. It amazed her how he was able to be so upbeat. Then again, good sex made for good moods.

"What are you smiling about?"

She looked up from her sewing machine. Cam had made a few final touches on the light feature on his gloves. She'd done the prime and paint for the gloves, chest plate, and helmet before the rest of the armor so that he could have plenty of time to work on the light effects. He'd been whistling while he worked, a sure sign that the lights were performing the way he wanted them to.

Was she smiling? Of course she was. Being with Cam, thinking of Cam, wanting Cam—he made her feel lighter, happier, better. It was long past time to tell him so.

She rolled her chair over to him, placed a hand on his thigh. "I'm smiling because I was thinking about how much I appreciate you. You're everything I need."

Delight suffused his features, so angelic she'd swear she heard angels singing. In that moment his smile became a treasure and she greedily wanted more of them. She'd add it to her memory hoard that included his sexy smiles, blissed-out after-sex smiles, and soft, secret smiles. With a treasure like that, she'd be richer than any dragon.

"I appreciate you appreciating me," he said, his voice for her alone. "I hope you know the feeling's mutual."

Impulse had her reaching up to cup his cheek. The stubble gave him a gruffly sexy air, reminding her of the beard burn on her thighs. She wasn't sure when she'd transitioned from PDAs for the cameras to PDAs for herself, but she didn't care. Why should she when she enjoyed giving them as much as Cam enjoyed receiving them? "I do."

He reached up to cover her hand with his own, his gaze soft and warm and full of promise. "KeKe, I—"

"You must be ahead of schedule, if you can take time for all of that."

Kenya jumped back in surprise and dread. She looked to the front door, her mouth dropping open. Sure enough, the judges had entered the shop and were avidly watching them. Rebecca, the one who'd spoken, looked as if she still hadn't removed the stick from her ass.

Nerves bounced like water bubbles on a hot skillet as she shot to her feet, dimly aware of Cam standing with her. "Oh my God. What are y'all doing here?"

"We've come to see your progress," Leon explained. "We're curious to see how well you're doing."

"And . . . we wanted to meet your partner!" Caroline exclaimed with a little excited hop. "Is this him?"

Considering that they'd caught her and Cam mid–emotional moment . . . Kenya reached for calm, found it in Cam's hand gripping hers. Together they walked to the front of the shop. "Cam, these are the *Cosplay or No Way* judges, Leon, Caroline, and Rebecca. Guys, this is Cameron Lassiter."

Cam shook their hands. "So nice to meet you, Mr. Lassiter," Rebecca said. "You have a lovely setup here."

"Thank you. We're real proud of what we've accomplished here."

Rebecca turned to Kenya. "How lucky are you to have someone with his expertise in your corner! It's no wonder you've made it to the final round."

Barely five minutes into their visit and Becky had her verbal knives out. The barb didn't surprise Kenya, but the sting of Rebecca's words did. Being home with Cam had softened her defensive shields. She couldn't allow Rebecca to steal her sparkle.

Cam spoke before she could. "Actually, I'm the lucky one," he said, draping an arm around her shoulders. "If not for Kenya getting me into cosplay and drama club in high school, Make It Worx wouldn't be here. We make great partners in every meaning of the word."

She leaned against him in silent thanks before addressing Rebecca. "Besides, isn't Ben's husband a stage manager for a community theater? Both of us have creative lives. I'd say we're evenly matched."

A thin smile sliced across Rebecca's face. "If you say so."

Cam tensed beside her. Kenya placed her palm on his chest, hoping to soothe him. She didn't need him to defend her honor over so slight a slight. If she'd learned anything about Rebecca, it was that there would be more coming. "Why don't we show you our project?"

Hand in hand with Cam, she led the judges and film crew to the worktables at the back of the shop. After Jane arranged them the way that she wanted, she signaled for them to begin.

Leon spoke. "What did you choose for your iconic duos cosplay?"

Kenya tightened her grip on Cam's poor hand, hoping to pull a little strength from him. The judges' scores still carried weight in this final round, and she wanted them intrigued and on board with their idea. "We decided to go with Iron Man and Thanos."

"A gender-bent Thanos," Cam added, squeezing her hand in return.

The judges looked at each other. Dread curdled in Kenya's stomach. Even Caroline frowned. "But . . . they're not an iconic couple."

"Iconic enemies, thanks to the movies," Cam said. "Think about it like Tom and Jerry, or Batman and the Joker."

"When you consider that one of the biggest movies ever pitted Iron Man's brain against Thanos's brawn, it fits the parameters," Kenya added. "Mainstream viewers will know those two."

Rebecca pursed her lips. "I find it fascinating that you chose to cosplay the villain."

Here we go. Kenya blanked her expression. "In what way?"

"Oh." Rebecca blinked, looked at Cam, then back at her. "Well, he's such a larger-than-life persona."

Cam gripped her hand so tight her fingers went numb. "Like Tony Stark's ego isn't?"

"Thanos isn't a likeable character," Rebecca continued, ignoring

Cam's words and his rising anger. "Which is something you've had to work on throughout the competition. Don't you believe it's a risk to cosplay such a ruthless character who will do anything to achieve his goals?"

"Just like a lot of us," she retorted.

Rebecca's gaze sharpened. "Really? So, you feel some affinity with the villain, willing to do anything to win?"

She knew exactly what Rebecca implied, and considering the way Cam tensed, he did too. No one outside of their friends and family believed that their relationship was real, and now that their relationship actually was real, the irony was so strong it burned like Two-Buck Chuck.

"We wanted to demonstrate a wide swath of skills," Kenya answered coolly, not wanting Cam to flip out or give Becky the satisfaction of getting a rise out of her. "We've said it before: Iron Man demonstrates our ability to create realistic-looking armor and light details. A gender-bending Thanos will still be Thanos, while highlighting our creative ability with prosthetics and makeup. We plan to showcase a wide variety of skills any costume department would look for."

"You're stretching your capabilities and taking risks," Leon said. "Exactly what we want final round contestants to do."

Kenya looked at Rebecca. "Go big or go home, right?"

She already knew that Rebecca wasn't going to be in her corner in this round, just as she hadn't been in any of the others. She wasn't going to let Bad Judge Becky dim her shine. The plan had always been to wow the other two judges and a majority of the viewing audience, and any costume designers who might be watching. Winning would be the best revenge.

Caroline turned to them. "I'd love to see your Arc Reactor. You 3-D printed it, right?"

"I did," Cam answered, his grip easing. Kenya pulled her hand free to work some life back into it, standing back so that Cam could explain as they walked the judges through the details of the armor build.

"An impressive amount of work," Rebecca said, surprising Kenya. Did the judge just give them a true compliment? "What did you do, Kenya?"

Of course. Kenya pulled her lips back from her teeth. "Keeping to the parameters, I cut the pieces for the armor, fit the Iron Man pieces together, and painted and primed it. Cam is handling the special effects work. All of our duties are split as denoted on our project chart here."

It was a slow roller coaster of questions and comments, positive words from Leon and Caroline, and not as many from Rebecca. It worsened when they moved to Kenya's table. Rebecca picked at every detail of the design in a prime example of concern trolling. The worst part was that it seemed to impact the other judges, based on their thoughtful yet concerned expressions.

Kenya had thought the competition was hers to win. Now she wondered if it was hers to lose.

can't believe you had to put up with that woman for two months!" Cam exclaimed as he snatched his toothbrush from the holder. "I mean, I thought that maybe she was being the mean judge for the cameras, but she's the same even when the cameras aren't rolling!"

"Yeah." Kenya shrugged, squeezing out toothpaste on her brush before handing the tube to him. "You get used to it."

"Babe." He touched her shoulder. "You shouldn't have to get used to shit like that. No one should."

A brief smile flickered at her lips. She grazed his fingers with hers before turning back to the mirror. "Microaggressions like that happen all the time. It's okay."

He watched her brush her teeth, trying to rein in his anger and frustration. It was *not* okay. It would never be okay to him that Kenya had to endure crap like that. The fact that there was nothing that he could do about it rubbed at him like coarse-grit sandpaper.

Outwardly she seemed okay. The judges had stayed at the shop for hours, observing them as they worked, questioning every decision they'd made. Or rather, questioning every decision Kenya had made. They'd switched to shop work after the judges and the film crew had left, but Kenya hadn't been able to focus. Instead, they'd come home, ordered a pizza, and piled on the couch to watch one of their new favorite shows, *Anubis Rising*, about a police detective possessed by the spirit of Anubis, who helps him solve crimes. They'd barely made it through one episode before Kenya declared her fatigue and headed to the shower.

It wasn't fatigue. He knew that to his bones. That judge with her fake sincerity and backhanded compliments had taken an ice pick to Kenya's confidence, and that was unforgivable. Their cosplays weren't easy builds, especially in the time frame they had. The judges needed to appreciate that, not chip away at it.

"Are you mad at your teeth?"

Kenya's quiet question sliced through the razor wire of his thoughts. He spit into the sink then rinsed his mouth and brush. "No, I'm still pissed on your behalf. I know I shouldn't be if you aren't, but it's hard to let the anger go."

"Welcome to my world." She wiped at her mouth with a washcloth, then replaced it on her rack. "The anger is always there, Cam. I just keep it locked down so that it doesn't burn me alive."

"How?" He pumped a couple of dollops of her lotion and began to rub it into his arm. Moisturizing his skin hadn't been a part of his nightly ritual until he and Kenya had begun sharing a bed and a bath. It had taken one comment about how she liked the way his skin felt to make him a convert. "How do you lock it down?"

She pumped some lotion into her palm, then moved behind him to apply it to his shoulders. "I remind myself of the positive things, the things that make me happy, the good things that I've done."

"Like what?"

Her hands slowed as she thought about her answer. "Like getting my degree. Like making it through this competition to the final round. Like Make It Worx making it happen."

His eyes slid closed as her fingers slowly worked down his back, easing his tension and anger with every stroke. He hung his head and gripped the edge of the counter, not wanting her to stop talking or touching. "My baby's doing good."

"Yes, it is."

He wasn't talking about the shop, but he didn't correct her. "Those are the things that you've done, but what about the things that make you happy?" He'd make a mental list to use later.

"Being able to be creative. Coffee dates with Janelle, making costumes." Her voice dropped as she smoothed more lotion down his back. "Dinner with you. Watching our favorite shows with you. Waking up with you. Everything . . . with you. Every day I'm grateful that I plopped down next to you during lunch period that day."

He spun around, then wrapped her in his arms. "So am I."

Her hands formed fists at his waist before she relaxed into him, wrapping her arms tight around him. A deep sigh shook her frame. "Maybe . . . maybe we should rethink my costume."

"Hey." He stepped back so that he could see her face. The doubt tore at him. "I'm not going to ask where this is coming from. I have a pretty good idea, and it's pissing me off. You can't let her get into your head, babe."

"I know I shouldn't, but she's a professional costume designer. You take away the snide remarks and she has some helpful criticism."

"Emphasis on 'criticism'." Wanting to soothe her the way she soothed him, he got some lotion and began to smooth it over her right arm. "If her criticism is making you consider killing a project halfway through our deadline, it's not really helpful, is it?"

"I know, but—"

"Answer me honestly." He began to lotion her left arm, moving his fingers in slow circles along her skin. "Do we really have time to create a new costume? And if so, do you have a costume in mind?"

Her shoulders slumped. "No. The only iconic duo choice to go with Iron Man is War Machine or Pepper Potts's Rescue armor, and we can't do either of them justice in the time that we have."

He moved behind her to rub her shoulders. Tension hardened them, making them feel like rocks beneath his hands. Protectiveness surged inside him. His heart ached for her, for carrying so much weight and stress. Although they had divided the work, she took on all of the emotional labor. Everything in him demanded that he take some of the burden from her.

"Call me biased, but I think we've got a fan-fucking-tastic idea," he declared, using his thumb to gently attack a knot between her shoulder blades. "For all the reasons you explained to the judges and then some. What we're producing in this time frame is nothing short of awesome, but that's to be expected from an awesome woman."

She gave him a heavy-lidded stare in the mirror. "I *am* pretty awesome, aren't I?"

"Listen. You are Kenya fucking Davenport. Smart, beautiful, sexy, creative, and awesome. You know your shit and you're not going to let Cosplay Karen dim your glow."

Finally, she laughed, then bumped against him. "See? This is part of why you have a permanent invitation to the cookout."

He wrapped his arms around her waist, lowering his head to press a kiss to her collarbone. "You can count on me to always be your plus-one."

"I'm going to hold you to that."

He certainly hoped so. "Okay." He stepped around her to grab the lotion. "Let's head to bed so I can do the rest."

She snorted. "You're just using this as an excuse to get into my pants."

"Maybe. But I'd also like to point out that you're not wearing pants."

"Oh my god!" She looked down at her grumpy pug tank-style sleep shirt, then back at him. "You're right! You know what else?"

"What?"

She turned to the doorway, stopped, lifted her hem, then mooned him. "I'm not wearing panties either."

CHAPTER TWENTY-ONE

Something wasn't right.

Unease prickled the spot between Kenya's shoulder blades. In the time since the judges had left, she couldn't shake the feeling of impending doom. She didn't want to admit it, but she was rattled, more rattled than she had admitted to Cam. He'd made a Herculean effort in keeping her spirits up, but the long days and stress were beginning to wear on them. They still had shop business to tend to, and even with Mack and Javier pulling more than their fair share, there were still duties that only she and Cam could do.

The only relief was in bed, even though lately they were too exhausted for more than kisses and cuddles before falling into too-brief sleep. She had to keep reminding herself that the win would be worth it. Cam would get an influx of cash for the shop, and she'd get to hang out her shingle as a costume creator. Their futures would be set. The win was everything.

She adjusted a hook-and-loop strap at his side, then stepped back. "How does it feel?"

"Pretty good, actually." Cam turned to her with a smile, arms spread as he showed off the armor. "I can move easily and there's good flexibility at the joints. How does it look?"

"Like real armor and not the foam it is." She stood back to observe the full effect. The only thing missing were the stones on his version of the Infinity Gauntlet. That and her own gauntlet were next on the to-do list. "The paint job is amazing. You did an excellent job with it."

"*We* did an excellent job with it," he corrected her. "Sanding that base coat took a lot, and don't forget the detail work you did."

"With just a little bit left, thank goodness." Pride blossomed within her as she assessed Cam's cosplay. The armor shone in the shop's lights, looking like actual metal instead of foam. The Arc Reactor gleamed in the chest plate. Then he slipped on the helmet. "Perfect! Light it up!"

The big test. Cam had a small switch on the inside of his left glove that powered the light kits in his palms, a button switch just inside the chin of the helmet for the eyes, and a separate switch for the Infinity Gauntlet. It had been a painstaking task for him to get the palms to light up simultaneously, and to make the helmet lights work without blinding himself, but the extra work could give them an edge in the competition.

"Here goes." He touched the switches. Kenya clasped her hands together, holding her breath as she waited. Flicker, flicker . . . on.

"Yes!" Kenya clapped her hands as she bounced in place, then broke into a song and dance. "Oh yeah, we got a light show, we got the eye glow, catch these hands, yo."

Cam's muffled laughter emanated from the suit before he switched the lights off and removed his helmet. "Love those moves, babe. I think we can officially mark this as a success."

"Hell yeah we can." She crossed to him, wanting to give him a hug, but not enough to risk damaging the suit. "God, Cam, you're amazing. This. Is. Awesome!"

He grinned at her, the tips of his ears reddening. "Awesome enough for a kiss?"

"A careful kiss now, or a thorough one once you're out of the armor?"

"Yes to both."

Happiness fizzed like soda in her veins, yet she carefully leaned forward and met him halfway for a kiss that didn't satisfy either of them. They couldn't risk her boobs crushing the armor with their usual tight embraces. It would take more time than they could risk to repair or replace any part.

He frowned as they parted. "Help me get out of this so I can kiss you properly."

"Yes, sir."

She helped him unbuckle and unhook the various pieces, carefully storing all but the Infinity Gauntlet glove into a hard-sided case that would protect the costume during transport to Los Angeles for the finale. He sighed with relief as he pulled the last piece off, revealing the tight black turtleneck and form-fitting black pants he'd chosen to wear beneath the armor.

Kenya appreciated the way the fabric clung to him, making a mental note to buy him more tight T-shirts and sweaters. Something soft and touchable that accented his eyes but was also easy to remove.

"I love that look in your eyes, sweetheart," he said then, standing so, so close. "Why don't you kiss me the same way you're looking at me?"

Anywhere else, with anyone else, she would have laughed off the sudden intensity. Even two weeks ago with Cam she might have thought about it. But two weeks ago felt like two years ago and in that time she'd done many things and felt so much more, all thanks to the man standing in front of her with hunger in his eyes.

So she didn't think about Javier and Mack wrapping up for the day. She didn't think about the camera crew leering over them. All she thought about, all she could see, was Cam. Moving into his arms as easily as iron to a magnet, she looped her arms around his neck, pressed her chest against his for a full-body hug, then kissed him.

His hands splayed across her spine as he kissed her back, a slight tremble flickering across his fingers. It was a deep kiss, a Cam kiss, the kind you remembered when you were alone in bed at night, the kind you bragged to your girls about. The toe-curling, blood-heating, heart-thumping kind, and she was suddenly furious that they were standing in the middle of the shop instead of their living room.

He pulled away with a low growl of regret. "I'm gonna go change into something a lot less restrictive, then come back to finish your helmet. I want to get you home as soon as possible."

It was her turn to shiver. "Then I guess I'd better get stoned—uhm, started on gluing the stones. On the gauntlets."

Laughter trailed behind him as he walked away. Then he stopped, looked over his shoulder. "Are you looking at my ass?"

"Damn right I am."

He grinned like sunshine. "Glad you like the junk in my trunk. Be back in a sec."

She shook her head as she turned back to her work space. She more than liked it, she was downright addicted to it. They were going to need to have a talk once the competition was over. Their relationship, their plans, their futures could go in a myriad of directions depending on the outcome of the contest. She was hoping that they would continue to travel that road together.

"Hey, Mack," Javier called. "Are you ready for happy hour? Looks like the bosses are ready to turn this into Shop After Dark."

"Yeah, man," Mack answered, switching off the lights in his area. "No need to stick around for that."

"Goodnight, guys," Kenya said, waving at them. "Don't let the door hit ya where the good lord split ya."

Only she, Cam, and Jane and her crew remained. Jane usually left earlier, probably to review the daily footage to slate things for postproduction. She didn't stay unless something interesting was happening.

Kenya snorted. Maybe making out with Iron Man Cam in the middle of the shop floor was interesting enough for them to stick around. Not that she wanted to put on a show, but if Cam gave her that look and asked for a kiss, how could she refuse?

Laughing to herself, she arranged the faux gemstones and pieces of the gauntlet on her worktable. She'd hand-drawn a template then cut each piece out of thinner foam for flexibility before heating and shaping them to fit her fingers. After priming and painting had been completed, she was now ready to glue the gauntlet pieces onto the base gloves she'd sewn out of stretchy black fabric. She had gone with copper-wire fairy lights beneath round metal frames on each of the gloves, with the power source in a pocket in the wristband. The plan was to stage a mock face-off, and at the end, she'd switch off the light kit on her gauntlet while Cam turned on his. Then she'd fall to one knee in defeat.

With the lights and the metal housings in place, all she needed to do was glue each stone into its socket with jewelry adhesive. Eager to get started so she and Cam could get home sooner, she spun in her chair and rolled toward her stack of supply bins. A light crash sounded behind her. She spun around and scooted forward to see what had fallen, but heard a crunching sound instead.

No.

Silence dropped like a hammer as she froze. If she didn't move, didn't look, then nothing was wrong and she could continue with her build.

She had to move. She had to look. She had to know if she'd just screwed herself. Barely daring to breathe, she carefully planted her feet, then rose. Then she lifted her task chair to place it out of the way. Another crunch. She looked.

Somehow she not only had managed to knock the largest piece of the gauntlet off her worktable, she'd rolled over it.

"No."

Panic seeped into her veins as she bent down to retrieve the part. A deep crease ran down the center where the chair wheel had rolled through it. That wasn't the worst part. No, the worst part was while she held the gauntlet part in her hand, the battery and housing for the lights still lay on the floor.

She let out a sound she didn't recognize, something between a bleat and a scream, as the enormity of her mistake crashed into her.

"What's wrong?"

She spun as Cam stepped up to her, his expression tight with concern. She held out her cupped hands, unable to control their violent shaking.

He cursed. "What happened?"

"I screwed up." She swallowed. "I turned too fast and knocked it off the table. Then I rolled over it. How could I be so stupid and not pay attention to what I was doing?"

Acutely aware of her voice rising with every word, she tried to think positively but her mind was quicksand. Blood pounded in her ears, spots flashed along the edges of her vision. "We're on a tight schedule. We're down to the wire. I can't believe I was so stupid!"

"Hey, hey." Cam gripped her biceps. "You know you're not stupid. This was an accident. We can fix this."

"How?" She pressed a hand to her forehead in an attempt to stem the burgeoning headache and the threatening tears. "If it was just a crease, I could use the heat gun to smooth it back out. But the wheel left a gouge in it, Cam. A gouge!"

His brows lowered with a frown before he knelt to pick up the other pieces. "The housing is broken."

"I know!" Her pulse fluttered in her throat as a phantom itch started between her shoulder blades. "I don't have anything here that I can use. We've got to get those gauntlets done so I can move on to the body paint and makeup and then I need to finish the collar on my vest and the details on my boots and I can't have any setbacks this close—"

"Babe." Cam tightened his grip on her arms. "Look at me. I need you to breathe with me, okay? Deep breath in, deep breath out. Good, let's do it again. Deep breath in, deep breath out."

Keeping her gaze locked to his, she matched her breaths to his until her heart no longer felt as if it would break free of her chest. A tiny tremor swept through her, and she managed to sound less hysterical when she said, "To have something like this happen this late in the game . . . it's—it's—"

"No, it's not." He slid his hands up her arms to cup her cheeks. "It's not too late. I'll go to the closest craft store and buy everything you need. I'll also grab something quick for dinner on the way back. We'll work on the gauntlet together tonight and be back on schedule in the morning. While I'm gone, you can try out the body paint and makeup. How does that sound?"

It sounded like a life preserver and she latched on to it with everything she had. "Thank you," she whispered, her voice warbling in relief as she rested her forehead against his. "I don't know what I'd do without you."

"Good thing you won't ever have to worry about that." He placed a comforting kiss to her forehead, diminishing her headache like magic. "I'll be back as quick as I can, okay?"

"Okay."

She watched him leave. Softer, calmer emotions percolated through her now that Cam had ridden to her rescue. That was the kind of man he was, talking her down from her freak-outs, offering solutions but making sure she was okay with them before taking charge. How could you not love a man like that?

The words rang like a gong in her head, echoing in her heart. How could *she* not love a man like that? She couldn't, which meant only one thing.

Not only did she love her best friend, she was also in love with her best friend. She was in love with Cam.

Her lips tugged up into a smile, and she hugged herself tightly to revel in the emotion and hold it close. It filled her spirit like sunlight after a storm, brightening all the dark corners and giving her an extra boost of desperately needed confidence. She could do this. They could do this.

In much better spirits, she returned to her workstation, carefully stored away the remnants of the glove and faux stones, then pulled out her tablet, purple body paint, makeup, and a tri-fold lighted makeup mirror. She'd found a website that sold fake body parts and had ordered several chins for backup in case she ran out of time to mold and create her own. Thanks to the Great Gauntlet Flipout, she didn't have the ovaries to experiment then, and she wasn't sure she'd feel differently in the morning.

She pulled up a headshot of Thanos on her tablet, then picked one of the chins. Not full enough. The second one was square enough, and with the roundness of her cheeks she could make it work. The third didn't feel right, so number two was the winner. She'd still have to build grooves into the chin but she'd save that for the morning.

Her next problem would be figuring out if she needed to put her regular makeup on the fake chin to match her skin tone before painting it over with the purple body paint. Probably, but she'd test that on one of the spare ones first. Before that, she had to get the right shade of purple. She didn't want to be strutting her stuff across a stage on finale night looking like Ursula instead of the Mad Titan.

She painted a couple of different stripes on her inner wrist, then grabbed a gummy worm when her stomach began to rumble. Lunch was a distant memory, so distant she couldn't remember what they'd had. Hopefully, Cam would arrive with her supplies and Chinese or pizza. Hopefully he'd show up at any moment.

As if on cue, the chime over the door rang. Happy excitement launched her to her feet, ready and willing to greet her returning hero. She froze.

It wasn't Cam who'd walked through the door. It was Jessa.

CHAPTER TWENTY-TWO

Jessa!" Kenya quickly made her way to the front counter to block Jessa from venturing further into the shop. "What are you doing here?"

The other woman glanced around the shop, her gaze landing on Jane and the camera crew. "Is Cam here?"

Kenya breathed a silent thanks that her gauntlet emergency had sent Cam out for a while. Now all she had to do was get Jessa to leave before he returned. "No, he isn't. Do you want to leave a message? I'm assuming it's the one that you couldn't say to Cam in front of me last week?"

Jessa's jaw tightened for a moment then relaxed. "That's all right." She plunked her keys and purse down on the counter. "I wanted to talk to you first anyways. Woman to woman."

Here we go. Kenya held on to the threads of her temper with sheer force of will. She did *not* have time for whatever drama Jessa wanted to start. She was too tired emotionally, mentally, and physically to deal with this, so she made another attempt to put an end to Jessa's stunt. "Woman to woman, I'm pretty sure we have nothing to talk about."

"Yesh, we do." Jessa lifted her chin. "We need to talk about Cameron."

"Wait." Kenya narrowed her eyes. "Have you been drinking?" This was the last thing that either of them needed, especially with a film crew avidly watching. Jessa would surely have regrets in the morning to go with her hangover. "Did you drive here? I'm going to call you a rideshare."

"No. Not until we talk."

"Okay, fine." Kenya suppressed a sigh as she folded her arms across her chest. "Go ahead."

"You need to break up with Cameron."

She'd figured that would be the point of Jessa's visit, but it still irritated her. "Did you really just fix your mouth to say that? I'm not going to break up with Cam just because you want me to, and he's not going to get back with you just because you want him to. Now that we've had this 'woman to woman' talk, it's time for you to leave. I have work to do."

"Then you leave me no choice but to tell him. He needs to know. The whole world needs to know."

"Girl." Kenya snorted. "This isn't an episode of a Shonda Rhimes show. Whatever you have to say, say it with your whole chest."

"Fine." Jessa sneered, pointing at her. "You're a liar and a cheat!"

Shock dampened her palms. How did Jessa . . . no. Kenya forced herself to stop and think. There was no way Jessa could know about the deal she'd made with Cam. Kenya hadn't told her, and she was pretty damn sure Cam hadn't either. Even if she had known, what had begun as a fake relationship was now very, very real.

Which meant Jessa had swung wildly like a kid with a piñata, hoping for a strike to get the goods. Or she could be thinking that

Kenya had lied and cheated with Cam while he and Jessa were still together. Either way, Kenya wasn't about to let someone accuse her of doing something dirty without defending herself.

"You have a lot of nerve coming up in my place of business being drunk and loud and wrong like this. You need to leave."

"I'm not leaving, and this isn't your place of business," Jessa retorted. "This is Cameron's shop. You just work here."

"Again, loud and drunk and wrong. I own a part of Make It Worx." A tiny part, but only because she'd refused to take the larger share Cam had offered when she'd contributed to his start-up fund. "Cam and I are partners in business and in life. And to make it crystal clear, we didn't start dating until after the two of you broke up. So no, he didn't cheat on you. That's not the kind of man he is. And if you can think that about him . . . well, maybe that's one of the reasons why you're his ex."

Jessa's eyes widened with a Molotov cocktail of anger, embarrassment, and hurt. "No, it's because of you! You lie and cheat and manipulate and play the victim to make Cameron help you!"

"Play the victim?" Oh, this was gonna be rich. She folded her arms. "Please, educate me on how I'm playing the victim in this scenario."

"You take advantage of him," Jessa said, her chin wobbling. "He's the nicest guy with the kindest heart, and for some reason, he can never say no to you. Every time you needed something, he would drop everything to help you out. That's why he agreed to help you with this show when he should have been focused on his business. In fact, he's been running to your rescue since high school."

Heat stung Kenya's ears as her temper began to fray. "You have no idea what you're talking about!"

"Really? He shares his apartment with you. He gave you a job. He helped you audition for this show and now, instead of focusing on running his shop, he's wasting time helping you with this competition. I mean, maybe you're holding something over him and he feels indebted to you for some reason. But I'm betting he just feels sorry for you that you can't do anything on your own. That's why I don't believe this 'relationship.' You're not his girlfriend, you're his charity case."

Kenya froze, her brain so overwhelmed by emotion that her body didn't know how to react. Anger scorched her muscles, demanding that she reach across the counter and snatch Jessa bald. Only her unwillingness to give Jane and the cameras the reaction they'd been wanting all season kept her from doing it. Instead, she did the only thing she could.

She laughed. Laughed at Jessa's intoxicated attempt to call her out. Laughed at Jane's desire to film an Angry Black Woman tirade. Laughed at the absolute absurdity of the day. Laughed at the little niggle of doubt caused by Jessa's words. Laughed so that she couldn't rage, or even worse, cry.

When her laughter faded, she pinned Jessa with a glare. "You're forcing me to take time for something so damn ridiculous, I should send you an invoice. Now, I'm sorry you worked yourself up like this, and I at least hope you weren't drinking alone and driving. I also hope that tomorrow you'll be in a better space than you are right now. But I need you to understand."

She moved closer, holding the other woman's gaze. "You've known Cam six months. I've known him more than twelve years. You will never know anything like what we've been through. You will never know anything like how deep our bond is. You will never be able to love Cam the way that I do, and he will never love you the way he loves me."

Rage sliced across Jessa's features. "You don't expect anyone to believe that the two of you are really dating, do you? Or better yet, do you really think people believe that you and Cameron are having sex?"

Kenya laughed at the irony. No one had a problem with her and Cam when they were pretending to be a couple. Now they actually were a couple and enjoying each other thoroughly, and doubts were coming out of the woodwork. "I don't give two shits what everyone else thinks. Cam and I know the truth."

"There's nothing true about your relationship! Because I'm not the only one who can't believe that Cam would give up all of this"—she gestured wildly to herself—"for all of that."

"You need to check yourself, Jessa." The other woman's tone and anger escalated, and Kenya had no idea what she'd do next. Just in case, she made a show of deliberately removing her earrings. Jessa was too drunk to receive the signal, but the cameraman closest to her did, judging by his excited expression as he trained his camera on her.

Frosty anger iced her veins, a frozen calm solidifying over churning rage. She did not want to give them the fucking show they'd obviously worked so hard to create, but what else could she do? Calling Cam was not an option—it would only escalate the spectacle and give Jane and her crew more footage for next week's episode. Thank God he wasn't here for this drama.

"I'm being nice because you are clearly drunk off your ass. You're already going to be hungover and embarrassed in the morning. There's no need to add to it."

"What do you have on him?" Jessa demanded, her voice cracking. "There must be something you're holding over his head to make him do this for you!"

Dammit. Now the tears? No matter what she did at this point, Kenya knew she would be viewed as the bad guy. Still she tried.

"You dated him but it's like you don't know him at all. I'm not holding anything over him, and it's insulting to Cam for you to think he'd let himself get played like that!"

"I love him!" she cried, slamming her hand down on the glass countertop. "I love him, and you took him away from me because you needed his help. You're always needing his help and he always comes to your rescue. Why?"

A rebuttal sprang to her lips, but Kenya held it back. How could she deny that when Cam had done exactly that earlier? "You need to leave."

"I'm not leaving!" Jessa wiped at her tear-blotched face. "I love him and he needs to know the truth."

How could her day have gone from so bright to so twisted? She wanted Jessa gone, and her drunken demands too. The only thing she could do at this point, besides physically throwing her out, would be to call the police. But what good would that do? They'd arrive, see a hysterically crying petite blonde facing off with a fat and angry Black woman, and before Kenya would be able to say anything, they'd have her in handcuffs, escorting her out of her own shop. The scene was whacked enough without adding humiliation to it.

"Look—"

"What the fuck is going on here?"

Anger shot through the roof as Cam surveyed the scene in front of him. Jessa crying hysterically. The full production crew trained on her. Kenya, standing stoically apart behind the counter, one cameraman hovering like a vulture.

No, not stoic. He saw the slight wobble of her lips, knew the Herculean effort it took to project a calm, cool, and collected demeanor. Whatever had happened, it clearly had been designed to hurt or anger Kenya. Neither was acceptable. Nothing mattered more than getting to her side and shielding her from all this.

Jessa blocked his way, tears streaming, arms up to embrace him. "Oh, Cameron, I'm so glad you're here! This is horrible!"

He ignored her to make a beeline for Kenya, gently taking her by her shoulders. "Are you okay, sweetheart?" he whispered.

Momentarily blocked from the cameras, she drew one stuttering breath, then another. "I'm fine."

Rage bubbled like lava in his chest as the need to protect her burned through him. He noticed her earrings on the counter, and the thought that she'd believed she'd have to physically defend herself incensed him further.

"Why don't you go on home? I'll deal with this."

"But—"

"We'll come in early tomorrow and knock out both gauntlets. You don't need to deal with this bullshit anymore. Let me take care of it. I'll be home as soon as I'm done here. Okay?"

She stared at him for several heartbeats as if trying to find a particular truth in his eyes. Finally, she sighed and dropped her gaze. "Okay. You need to call Jessa a rideshare. She's been drinking."

He waited until Kenya headed to the back exit before turning around to face Jessa and the crew. "I'll ask again. What is going on here?"

"I—I came here to talk to you," Jessa said through her tears. "B-but she got so angry and I got so scared—"

He held up a hand to stop her. That didn't sound like Kenya at all. Her anger, like her hurt and her fear, was an emotion she kept tightly controlled because she hated showing vulnerability. It took a lot for her to erupt, a lot more to show it. "What did you say that made her angry?"

"I didn't say anything that wasn't the truth!" Jessa insisted. "I told her the truth."

Cam gritted his teeth. He wanted to get home to Kenya, to hold her, to make sure she was all right. But he needed to find out what had happened so that they could talk about it. "What. Did. You. Say?"

"She's using you to get what she wants! Can't you see that?" She leaned closer. "I can help you see it. I can prove she doesn't love you. Not like I do."

"You're right."

His words dropped like a gavel demanding silence. Everyone looked at him in shock. The cameras quickly focused on him, and he had a sneaking suspicion that Jane was somehow behind Jessa's appearance, maybe even the gauntlet issue. Anger tightened his jaw. He needed to get everyone out of the shop before he said something that he'd regret, or worse, would harm's Kenya's chance to win.

Jessa wiped at her eyes. "So . . . does that mean you agree with me? You're breaking up with her?"

"No." He laughed. "I'm not breaking up with Kenya. That's never going to happen."

"But you said—"

"I said I agree with you, and I do. Kenya doesn't love me the way you think you do. Her love is so much more."

His voice softened. "I've known her for half my life, and she has had my back every minute of that time. She's my cheerleader, my partner, and my lover, and I try my best every day to give her all that and more because she deserves it. I love her, and I'd sooner stop breathing than stop loving her."

"She's using you," Jessa said, her voice small and tight with un-shed tears. "How can you not see that?"

"How is she using me when I'm helping her like she helps me? When I support her the way she supports me? We're partners and we're in this equally. Together. I don't know how else to explain it to you, and I'm done trying."

"This isn't fair. It isn't fair that you chose her instead of me. Look at me. How can you give all this up for her?"

"I didn't hear anything from you for months after we broke up," Cam informed her as he pulled out his phone, patience wearing thin. "As soon as you hear that I'm dating Kenya, now you're concerned? I don't think your problem is that I'm dating someone else. I think your problem is *who* I'm dating."

Red blotches mottled Jessa's face. "That ungrateful bitch doesn't deserve you!"

Snap! "My girlfriend was concerned about you getting home safely tonight, so I'm going to respect her kindness, which you definitely don't deserve, and get a rideshare for you. You can wait for it out front."

Her mouth dropped. "You can't just throw me out!"

He crossed to the front door. "Do you want me to have you arrested for trespassing instead? You have until noon tomorrow to come back for your car, or I'll have it towed. We need the space for customers."

"But—"

"Good-bye, Jessa." He held open the door. "I hope you have a good life."

She stared at him for a long moment before snatching her things and pushing past him. "You're going to regret this, you bastard."

Cam sighed as he closed and locked the front door. He saw Jessa's friends get out of her car and canceled his rideshare request. He couldn't help wondering if they'd pushed her into doing this or if it was a coordinated effort with Jane to attack Kenya while she was alone.

Anger surged again as he spoke without turning around. "All of you, get the fuck out of my shop."

"We're still filming—"

"The hell you are!" he snarled. "*We* are done for the day. You wanna keep filming, you can go out the front door and finish what you started with Jessa. I'm going home to my girlfriend."

He didn't say another word as he waited for Jane and her crew to pack up and leave. Didn't look at them when he set the alarm and made his way to his truck. Didn't give them the satisfaction of further reaction until he was safely in his gated complex.

Kenya's car wasn't in its usual spot. Anger evaporated into concern. Why wasn't she home? Where did she go?

He dug out his phone to call her and discovered a text message instead. NEEDED TO CLEAR MY HEAD. BE HOME SOON.

What he'd experienced with Jessa had been unpleasant, but it had to have been much worse for Kenya. He recalled that look of vulnerability she only allowed him to see and curled his hands around the steering wheel so he wouldn't chew his nails to the quick. She was hurting but she wasn't there and there was nothing he could do about it except wait until she returned so that he could help.

And tell her how he really felt. Then spend the rest of the night proving it.

CHAPTER TWENTY-THREE

Emotion churned with hurricane force through Kenya's body, generating nervous energy she couldn't alleviate. Not ready to go home and wait for Cam, and knowing Janelle was out with her man, Kenya headed to the only other place she could go that the film crew couldn't follow: her parents' house.

Lights were still on when she pulled into the driveway. She rang the doorbell before she could change her mind. Her parents knew Cam almost as well as she did. They would be able to give her advice on how to talk with Cam, how to sort through the jumble of emotions that buffeted her. She hoped.

Her father answered the door, mouth dropping open in surprise. "Kenya? What's wrong? Where's Cameron?"

She glanced behind her. Silence blanketed the street, but this wasn't a conversation she wanted to start on the doorstep. "Can I come in?"

Her father stepped back to allow her in as her mother made her way downstairs to join them, tying the sash on her robe. "Kenya? Is everything all right? Is Cameron hurt?"

"No, he's all right. I mean, he's physically all right, but—"

"Okay." Her father took her by the shoulders. "You're obviously upset, which means this isn't a conversation for the foyer. Let's go to my study."

Kenya followed her parents down a side hallway. Two doors stood opposite each other, one her father's study, the other her mother's office. Neither of which any of the kids had ever been allowed into before, not even as adults.

Her father called it a study, but Kenya called it a professor's man cave. Solid oak bookcases lined one wall, laden with books. The other walls were painted a deep forest green. A flatscreen sat on one wall, with a record player and a collection of records in cubbies below and a pair of leather recliners in front of it. The third wall anchored a massive desk covered in books, study journals, notes, and a laptop. Next to it was what appeared to be a minibar.

Her father gestured to her to take one of the recliners while her mother took the other. "You said that Cameron is all right, then you qualified it to say physically fine. So, what happened, and why isn't he here with you?"

"He had to deal with Jessa."

"Jessa?" her mother echoed. "His ex-girlfriend Jessa?"

Kenya nodded. "He had to go out for some supplies. While he was gone, Jessa showed up. She was drunk and angry and wanted to confront me. I have a feeling the producer put her up to it."

"What?"

The story spilled out of her in choppy bursts. Her father crossed to his minibar, opened the cabinet to extract three shot glasses, then poured golden liquid from a crystal decanter into each glass. Stuttering her thanks, Kenya drank the shot, gasping as the liquor burned down her throat.

"It was so awful," she said, digging into her tote for a pack of tissues. "And the production crew was there to film every moment of it. I should have known something was up when they didn't leave at their regular time."

"How did Cameron take it?" her father asked.

"He was so furious," she confessed, dabbing at her eyes. "He came back during the last bit of the argument and Jessa tried to play victim. He told me to go home and that he would handle it, but I was too keyed up to go, so I came here."

Her fingernails dug into her palms as she fisted her hands. "I'm still furious. The crew clearly wanted to see a fight between me and Jessa. She said some pretty heinous stuff, and I can't help thinking that one of the production assistants took her to a bar and talked enough smack to get her to charge over to the shop and show her ass. I'm glad Cam wasn't there for most of it, but he heard enough."

She pressed her knuckles against her forehead. "I hate that he was exposed to that. I hate that this hurt him. I hate that we have to figure out how to manage this before we go back tomorrow."

"If you hate it so much, why keep doing it?"

Her hands, her heart, and her mouth dropped as she stared at her father. "Dad?"

"It's not a rhetorical question." He poured himself another drink. "You come over here upset, telling us this story, saying how much you hate it—is doing this competition worth everything it's costing you?"

The thought of giving up the show and what that meant for her future clammed her palms. She rubbed them against her thighs. "I don't hate the competition. I don't hate what we're creating. We work well together. It's just the producers trying to create drama where there isn't any."

"Isn't any drama?" her mother echoed. "You're here and Cameron's with his ex-girlfriend after she got in a shouting match with you at the shop, cameras rolling. How is that not drama?"

She flinched in the face of her mother's logic, reverting back to her childhood defense of staring at the floor and swallowing an emotional outburst. "We don't have to give the production crew what they want. We can just focus on finishing the costumes and going back to Los Angeles for the finale."

"Do you think Cameron can do that?" her father asked. "Do you think he should do that, just pretend this incident didn't happen?"

"I did not say that," she replied, flattening all emotion out of her tone. "I said we'd talk about it and decide how to move forward together."

Her mother placed her shot glass on the table with precise movements. "Baby, have you considered that Jessa might be right?"

Did her mother just . . . "What?"

"Maybe you're not using him the way she meant it, but you must admit that you do lean on Cameron far too much."

Her hands numbed as icy shock streaked through her veins. Her mother . . . *her mother* agreed with Jessa. "Mama."

Her mother's expression balanced between concern and sternness. "It's time for you to give up this foolishness. It's time for you to stop depending on Cameron to bail you out. You're a grown woman. Act like it and stop taking advantage of that poor boy."

Kenya drew back, stung. "I'm not taking advantage of Cam."

"Really? You've talked him into backing one far-fetched scheme after another for years. Now you have him doing the biggest, most expensive scheme ever. He promised to look out for you, but you're taking advantage of his feelings and going too far."

Shock chilled her veins. It was as if her mother had given Jessa the words to say, they were that eerily similar. So many things punched into her brain at once, she had difficulty focusing on the whole of her mother's words. She picked the first thing that rose up from the noisy confusion in her head. "Cam . . . promised to look out for me? He promised you and Dad?"

"We asked him to," her mother answered. "We knew high school wasn't going to be easy for you, even more than normal, and you wouldn't have your brother or sisters there to look out for you. So, we asked Cameron."

Kenya squeezed her forehead, disbelief racing through her. "You asked a thirteen-year-old boy who'd just lost his mother and had an alcoholic father to be my what? My babysitter? My bodyguard?"

"Cam needed something, someone to connect to," her father explained. "He needed to be needed."

"With your repeated flights of fancy, someone needed to watch out for you," her mother retorted. "Who knows what sort of trouble you would have gotten in if Cameron hadn't been there."

"You're blaming me for being a teenaged girl?" Another chilling thought nearly stopped her heart. "Did you pay him to protect me?"

"No, of course not. As your father said, he needed to be needed, and protecting you gave him purpose. We nurtured him, treated him as if he was our own—helping him with his studies, helping him plan his future, writing recommendations for college, teaching him responsibility—something we apparently failed to instill in you. Your father even talked to his father during one of his sober periods and he agreed to have us designated as Cameron's guardians if necessary. Cameron appreciated the stability we gave him."

"In exchange for looking out for me." Kenya staggered to her feet, horrified. "How could you do that to him?"

"We assumed that you would grow out of your hobbies and focus on college and a real career as you got older."

Her mother's lips pressed into a thin line. "Unfortunately, you continued to cling to this ridiculous costume-dream, so that boy has continued to indulge you, even if it means taking a financial hit."

"Stop calling him boy," she snapped. "Cam is a grown-ass man."

"And you are a grown-ass woman," her mother shot back, clearly exasperated. "It's time for you to own up to the responsibilities of adulthood and stop using Cameron as a crutch."

"I'm not using him! He loves me, and I—"

"Oh, Kenya," her mother interjected, her words all the more powerful for their softness. "I think he thinks he loves you. I think he may even want to love you. Because you've known each other forever. Because you're safe together. That's why you need to let him live his own life, free of continuously coming to your rescue. It's not fair of you to hold him back from his dreams so that you can follow yours."

Each word her mother spoke was another brick on her back, crushing her hopes, dreams, and confidence until only doubt, disillusionment, and distress remained. She clenched her hands, trying to hold back her words, hold back her tears, hold back everything that would weaken her further in their eyes.

Did Cam have dreams he hadn't shared with her? Was he spending money on her that he needed to put into the shop? Was she holding him back from going after his true goals because he felt obligated to look after her? The thought that she was a hindrance to Cam slashed deep. Jessa's opinion she could have passed off as jealousy. The thought that her parents believed she was a burden to him slashed deeper.

"God." She didn't want to say the words, yet they clawed their way up her throat like a feral cat, desperate to be released. "Y-you don't think I'm good enough for Cam, do you? You really think I'm holding him back?"

"Kenya." Her mother's voice softened. "I know this seems overly harsh, but it's past time for you to face the truth. Give up this foolish dream that's done nothing but cost both of you money and time that you could have spent building a real career and cost Cameron—"

Kenya threw up her hand. "Don't," she whispered, her voice thinned with the effort to speak normally past the scream welling in her throat. She wanted to believe that her mother didn't know how much her words hurt. Or maybe she did but didn't care. Tough love and all that. "Please don't say another word."

Her father, ever the peacekeeper, stepped forward. "Kenya, we just want both of you to be happy."

She laughed, the taste of it bitter on her tongue. "No. No you don't. Because if you did, you would let us live our lives the way we want, doing what we want to do. You'd trust us to know what's best for us, what makes us happy. But no, what you want is what you think is best for us. Who gives a fuck if what you want makes us happy or not?"

"Don't you dare use that language in this house, young lady!" her father demanded. "Apologize!"

"I'm sorry." Kenya backed up a step, her heart shredding. Why didn't her parents understand? Why did they think she was so incapable of making decisions for herself? "I'm sorry that you think me saying the word 'fuck' is the worst thing that happened tonight. I'm out."

She lunged for her keys and tote, then spun for the door, needing to escape her mother's harsh words and the heavy truth that laced them.

The ride home passed in an emotional blur. Kenya pulled into her parking spot, noting that Cam's truck was already there. She killed the engine, gripping the steering wheel. Silence wrapped around her but it did nothing to quell the thoughts stampeding through her brain, threatening to become an avalanche she couldn't hold back.

Her relationship with Cam was a lie.

Yes, their romantic relationship had begun that way, but it had grown into something real. At least, she'd thought it was real. But the friendship, the decade of being in each other's lives—was that only because her parents had made it worth his while? Did Cam even see it as friendship, or as protecting a flighty teen girl who wasn't practical-minded enough to take care of herself?

Ice clammed her hands, causing them to shake as she gripped the steering wheel. She'd known her parents had barely tolerated her artistic expression, but the idea that they'd had so little faith in her, that hurt. Saying she was a burden on Cam—that she'd been holding him back—stabbed deep, crumbling her foundation, chipping at her confidence. She wasn't sure of anything anymore.

Earlier, she'd thought she'd fallen in love with him. Now she doubted herself. She'd thought she'd fallen in love because of how he made her feel, but now she wondered if it was because of what he'd done. She'd thought of him as her knight in shining armor after he'd ridden to her rescue over the gauntlet. She'd flipped out, and he'd taken care of things. When he came back to the shop, he'd sent her home so he could take care of that too. She'd thought it part of what made him loveable, instead of being in love with him just because.

Another bolt of thought left her gasping. What if . . . what if Cam wasn't in love with her? She'd told her parents that he was, but she'd never heard him say the words, had she? There she was, thinking of love and their future and soft, squishy things. What if none of that had ever crossed his mind? What if he was satisfied with

Friends 2.0 because he was finally getting something out of their relationship?

No. Her heart twanged hard at the thought. Cam wasn't that kind of guy. He just wasn't.

More doubt slithered in. How could she be sure? She'd been sure that they were lovers moving forward together. She'd been so sure they were ride-or-die partners, them against the world. But the truth was she was needy and he needed to be needed.

She dug into her bag for her tablet, powered it on. It only took a few moments to access the shop's accounting software, to find the proof that would confirm or deny her mother's accusations.

Numbers didn't lie. The shop wasn't in trouble, but it was a close thing. If one of their regular customers bailed, the shop would take a hit. Cam would take a hit. The only certain cushion he could have was taken up by her being on the payroll.

Did he think she couldn't handle anything on her own? Had he spent so much of his life looking out for her and she'd spent so much of her life expecting him to that it had twisted into some codependent thing?

How was she supposed to face him now, knowing all of this?

Breathe in, breathe out. She couldn't pretend nothing was wrong, not with Cam, but she could pretend it was the shit-show at the shop that bothered her, and not the revelations her parents had dropped on her.

The thought of being fake with Cam churned her stomach. This was Cam—her best friend, her ride or die. Her lover, her partner, the love of her life. The one who had made high school bearable. Except instead of doing it as her friend, he'd been her protector, coerced into the role by his own sense of duty and her parents' concern. And she, she had taken advantage of that, and of him. It had to stop.

Her lips split open in a silent scream, her lungs too constricted for air, the pain too deep for tears. She couldn't keep doing this to Cam. He'd been through so much and he deserved a life free of the burden she and her parents had placed on him. Moving on was the least she could do for him.

She had three options. She could go in tonight and tell him she was quitting the competition. It wasn't worth the price they were paying. She'd then clean out her savings account to give to him, put in her notice and move out, then work out some sort of arrangement to pay him back for everything he'd done for her over the years.

If he didn't want to quit, the second option was to stay in and win the competition. She would give him all of the prize money, then insist they were a team for whatever costume department she'd get to work in. She'd forge connections, work her ass off, prove she was more than a publicity stunt. Maybe Cam and his shop would get hired for different sets, and they'd naturally grow apart as their work took them in different independent directions.

If she didn't win . . .

If she didn't win, she'd be left with the nuclear option. She'd give every penny she had to Cam and move out, but not back to her parents. She'd get a job using her degree, get a place to live, get an independent life. Maybe she'd even find a job out of state. She would prove to all of them that she wasn't a burden.

None of those options included being with Cam, living with Cam, or even maintaining a friendship with Cam. They couldn't. She had doubts that their friendship would survive in any of the three scenarios. How could it if what her parents said was true? He'd be hurt at the outset, maybe even angry, but eventually he'd accept it. He might even believe that she'd done him a huge favor. He'd get to find the happiness he deserved without having to worry about her.

And if she shriveled and died a little inside because of it, that would make it hurt less, right?

Her hands shook as she opened the visor mirror. She looked exactly how she felt. Digging into her tote, she extracted her makeup bag and did a careful touch-up job. Nothing she could do about the redness of her eyes, but hopefully Cam would think her upset was about being ambushed, not about what Jessa said. What her parents said.

She tried to force her lips into a smile, but could only manage a grimace. "Get it together, girl," she whispered to her reflection. "Don't let anyone see your hurt. Don't give any of them the satisfaction."

Another attempt, much better results. She could do this. She could fake her way through the next few days, wearing the confidence mask she'd worn throughout the competition. She just hadn't planned to wear it for those she loved.

More or less together, she exited her car and made her way to Cam.

CHAPTER TWENTY-FOUR

Cam leapt to his feet as soon as he heard Kenya's key in the lock. He rushed to her, reaching out, needing to touch her to know she was okay even as he asked for verbal confirmation. "Are you all right?"

"Yeah." She hugged him hard, harder than she ever had, then gently pushed him away. "I just needed to clear my head away from everything for a while."

Based on her expression, it didn't seem to have worked. She looked furious and devastated and heartbroken and far from okay. "I got some Chinese for dinner. It'll take just a few minutes to warm it up."

"I'm not hungry." She moved past him, heading for the fridge. "What happened after you sent me away?"

Her tone, so calm and even, didn't match her expression. Worry crawled through his gut. He chose his words carefully in the hopes of reassuring her. "Jessa tried to convince me to leave you and get back with her while Jane and her crew filmed every moment from every angle. I would have felt sorry for Jessa if I wasn't so pissed off.

After I told her that there was no chance in hell of us getting back together, I told her to leave. Come to find out, those same two friends from game night were in the parking lot waiting for her."

"Oh." She uncapped a bottle of hard cider. "So, they got her tipsy and put her up to it? I thought . . ."

"You thought Jane or her assistant got Jessa drunk, hyped her up, then sent her in so they could film the damage. Yeah, I thought so too. I still do."

"It's hard not to jump to that conclusion." She paused to take a deep swallow of her cider. "I mean, the timing couldn't have been more perfect. It's like they knew I'd have a meltdown about the crushed gauntlet and you'd volunteer to save the day. Which creates the perfect opportunity for the ex-girlfriend to confront the new girlfriend, and it conveniently gets caught on camera in all its dramatic ugliness."

She snorted. "And the pièce de résistance is when the white knight returns. Who will he save? His hysterical former flame or the conniving queen who made her cry?"

Bitterness and pain laced her words in a thorny weave, thick enough to hurt. Yet he pushed through the verbal barbs, reaching for her. "You *are* a queen. My queen. But conniving? Ain't no way."

Vulnerability flooded her eyes, but she blinked the threat away. "That's not what she thinks. That's not what any of them think. Didn't she tell you?"

Reluctance pulled at him. He didn't want to tell her, didn't want to repeat the awful words. The night had been awful enough, and he didn't want to inflict more pain on her. "It doesn't matter what she thinks. It doesn't matter what the film crew thinks or what trolls think. Nothing's changed with us."

"Trolls?" She cut a glance at him. "You've been going onto the message boards?"

Shit. Still, he couldn't lie to her. "Yes."

"When did you have time to?"

"While you were in Los Angeles. I used a burner account. I wanted to know what you were up against and support you how I could from here."

"You shouldn't have. Those forums are horrible."

"I know." He swallowed the string of curse words that rose like acid in his throat. There wasn't enough eye bleach in the world to unsee what he'd read on the boards. The glee with which people spewed their trash takes in online anonymity was the epitome of vile. It had only hardened his resolve to protect her and love her and help her win. "People just saying whatever they want to get a rise out of others. It's fucking sick!"

"There you go, defending my honor yet again. It's like a second full-time job for you."

He wasn't sure what to make of her tone. Her obvious upset stabbed him with twin knives of anger and guilt, calling up his own bitterness. "A job I'm obviously failing at. I'm so sorry, babe."

She tilted her head at him. "What are you apologizing for?"

"I shouldn't have left you alone with them." He balled his hands up. "I should have been there to protect you!"

"It's not your job to protect me, Cam."

"I know that, but I want to do it," he insisted. "I have to do it. It's important to me."

His words didn't have the reassuring effect that he'd hoped for. If anything, dismay and anger pursed her lips. "I don't need you to protect me," she said again, an edge to her tone as she backed away. "I dealt with them out in Los Angeles and I dealt with them in my own way tonight."

She sighed. "If anything, I should be the one to apologize."

"What the hell for?"

She gestured with the bottle. "This. Everything. None of which you signed up for. You shouldn't have had to deal with that, and honestly, neither should Jessa. Neither of you should have been used like that."

He leaned forward, temper spiking. "Jessa wouldn't have been in this if she had stayed home. Instead, she drank some shots to get up the courage to say shit she wouldn't dare to say sober."

"It doesn't make a difference," she muttered, fiddling with the bottle before taking another sip. "She said it, said what everyone else is saying or thinking or posting."

"That doesn't make it right," he shot back. "Haters gonna hate. You said so yourself."

"It's different when it's just me. I totally expected the haterade. You didn't." She polished off the rest of her cider, then looked at him. "That's why I think we should quit the show tomorrow."

Kenya hadn't intended to blurt the words out so soon into this conversation, but she felt cornered and out of options. She'd known that achieving her dreams required hard work and harder nerves. She'd known that and had been willing to sacrifice blood, sweat, and tears. Hers, not anyone else's. Even still, she hadn't accounted for this emotional burden.

Her heart ached for Cam, for her, for them. He hadn't signed up for any of this, but he'd been willing to help her any way he could, protect her any way he could. His e-mails and DMs had probably been flooded since they'd started filming in the shop, and based on what she'd seen of hers, she could imagine that his were probably awful and likely along the same lines of what Jessa had shouted during her drunken rant.

That shady drama-hunting scheme wouldn't have happened if

she hadn't gotten on the show. It wouldn't have happened if she hadn't been so needy for a friend that she'd latched on to the new kid who had desperately needed someone to protect after losing his mother. All he'd agreed to all those years ago was to be her friend, not all the stress she'd brought to him by calling his name on live TV. Not all the drama, the verbal attacks, the trolls. His misery now was because of her.

So was his anger. "The fuck we're quitting!"

She appreciated his anger, anger that she didn't dare give vent to because if she set it free it would raze everything to the ground, and she needed to save something. Save him. "You didn't sign up for this, and neither did Jessa. I don't appreciate them using both of you like that."

"They used you too, and don't you dare accept that treatment as part of playing this game." He leveled a finger at her, features fraught with fury. "And another thing. Don't even think about withdrawing. That's what they want, and we're not going to give them that satisfaction. Like hell we're quitting this close to the finish line."

She tried again. "But this stunt—"

"Was a ploy to make us fail. You've come too far and I'm not going to let you throw away your chance when you're this close to everything you've ever dreamed of."

Once again, he was taking on more than he should have, just to help her. "It's my dream, Cam. Not yours. This is too much on you."

He gripped her arms. "Sweetheart, I know it's your dream. I've been with you every step of the way. I want to see your dream come true, and that means doing what I can to make sure no one else comes between you and that goal. To hell with all of them! I owe you and your parents too much to let that happen."

Anguish gripped her lungs like a vise. She'd still had a small hope that he'd helped her because he loved her, really loved her, and not because of some sense of duty pressed on him by her parents.

"You . . ." Her voice wheezed out, her lungs and heart still constricted as if she'd run a marathon and her body failed her just before the finish line. "You don't owe us, Cam. You don't owe us anything. Especially me."

He leveled a gaze at her, his expression grave. "I owe you most of all."

"Don't say that!" She jerked back from him, needing to distance herself from the guilty hurt that his words caused. If he owed her, how much did she owe him? How could she possibly repay him for everything he'd done? "Don't say that, please."

"Okay." He reached for her again and this time she went, wanting the warmth of his palm running down her back. "I'm sorry. I don't want to upset you more."

Her hands tightened on his shirt and she breathed deep and loud, needing him and hating herself for being so fucking needy. She shivered, her shoulders slumping beneath the weight of exhaustion, worry, and heartbreak. She wasn't sure how much longer she'd be able to hold it together, but she didn't want to cry in front of Cam. Not now. Not ever again.

"I'm exhausted, but I need to figure out how to deal with all of this before we get to the shop tomorrow. You know they'll be waiting."

"Like the vultures they are." He kissed her forehead. "We can figure something out over dinner. I got your favorite."

"I can't . . . I can't do this."

He froze, his arms tightened around her. "It's okay," he whispered against her cheek. "It's been a long day and you've been through a lot. We can sleep on it tonight. We can think things through and come up with a plan in the morning."

That wasn't what she meant, and she had a feeling that he'd deliberately misunderstood her. "Of course. You should take some time to think about this, too."

He stepped back just a hair, still within touching distance. Still close enough to crack her façade if he pressed. "What do you think I should think about, other than how to deal with those vultures at the shop?"

The tight caution in his voice almost broke her. She could say the words, and it would be done. The competition would be over, her dreams would be over. They would be over. As much as she'd reluctantly accept the first, she wasn't ready to accept the last. She'd never be ready.

The true words stuck in her throat. She coughed, trying to loosen them, trying to get enough air in her lungs. Instead a lie slipped out. "I owe you a serious vacation when this is all over. You need to think about where you'd like to go."

Again that careful perusal, and she knew he'd heard the lie and the deflection. He blew out a harsh breath, obviously trying to find calm. "I know we have a lot to talk about. Let's just focus on dealing with tomorrow, getting through the competition, and taking home the prize. Okay?"

She nodded, grateful for the exit ramp away from the difficult conversation. It didn't matter that it was a postponement and not a resolution. She didn't have the bandwidth to deal with her parents' revelations, or the sense that everything was conspiring against her achieving her dreams. All she wanted to do was go to bed.

Everything was different now, and the only thing she knew for certain was that her heart was breaking in slow motion.

CHAPTER TWENTY-FIVE

Cam quickly silenced his phone's alarm, then turned back to Kenya. Thankfully, she was still asleep, curled up and facing him. She'd lain awake for hours, they both had, thoughts too heavy for sleep to come easily. He'd cycled through fear, rage, and hurt on an endless loop, the fear lasting the longest.

I can't do this.

Four little words that had squeezed his heart to the point of breaking. He'd known she didn't mean continuing the competition. He'd known she didn't mean going into the shop today with a brave face and a middle finger for the production crew.

She'd meant being with him.

He'd lain awake beside her, torturing himself, waiting for her to say she wanted to have "the talk." Waiting for her to say that after everything Jessa had said to her, after everything trolls had said, pretending to be with him and then being with him in truth wasn't worth the pain. It wasn't until she'd pressed against him and nestled his hand over her heart that his heart had finally stopped its frenetic pace.

The fear had lingered, though, even in sleep and now in the predawn. He had to admit, if only to himself, that if she'd come to him for friendly advice about this situation with another guy, he would have told her to cut her losses and run. It wasn't another guy, though. It was him, and he wanted to prove to her that their relationship was worth it. That he was worth it. That he would always be with her and beside her, ready to help and, if necessary, to shield.

He wanted to tell her that he loved her. Really loved her, and not as a friend. If he told her now, he was sure she'd blow it off, thinking it was his reaction to the drama with Jessa. All he could do was stick to the plan and wait until the competition was over before telling her exactly how he felt, how he wanted to spend the rest of his life with her.

Kenya stirred. She gave him a sleepy smile, her eyes soft and sweet. He cupped her cheek and saw the exact moment that the storm clouds of memories filled her gaze.

She drew back.

He buried the hurt behind a smile. "You ready to kick today's ass?"

She wiped the sleep from her eyes. "Not yet, but I will after a shower and some coffee."

"Okay." He kissed her forehead, then sat up. "I'll go put on a pot while you get ready. I also want to give Mack and Javier a heads-up."

"God." She scrubbed her hands down her face, then swung her legs over the side of the bed. "I guess they do need to know, don't they?"

"I won't give them a play-by-play, but they need to be prepared just in case."

"In case I act the fool with Jane and her crew when they try to interrogate me about last night?"

"You wanna wild out, I'll be right there with you," he said, quitting the bed. "But since they went low, maybe we should go high."

She snorted. "I know shit's real when you quote Michelle Obama at me."

The wryness in her voice was miles better than bitterness. "So, are we still doing this?"

"Hell yeah, we're doing this." She got out of bed, stretched. "We're going high. So high they'll need radar to track us."

"So high even Snoop Dogg will be impressed."

"For sheezy." Laughter, real laughter, rolled from her, prompting him to laugh too. She crossed to him, then pressed a kiss to his cheek. "Maybe we can finish ahead of schedule at the shop, then go someplace nice for dinner. I owe you for helping me like you did yesterday."

He dropped his hands to her hips. "Yes to a nice dinner, no to you owing me. We're a team, remember?"

"Teamwork makes the dream work." Her expression softened. "I would love to go on a date with you, Cam. Just the two of us, being us."

"I say we make that happen as soon as possible. And then come home for dessert."

"You're cute when you're horny." She patted his cheek, then headed for the bathroom. "We've got a plan and a business to run. Let's do what we do, then make sure we have even more reason to have that dinner."

After she left, Cam got dressed and headed into the kitchen to make the promised pot of coffee. As he waited for it to brew, he sent a group text to Mack and Javier asking for a quick call before they headed to the shop.

Mack wasted no time as soon as he got on the line. "Why the hell did Jessa show up at the shop last night?"

Ice slid through his veins. "How do you know about that?"

"A video got posted to the show's forum. My lady's addicted to the show and goes out into the forums every day to support Team KenCam," Javier said. "This morning she got a notification about a surprise showdown and logged on to see what had happened."

"The whole country knows," Mack answered. "It's a thirty-second video that shows Jessa crying and Kenya taking off her earrings. Looks like they're teasing a fight for the next episode."

"Fuck." Cam bit at his fingernails, his mind racing. He had to tell Kenya about this development and hope it wouldn't send her spiraling again. "There wasn't a fight. Jessa got wasted and went to the shop to confront Kenya while I was out on an emergency supply run."

Javier snorted. "Mighty convenient, if you ask me."

"You're saying what we're all thinking." Cam relayed the sequence of events, glossing over the painful conversation he'd had with Kenya.

"How's our girl doing?" Mack asked.

"Better this morning. Last night was hard for her." Hard for him too. "She's decided we're going to take the high road."

"She's a better person than I am."

"She's a better person than all of us." Cam pulled Kenya's favorite travel mug, hot pink with the word *Queen* and a crown emblazoned on it in gold, out of a cabinet. "So let's just follow her lead today when it comes to the production crew, give them as few sound bites as possible, and help our girl win this damn thing."

He disconnected the call, then scrounged in the freezer for some breakfast sandwiches to throw in the microwave. By the time he sliced a couple of oranges and plated everything, Kenya emerged from their bedroom.

She wore a fuchsia blouse with ruffles at the wrists and a low-cut neck that called attention to her divine cleavage, black jeans that sung the praises of her hips, and the hot-pink Timbs that warned everyone that she was ready to kick ass without taking names. Around her neck she wore a gold chain from which hung a shooting star with the tiniest diamond accent ever, a gift he'd given her the Christmas after his father had died. She looked . . . she looked . . . his brain couldn't find the right words.

"I . . . uhm, you . . ." He pointed at her.

Her soft laugh was a balm to his stress. "I'll take your reaction as a compliment."

"Yes. Good. Uhm, coffee?"

She joined him at the table. "You sure know how to make a girl feel good," she said, glancing at the table. "Thank you for doing this."

"You're welcome. I just want to make you happy."

"It's helping." She added cream and sweetener to her coffee. "What did Javier and Mack say?"

He didn't want to jump into it so soon, but it was best to share the news and get it over with. "Javier's girlfriend saw a short video posted on the show's forum. They're teasing the argument as a fight and plan to show it for the next episode."

Her hand shook as she returned her mug to the table. "That was fast," she finally said. "They must have worked through the night to make the clip."

"Maybe they'll be too tired to worry about filming us today."

"Yeah, right." She picked up an orange slice. "You know they want to film us walking in, see if there's any kind of strain between us, and talk to us about last night."

"Bastards. I'm not giving them the satisfaction."

"We're going high, remember? We go in, supremely unbothered, behaving exactly the same way that we did yesterday morning. Just because they want drama, doesn't mean we have to give it to them."

"You're right." He studied her over the rim of his mug. She projected an air of cool, calm, and collected, not to mention smoking hot. He wondered, though, how much was real and how much was pretense.

"If you don't mind, I'm going to have lunch with Janelle today," she said, picking up her sandwich. "I want to let her know what's going on, and I don't want to do it over the phone."

"Of course I don't mind. It'll be good for you to get away from the shop for a while. Just make sure they don't know where you're going."

"I figured we'd come back here. The film crew can't get through the security gate and Janelle never signed a release form."

"Good thinking." He should have known she'd thought everything through. "I guess this means you don't want to ride in together?"

She shook her head. "No, we need to arrive together. It doesn't matter that we've driven in separately before. Today, they'll try to make something of it. We need to look like a united front."

"We *are* a united front," he retorted, his tone harder than he'd intended.

She blinked, and he instantly regretted the harshness of his tone. Then she smiled, reaching over to squeeze his hand. "Of course we are. I meant that we need to look united to the crew and any other gawkers who might be hanging around."

"Okay." He stood, pushing back his chair and a sense of disquiet, then gathered their dishes. "You ready to seize the hell out of this day?"

"Let me refill my coffee and I'll be ready to go."

Admiration and awe filled him at seeing Kenya's ability to put up a good front. Yet he couldn't shake the feeling that she was fronting with him, too.

Thanks for having lunch with me, Janelle."

"With everything you've been through last night and this morning, I would have been pissed if you hadn't called me."

Kenya picked at her noodle bowl, gathering her thoughts. As she'd expected, the production crew had been on them the minute they'd pulled into the parking lot. She'd ignored them, instead talking with Cam about consultations and order requests that needed to be slated for their work queue. Javier and Mack had been equal parts angry and protective, but they eventually had to begin work on their projects, and Cam had clients to call, leaving Kenya alone on the floor with Jane and the cameras.

Kenya had focused on the finishing touches to the helmets. Any question Jane asked, any attempt to delve into the previous night's drama, Kenya had turned into commentary on the costumes. Eventually Jane had gotten the point, but that hadn't stopped Kenya's stomach from churning, fearful that Jessa would return to the shop for another round in front of the cameras.

"Okay." Janelle put down her fork and placed her palms flat on the table. "I need you to tell me what happened and whose edges I need to snatch."

"I'm so glad you're on my side. Okay, here's part one." Kenya gave her friend a play-by-play of her freak-out, the confrontation with Jessa, and Cam's knight-in-shining-armor appearance. "I'm not sure exactly what happened after I left, but I know Cam was still pissed when I got home."

"I would have been too, if my ex had ambushed my current girlfriend. And she's got a lot of nerve accusing you of using Cameron like that!" Janelle huffed. "You should have called me. I may be a professional who spends most of her time behind a computer, but I would have been more than happy to roll up on Jessa and her friends and put the fear of Jesus in them."

Kenya let out a much-needed laugh. "Have I mentioned how I'm glad you're on my side?"

"It doesn't hurt to be reminded." Janelle winked, then paused. "Hey, if you left the shop before Cam did, why did you get home after him?"

"That's part two. I was too upset to go directly home, so I went to my parents' house." She drew in a stuttering breath. "I told them everything that happened, everything Jessa said, and they . . . they agreed with her."

"What?"

"They . . . said I've been leaning on Cam my entire life, that I always depend on him to bail me out of one wild idea after another. Then they told me that they had asked him to watch out for me during high school, like a bodyguard or something, and that's what he's been doing all this time. They said he's been doing it because he felt obligated to our family, that it's not fair to him to keep on doing this to him and not let him live his life." She choked. "Without me."

"Damn." Janelle stared at her, eyes and mouth wide. "That's . . . What did Cameron say about all this?"

"I haven't told him. I can't tell him."

"Why not? You can't keep something like this from him."

"I have to. At least for a little while."

"Okay. I'm going to need you to give me one good reason why."

"That's part three." Kenya tried for a smile. "But before I get to that, I have to make a confession."

Janelle looked at her tea. "It's too damn bad it's too early for alcohol. Okay, spill."

"When I announced that Cam was my significant other on the show, it was a surprise to everyone, including . . . Cam."

Janelle's mouth dropped open again. "Wait. Y'all are just pretending to be a couple?"

"Yes. I panicked when I blurted out his name on the show, because I really need to win. When I came home, I promised that I'd split the prize money with him if he'd help me by pretending to be my boyfriend, and he agreed with no problem. He was actually already into it because he met me at the airport with balloons and flowers and kisses. That lasted all of a week before things got real. Really real, and really, really good. Yesterday, it finally hit me. I went from loving Cam to being in love with Cam. Then everything went to hell."

"But y'all are good now, right?" Janelle demanded. "You told him how you feel, he did the same, and you two are going to be even more cute together now."

"I didn't tell him." She looked down at her tangled fingers. "I can't tell him."

"Why the fuck not?"

"Because when I told my parents that I love Cam and he loves me, they said it wasn't love." God, it still hurt to recall their words. It wouldn't ever not hurt. "They said we might think it is, but it's just him needing to be needed, and me taking advantage of it."

"Oh, Kenya, that can't be true. How can you believe that?"

She reached for a napkin to dab at her eyes. "Last night, when I offered to quit the show, he refused to let me. Said that he owes me too much to have me give up on my dream. He . . . apologized for not being there to protect me when Jessa ambushed me. He was angry with himself for failing to be there for me. That hurt so much I knew there was no way I could tell him how I felt."

Taking measured breaths, she waved her hands in front of her face to dry the tears that threatened to become a torrent. "My parents are right. Our whole relationship is one big codependent clusterfuck. If I win, I can at least try to even things out by giving him the prize money and whatever business might come out of it. But if I lose . . ."

"Nothing. I bet Cameron doesn't care about the prize money. Y'all will have time to work things out without the cameras and pressure of the show on you."

"No." Kenya sniffed. "We won't."

"Why not? And I'm gonna need a better reason than you thinking you're using him."

"I made a deal with my parents before I went to LA. If I lose, I have to quit cosplaying, and get a job using my degree. I also have to leave Cam to give him the chance to live his life and run his business without him worrying about having to take care of me."

Janelle shot from her chair, then rounded the table to pull Kenya into a bear hug. "Oh God, Kenya, I'm so sorry."

She leaned into Janelle's embrace, shaking and grateful to have the story out, the burden shared. "I've been doing the whole unbothered thing all morning, and I hate that I have to do it with Cam."

"Then don't." Janelle grabbed her by the shoulders. "Do you even see the way he looks at you? Cam loves you. He has for a long time. You need to tell him everything that's going on, especially that bullshit with your parents."

"I know Cam loves me," she replied, dabbing at her nose. "We both love each other. But I don't know if he's in love with me, or still just feeling as if he needs to look after me. I mean, think about it. He was my protector throughout high school, and we became his second family. We were only apart for a couple of years during college. We moved in together after his father died. And somehow, I ended up working at the shop with him.

"God." She clenched her fists. "He's been supporting me all this time. Even auditioning for the show was his idea. He even created a sock puppet account to defend my honor on the show's forums. There's no way I'm ever going to be able to pay him back for everything he's done for me."

"Has he asked you to?"

"You know he wouldn't. But what if I'm nothing more than an obligation to him? That he's been my friend because my parents asked him to look out for me, and he feels it's his duty because we gave him an escape from his dad? What if the only way I can repay him is to leave so he doesn't have to worry about me anymore?"

"I think you're wrong," Janelle insisted. "I hope you're wrong. And if by some wild twist of fate you're right, I still think you need to talk to him about this."

"I will. After the competition." She pressed her fingertips beneath her eyes. "There's a couple of days left before we fly to Los Angeles for the finale. If I win, giving him all of the prize money will help the shop a lot, and can be a down payment on what I owe him. If I lose, I'll dust off my resume, maybe do some contract work until I land a full-time job. Either way, I'm going to have to move out. There's no way we can go back to just friends after all of this."

She stood. "I need to go fix my makeup and my game face. All I have to do is fake that everything's all right for a few more days. One way or another this will all be over soon, so I'm going to enjoy what I can with Cam while I can."

CHAPTER TWENTY-SIX

Are you excited?"

Cam turned to Kenya with a wide smile. "How can I not be excited? I'm in Los Angeles for the first time. I'm with my girl, and I'm about to see her become the first *Cosplay or No Way* champion!"

Kenya returned his grin, his excitement infectious. Here in LA, it was easy to put the stress and heartache of the last few days in Atlanta behind them and simply soak up this moment, the pinnacle of all their hard work, together. She'd spent those days focused on their project and the nights wrapped in Cam's arms, showing him everything she was afraid to put into words, enjoying every moment while hoping it wasn't the last.

She pressed her arm against his since she couldn't thread her fingers in his. They were in their costumes, waiting for one of the production assistants to wave them onstage to present their cosplays to the judges and the live audience. "From your mouth to God's ears, I'm crossing everything and praying for the win. But we haven't seen Ben and his husband in their cosplays yet."

Hope and dread were the twin echoes of her heartbeat. Hope flourished, fed by her love for Cam. Hope that they'd win, that she'd get to relaunch her business, that they'd get the money to infuse into Cam's business and allow her to repay a small portion of everything he'd done for her over the years. Dread that they'd lose, that it would cost her a career, a friend, and a love.

She couldn't focus on that. Not now. Now, they had to wow the audience and the judges one final time. Everything, literally everything, depended on that.

The lights dimmed as the show's intro music blared. Mark, the host, stepped onto the stage to applause. "Welcome back to the finale of *Cosplay or No Way*, the show that had cosplayers across the country compete against each other to craft amazing costumes. It's been a wild ride and we're finally down to our last two contestants, Ben and Kenya. The winner will receive $100,000 and the chance to work in costuming for a major blockbuster production!"

Applause and cheers thundered through the theater, the energy of it reaching backstage.

"Our two finalists have been at home for the last few weeks working on not one, but two costumes with their partners, and they're back to show us what they've done. First up, we have Kenya and her partner, Cameron. Are you ready to see the iconic duo that Kenya and Cameron created?"

The audience screamed again. Cam sucked in a breath, so loud that she turned to look at him. He gave her a thin smile, then lowered his helmet. She gripped her battle blade and channeled her inner Titan conqueror. *Game on.*

"All right then, let's welcome Kenya and Cameron to the stage!"

The assistant turned to them. "Okay, go exactly as you did in rehearsal. If you have any issues, Mark will handle it. Go, go!"

Heart pounding, Kenya stomped out onto the stage to dramatic, ubervillain music. She'd tucked her hair beneath a bald cap that she'd painted the same purple hue as her skin, though it was hidden by her helmet. Deft application of the body paint had also created the illusion of ubermuscular biceps. She was supremely proud of the prosthetic chin. Of the whole look, actually. She really did look like Thanos with boobs.

Four inches taller than usual, she used her battle sword for balance as much as for show, but this was her moment, and she gave herself over to it. She raised her hand, and the crowd went nuts when her gauntlet lit up in the colors of the Infinity Stones. Brandishing her blade and the gauntlet high, she was in all her Titan glory, powerful and unstoppable.

The music changed, swelling from dark to light. Cam strode onstage, armor gleaming under the lights. The Arc Reactor glowed bright as the audience cheered. She pretended to swing her sword at him, then faked a stumble. As the music swelled, she raised the Infinity Gauntlet for a snap.

Silence. Then, Cam raised his fist, and the Nano Gauntlet gleamed with the colored lights of the stones. The crowd went nuts as he snapped his fingers. Using the sword, Kenya sank to one knee, defeated. The stage went dark.

For a heart-stopping moment, silence reigned. Then the crowd exploded with cheers, shooting to their feet with applause and whistles. The lights came back up as Cam came over to help her to her feet and they were joined by the host.

"Wow, that was amazing," he said. "Everyone, give it up for Kenya and Cameron as Thanos and Iron Man!"

The audience applauded again as Cam removed his helmet. His smile was everything she'd hoped it would be, boyish and excited and ecstatic. She grinned back at him, then hugged him as tightly as she could, careful not to damage their costumes.

A stagehand handed Mark a microphone as several cameras captured their costumes from every angle. "How are you guys feeling right now?"

"Thrilled," Kenya said, certain the audience could hear the bass drum of her heartbeat. "The reaction you guys gave us is everything we could have hoped for. Thank you!"

The audience cheered again as Mark turned to Cam. "And what about you, Cameron? How does it feel to be on the *Cosplay or No Way* stage?"

"Awesome," Cam replied, his grin still in place. "Being here with my girl is the best thing ever, and she makes Thanos look good."

"That she does," Mark agreed to laughter and cheers. "Well, let's take a quick look at how you created these two larger-than-life characters."

They turned to the massive screen as the lights dimmed. A video played, showing a montage of their work, from cutting and molding foam to painting and buffing armor, to Cam working on the armor lights while Kenya performed detail work, to Cam helping her with her purple body paint, and finally, them standing in the shop in their completed costumes.

Mark turned to them as the lights brightened. "Looks like you guys put a lot of work into your projects. Now, let's get close-ups of your cosplays, then it's time to see what the judges think."

As rehearsed, they stood roughly three feet apart so that the camera could move around and between them, the minute details of their costumes displayed on the jumbo screen. When the camera pulled back, Cam reached for her hand as they turned to face the judges at their raised table. As always, Leon basked in his inscrutableness, Rebecca stewed in displeasure, and Caroline vibrated with excitement. It felt like being in front of a tribunal composed of the lion, the witch, and the manic pixie.

Caroline spoke first. "That was amazing! The detail work on both your costumes blew me away. And a female Titan? I think you've just inspired thousands of women and girls everywhere. Five stars!"

"Thank you," Kenya and Cam said in unison, then smiled at each other.

"I really like your take on Thanos," Leon said. "You managed to make it menacing yet sexy at the same time—no offense."

"None taken," Kenya answered. That was the intent, after all.

"Also, building two sets of armor from scratch in the time frame we gave you was very, very ambitious," he continued. "Some would say overly ambitious."

Everyone avoided looking at Rebecca, but Kenya had heard those words and more during the judges' site visit. "Getting the light effects just right on Iron Man can be a daunting task, but to also illuminate the Infinity Stones? It was a very risky gamble—and it paid off beautifully. Well done."

More audience applause. This was going just as well as she'd hoped. This was what they'd worked their asses off for, and it had finally come to fruition. America could see their efforts, their talents, and hopefully that would turn into level-ups for both their careers. The thought made her giddy.

Cam bumped her shoulder, his grin as bright as the overhead lights. She pulled off the Infinity Gauntlet to clasp his hand, needing that contact.

Of course they saved Rebecca for last. Kenya ignored the acid rising in her stomach, instead focusing on the feel of Cam's hand in hers. It was much easier to stand there with him beside her. The audience fell silent as they waited for her to speak

"A gender-bent Thanos," she began. "Kudos for throwing yourself wholeheartedly into the role. It looks like you bulked up some to really highlight the size difference between your character and Cameron's."

Kenya drew a breath as the crowd tittered in unease. No one was sure how to take the remark, least of all her.

"Kenya did a great job blending the makeup and the prosthetics on her arms and legs to look natural," Cam said then. "And of course, nailing the chin. She's a wiz at it."

Judging by her frown, Rebecca wasn't thrilled by Cam's response, although the audience loved it. The judge leaned forward. "I'm rather surprised that you took on the role of the Mad Titan," she said. "Becoming the villain is a risky move."

Again, a tense moment of trying to decide how to take the judge's words. "I'm cosplaying a female version of a villain who's a hero in his own mind," Kenya countered. "He had a goal and sacrificed everything to achieve what he thought was best for the universe. He accomplished what he set out to do and inadvertently gave Tony five years as a family man."

"He killed half the universe."

"He did. Then our heroes got the Infinity Stones and killed him and his minions. Maybe that wasn't half a universe, but it was a lot."

"So you're saying that the heroes are the same as the villains? That's a controversial take."

"It is," Kenya agreed. "Who's the villain and who's the hero always comes down to which side you're on. That's what makes Thanos so fascinating. He's got reasons for being the way he is, like we all do. Which is why I thought it would be interesting to cosplay him. Besides, Cam will always be my hero. Of course I didn't want him to be the bad guy."

A collective "Awww" rose from the audience. Rebecca ignored it. "Let's look at some more of your time at home."

Kenya didn't have time to steel herself as the giant display screen showed a tearful Jessa ranting, and a pissed Kenya taking off her earrings. She hadn't watched the episode when it aired, and had basically ignored social media, not wanting to relive the emotional upheaval. She hadn't expected that the producers would be so conniving as to air the footage during judging, with them standing right there.

Cam squeezed her hand, and she realized that she held his in a death grip, so tight her arm trembled. Breathing slowly, knowing the cameras were on them, she forced herself to loosen her grip and blank her face, drawing on her conception of Thanos. The helmet helped.

They continued their retrospective—or rather, their edited version of the weeks leading up to the finale. All the hard moments— the times she nearly cracked under the pressure, became snippy or frustrated with her progress—scrawled across the screen in high-definition detail. Kenya's heart sank, dread eclipsing hope. Despite her best efforts they had cast her as the villain, and she'd reinforced their attempt with her cosplay choice and her reasoning behind it.

The lowlight reel finally ended. "You've gone through a lot in this competition, Kenya," Rebecca said as the screen returned to the show logo. "Each time, you've overcome and let your cosplays speak for themselves. You're known for taking chances and thinking outside the box for your designs. You've obviously wowed people, or else you wouldn't be here."

Kenya held her breath and Cam stiffened beside her, apparently as shocked as she was. Was Rebecca being nice to her?

"Unfortunately, I think you played it safe for this final round, which is surprising given that you chose a partner who owns a fabrication shop. I wanted to be wowed, but I wasn't. I'm sorry."

Blood flooded Kenya's face, the pressure filling her eardrums and drowning out the disappointed groans of the audience, the argument Leon directed at Rebecca. That damn immortal hope that would not die might have just been extinguished for good. Yeah, Rebecca was only a third of the judging panel, but her critiques carried a lot of weight. That last bit of concern trolling might have torpedoed their chances with the voting audience.

The host stepped forward as the jumbo screen returned to the show logo. "America, let's give it up one final time for Kenya and Cameron. We'll be right back after this!"

Kenya gave Cam a smile as she squeezed his hand, then released it to smile and wave at the cameras and the audience. The crowd applauded and yelled as a production assistant guided them to a tiny waiting area just offstage. Kenya barely heard it. It took everything she had to keep her emotions dialed down so she could make it through the next portion. The way the judges reacted to Ben and John's cosplay would determine everything.

Cam turned to her, cupped her cheek. "Are you all right, sweetheart?"

She wrapped her fingers around his wrist, grateful for the contact. "Just nervous," she said, then decided to be real. "Scared to death, actually."

"Same. These gloves are keeping me from biting my nails to the stubs." He bared his teeth, his displeasure obvious. "I'm also a little pissed. That judge—"

"Is one of three," she whispered in his ear. "I don't know if there are any microphones over here, but let's assume there's at least one camera trained on us at all times."

"Gotcha." His lips brushed her ear, then lingered at her jaw. "Besides the obvious, I think our odds are good. The crowd loved us."

"They did." She hoped it would be enough. She didn't want to think about losing, didn't want to put it out into the universe, but she had to be realistic. Had to decide how and when she would break things off with Cam before her parents took the decision out of her hands. She wanted to spend as much time with him as possible before everything went to hell. One more chance to enjoy the illusion before reality took it away from her.

"Hey. When this is over, let's do a getaway, just you and me. Somewhere where we can forget everything but each other for a while."

"A just-us vacation?" He waggled his eyebrows. "I like the sound of that."

"Good. Think about where you want to go. Maybe someplace that doesn't require a lot of layers and has a nice view we can see from bed."

"My mind is taking me in directions I shouldn't be considering, but I appreciate having something else to think about. Thank you."

Her shoulders sagged in relief. The vacation idea would hopefully give them enough to talk about on the long flight back home if the voting didn't go the way they hoped. Her stomach churned at the thought of losing. If Ben's iconic duo cosplay went well, she and Cam were in serious trouble.

"Welcome back to the *Cosplay or No Way* grand finale. You've seen finalist Kenya with her partner, Cameron, doing a fantastic cosplay of the iconic duo of Iron Man and Thanos. Now, we're ready to see what our second finalist has in store for us. Let's welcome Ben and his partner, John, to the stage!"

A dramatic drumbeat rolled across the stage. Kenya watched as Ben glided out in the black garb of a certain blonde dragon queen, complete with intricately styled wig. He'd nailed the look perfectly, but where was his husband, and what character was he cosplaying?

Ben turned to the backstage area, then stretched out a hand. Dramatic music swelled as glowing eyes filled the darkened area. The music crescendoed, then a black dragon stepped out onto the stage. John manipulated the dragon's frame like a puppet master, walking the dragon up behind Ben before unfurling its wings. The audience went nuts.

"Sonofabitch," Cam whispered, his voice thick with the same shock that flooded Kenya. She knew that the other contestant had gone with Daenerys and Drogon cosplays, but she had no idea how they would have been able to pull off a full-on dragon costume in the time frame they'd had. Even in Cam's shop, just the head alone would have taken months of work to perfect.

The judges obviously wondered the same thing, because that was the first question they asked. "That's a really impressive dragon," Leon said. "Tell us how you were able to pull this off."

"We knew the dragon was going to be the hardest part of the cosplay, so we decided to put the bulk of our time into it," Ben explained. "John does set and costume design for theater productions, so we leaned on his skills to source most of the components. Our focus went into molding the head and making sure that was accurate. We then modified, assembled, and finished the detail work ourselves."

Sourced, not made from scratch. Kenya grunted. It wasn't necessarily against the written rules, but in her opinion, it went against the spirit of the competition. With the wings folded in place, it was difficult to see the dragon body, but what Kenya could see let her know that it wasn't in proportion to the head. In her opinion, it was more a dragon for a theater production instead of a cosplay competition and should have cost Ben some points.

Apparently, the judges didn't see it that way. "The detail work on the dragon's face is amazing," Caroline said, trotting out her favorite word yet again. "And I love your Daenerys portrayal. Your hair is popping!"

It was. Ben had invested in a great unit and nailed the intricate hairstyle perfectly. Based on the audience applause, they agreed wholeheartedly.

Kenya curled her fingers, the tips digging into the thick fabric covering her thighs. Beside her Cam raised his right hand to chew on a nail, realized he still wore his gloves, then lowered his hand. She reached over to lace her fingers with his. This time he didn't smile. Neither did she. Not with Rebecca coming next.

Mark spoke. "Before we get to Rebecca's feedback, let's take a look at Ben and John at home."

Ben's highlight reel was much shorter. He and John had a scattering of tense moments, but no former lover showed up at their house to start a fight. At least, if their location crew had filmed any, it hadn't made it to the highlight reel.

Acid filled Kenya's belly, rising to eat at her hope. While she felt that her and Cam's costumes were superior, a lot of people voted based on who was more likeable. Thanks to these video recaps, it was clear who the show thought had the likeability factor.

Rebecca leaned forward. "Ben, being in the final round means that you have to bring it. You can't play it safe and you have to wow us. You took a risk with the dragon costume. I think it paid off. Great job!"

In that moment, Kenya knew she wasn't going to win, especially if Rebecca had her way. She saw the truth confirmed in the smugness of Rebecca's expression. It rocked her back on her heels. Cam drew her closer, concern lining his features. She dredged up a smile for him, then let it fade, certain she'd need to save her energy for the decision.

CHAPTER TWENTY-SEVEN

During the commercial break, an assistant brought them back on-stage. "Hey," Kenya greeted Ben, giving him a hug. "Great job."

"You too." He waved at the dragon. "That's my husband, John, underneath there."

"Nice to meet you, John. My boyfriend, Cameron, is under the Iron Man helmet."

Cam shook hands with Ben then waved at the dragon. Ben rubbed his hands together. "This is it. I'm so nervous I can barely stand it!"

"Me too."

He leaned closer. "What was the deal with that woman that argued with you in the shop?"

"We don't know," she deflected as Cam tensed up. "They broke up a while ago. It didn't make sense for her to show up when she did, but we weren't going to let her or anyone else stop us from reaching the finish line."

Cam touched her arm. "And here we are."

"Here we are," Ben agreed with a smile. "Let's do this!"

Mark stepped forward. "We all know putting costumes together is just one part of cosplaying. Another part—the largest part—is actually showing them off. Unfortunately, there's not a convention in town right now, but we're going to give our audience a treat. Our finalists are going to walk the runway in their costumes right now!"

The audience cheered as Kenya and Cam moved stage left to the start of the huge U-shaped walkway that protruded deep into the audience. Ben and John moved stage right. "All right, America, it's time to get your vote on! While our studio audience gets up close and personal with our contestants, you can use these toll-free numbers to vote for your favorite cosplay!"

Music blared throughout the auditorium. The bass bounced off her chest, pounding away the doom and gloom to reveal a simple truth: her love of cosplay. She and Cam had made killer costumes and now they had a chance to show them off to a large group of people, same as they did for every Dragon Con, Anime Weekend Atlanta, Comic-Con, and every other regional convention they could get to. This was the fun part, and she wanted to thoroughly enjoy it.

It seemed that Cam had the same idea, strolling the walkway with all the confidence of a genius tech billionaire. Channeling her inner Titan, she stalked him, brandishing her sword and the gauntlet, pausing every few feet to growl at audience members who wanted to snap pics. Somehow she stayed in character when all she wanted to do was laugh her head off. All the pressure, the stress, the drama and threats faded away. Only the joy of cosplay remained.

Her heart dropped when John and Cam passed each other. Although the walkway was wide, neither of them could see very well through their headgear. Cam had almost no peripheral vision and Kenya couldn't tell how much of a view the dragon mask gave John. He flapped the dragon's wings, almost clotheslining Cam in the process.

Cam ducked, then made the best of it by dropping into a super-hero crouch, lighting up his palm as if to blast the dragon into smith-ereens. More people rushed over, phones held high to record the exchange. When the dragon shuffled on, Cam rose to his feet, then punched the air in triumph, nodding to the audience. They ate it up.

Pride and love blossomed in her chest, and she took a step to-ward him before remembering she wasn't cosplaying Pepper Potts. She settled for brandishing her double-edged sword and scowling in Drogon's general direction.

The show went to a commercial break as Kenya and the others finished their walk of fame, returning to center stage. All at once the tension crashed back into her as she stood in place with Ben and his spouse on one side of her and Cam on the other. Blood pounded in her ears, muffling sound. Anxiety squeezed her lungs, constrict-ing air.

Cam took her hand, and she could breathe again. Drawing on the attributes of her character, she pushed her emotions down deep, blanking her expression to one she hoped exuded pleasant indif-ference.

"Welcome back to the finale of *Cosplay or No Way*! Tonight, one of these finalists will win $100,000 and a chance to design cos-tumes for a major film! You've voted, America, and while we wait for the final results, let's look back to see how our top two com-petitors got here!"

The jumbo screens replayed scenes from earlier in the season, from Kenya's and John's audition tapes to their first day in the group house to their first challenge. *Look at how excited and happy I was. I miss that.*

The retrospective continued, showing each contestant returning home. The audience cooed and clapped in delight as Cam swept her up in a balloon-and-flower-filled embrace and gave her the smooch that curled her toes. *Look at us. I think I was already in love with him then.*

I think I've been in love with him all this time.

Like turning to a lodestone, she turned to look at Cam. He was already turned to her, the front piece of his helmet pushed up. The intensity of his gaze jolted her heart. *Maybe my parents are wrong. Yeah, loving someone is different than being in love with someone. Maybe Cam is in love with me, has been in love with me for a while. I have to ask him. I have to know before I yeet everything into the sun.*

Maybe there was a question in her eyes, because he squeezed her hand and mouthed words that looked a lot like *I love you.*

Whether he said it or not, whether he meant it or not, she couldn't let the moment pass without acknowledging it. Squeezing his fingers in return, she let down her defenses long enough to feel all of the love and joy in her heart. "I love you."

His answering smile was a prize in itself. No matter the outcome, she was glad that Cam had been with her every step of the way. This was as much for him as it was for her.

She didn't give attention to the rest of the retrospective, didn't come back to the moment until Mark spoke. "Before we announce the *Cosplay or No Way* winner, let's have a final word from our contestants. Kenya, do you have anything you'd like to say to our audience here and the millions watching?"

"Yes, yes I do." She gripped Cam's hand to steady herself. "I'd like to say thank you to everyone who voted for me, from the beginning to now. Your encouragement and support mean the world, and—and . . ."

She stopped, twisting her lips and blinking rapidly to hold back the floodgates. *Just a little bit more. Get through this and then you'll be able to break down in private.*

Cam squeezed her hand and whispered, "You got this, babe. I'm right here with you."

Then someone in the audience screamed out, "We love you, Kenya!"

Lifting her chin, she blinked rapidly, then managed a smile. "No matter what happens, this has been an incredible journey and I'm glad I had the chance to show the world what I can do. I'm glad I got to show the world why Cam is my own personal superhero. Because of his faith in me, I'm already a winner."

Appreciation poured through her as the crowd roared in enthusiastic support. Yes, she still wanted the win. Still needed the win. But this moment, this present time balanced between hope and reality, was perfect.

"Ben, do you have anything you'd like to say?"

"I do." Ben nodded then turned to the audience. "This competition has been one of the best times of my life, and I've enjoyed stretching my capabilities and being inspired by my fellow contestants. Thank you, everyone, for supporting us. I'll never forget this."

Kenya grinned at Ben and applauded along with everyone else. She and Ben had gotten along well despite being competitors. Another place and time, they might have become friends.

"The moment is finally here!" Mark declared as a stagehand handed him an envelope. He held it up. "In my hand is the name of the first winner of $100,000 and the chance to work on a blockbuster film!"

She and Ben gripped each other's hands, although they both

still held on to their partners too. *This is it. This is the moment that decides the rest of my life.*

"The first *Cosplay or No Way* winner is . . ."

Ben!"

Kenya gasped as shock doused her in icy realization. Despite expecting it, she had still held out a slim hope that she'd be declared the winner. Trembles shook her body as her vision grayed at the edges, the weight of reality almost too much to keep her upright. Somehow she forced herself to turn to Ben, congratulate him with a hug before his dragon husband swept him up in his wings.

Lost, bereft, she floundered briefly beneath the bright lights, unsure of where to go or what to do. Cam grabbed her hand and held it high, gesturing to her with his free hand. Right, she still had a part to play. So she smiled and blew kisses to the audience, silently thanking them for their support, placing her hand over her heart in an attempt to convey how much she appreciated them.

One of the production assistants, Amy, came up to them to lead them offstage. Kenya followed, smile locked in place, emotions locked down, full defensive mode engaged. Cam stomped off with her, and she didn't need to see his face to know he was upset and stunned by the loss. She couldn't afford to feel either emotion. She couldn't afford to feel anything. Not yet.

"We have a car that will take you to the after-party," Amy said as they made it back to the dressing room. "A bunch of different media outlets will be there, including network affiliates. The PR team also set up an interview with your local affiliate on a show called *Good Morning Atlanta*, the day after you get back home."

"That's great." Another reason not to yield to the despair clawing at the edge of her control. Being gracious in defeat and still putting on a good face for interviews gave her more chances to talk up Cam and the shop. Having to do an interview with the local station in a couple of days meant she could put off the inevitable that much longer, and gave her time with Cam, which she was now desperately greedy for. If she couldn't give Cam the prize money or stay with him, at least she could give him good press.

"We'd like to go back to the hotel first, if that's okay," Kenya said, hyperaware of Cam's fuse growing shorter by the moment. "We wore our street clothes in, and we want to pack up the costumes and take them back to the hotel anyway."

"Oh, of course!" The other woman leaned forward. "I'm really sorry you didn't win. Both of you have really awesome costumes. I can't believe you made those yourself!"

"Thank you." Her voice wobbled, prompting Cam to take a protective step forward. She dragged her emotions back behind a pleasant mask of a smile. "We'll be as quick as we can, I promise. I don't want to walk through the lobby all purple."

"Understood. Just call me when you're ready."

Amy left, closing the door behind her. Kenya sighed as she turned to Cam. He'd already removed his helmet and gloves. "God, I need to get out of these boots, and I'm sure you want out of that armor."

He stepped close to her, concern heavy in his eyes. "What I want is to know how you're doing."

Automatic-answer time. "I'm fine."

She reached for the chest-plate closure on his left side, but he took her hand, stopping her. "KeKe. How are you really?"

The soft question probed at her defenses, but she couldn't let it through. Not yet. "Ask me again when we're safely back at the hotel, okay?"

"Okay." He backed off, giving her the space she needed to compose herself.

They shed their costumes as quickly and carefully as they could, breaking down the pieces and packing them carefully into the padded suitcases they always used for transporting their costumes. She applied a liberal amount of cold cream to her face and arms, and Cam helped her wipe it away. Her breath quickened. Removing the purple makeup felt as if she was stripping a layer of protection away, protection she clung to like a life preserver as she floated in a choppy sea of surging emotion.

"Mental yoga."

She looked at him, her breath coming way too fast, panic creeping whitely at the edges of her vision. "W-what?"

"Visualize yourself doing your yoga stuff," he clarified. "It will help."

She did and it did, helping her manage walking through the remnants of the production, loading everything into the car, making it to the hotel, and finally crossing the threshold into their room. "Thank you for that advice. You're always h-hel-help, help—"

Her façade cracked, then burst, her emotions flooding past the broken barriers of her control, her will crumbling beneath the deluge. Her knees buckled from the weight, but Cam was there, holding her up as the maelstrom of heartbreak and pain and disappointment buffeted her. "I'm sorry, Cam. I'm so sorry . . ."

He wrapped her in his arms, wanting to shield her from hurt and disappointment and anyone who caused her pain. She trembled like a leaf in a storm, her tears soaking his shirt.

"It's going to be all right, KeKe," he whispered into her hair. "I promise."

"No, it won't. It's over. Everything's over."

Panic clutched his chest. He hoped she didn't mean *everything* everything. "No, it's not, baby. You still have a lot of people who support you and your work. You'll still have a lot of interest in your business even without the *Cosplay or No Way* winner badge. We've already had more traffic and project requests at the shop. We'll be okay. I promise."

She shook her head, then pulled away from him, wiping at her eyes. He watched as she pulled herself back together piece by heartbreaking piece, then gave him a watery smile. "I desperately need to shower the rest of this purple away and put on something pretty. We're gonna have to mix and mingle at the after-party for a couple of hours."

"Do we have to?" He didn't want her to expend any more energy on something that hurt her so deeply, and frankly he wanted to punch a judge or three.

She linked her fingers with his. "There will be a lot of media there," she answered, kissing his knuckles. "It'll be one more opportunity to get some publicity for your shop."

Alarm spasmed in his chest. "*Our* shop."

Cool fingers cupped his cheek. "Okay, *our* shop. We'll go out there and smile and chat about our future plans for the shop. I'm sorry that's all I can give you to thank you for helping me with this."

"Hey." He gave her a tight squeeze before stepping back enough to see her face. "You've got nothing to apologize for. You had a kick-ass idea and you made it happen. If anything, I should be apologizing to you."

"What? What for?"

A flare of anger heated his ears. "You picked me for my fabrication skills, and I let you down. I know how important this win was to you."

She shook her head, then cupped his cheek. "I'm not going to let you blame yourself for how this turned out. Besides, I picked you because there's no one else I wanted on this journey with me. I just wish . . ."

Her bottom lip trembled. "I just wish things could have turned out differently. Maybe one day I'll be able to make it up to you."

An undercurrent ran through her words, one that made his stomach churn with unease. Hoping he was wrong, he offered up a distraction. "Let's go to this party and network our asses off. On the way back, we'll buy a giant bag of gummy worms, climb into bed, and plot our next plan for world domination." He waggled his eyebrows. "And maybe bang the headboard a couple of times."

As he'd hoped, she smiled. "Since the headboard is attached to the wall, that will take some doing. Still, I really like the sound of that."

"Good. Why don't you go on and shower . . . unless you need some help de-purpling yourself?"

"You know what? I think that's a great idea," she said, surprising him. "That'll be a good memory to have."

Again, a bit of unease rippled through him. He tried to stamp it out. Kenya still needed time to deal with being runner-up. He did too. But he was determined to give her plenty of good memories to outweigh the bad. Things would get better once they returned home.

He hoped.

CHAPTER TWENTY-EIGHT

TALK TO HER. MAKE HER TALK TO YOU.

Cam glanced at the text from Janelle, then at Kenya's silent
form. The unease that had crawled through him since their flight
home dug its claws deeper into his psyche. He wanted Kenya to talk
to him, but Janelle knew getting Kenya to talk when she didn't want
to wasn't easy on the best days, and he had a feeling this wasn't one
of those days. DO YOU KNOW WHAT'S GOING ON?

I TRIED TALKING SENSE INTO HER, BUT SHE'S NOT ANSWERING
ME. IF YOU LOVE HER LIKE I THINK YOU DO, DON'T LET HER DO
ANYTHING STUPID.

Dread iced his veins. What the hell was Kenya planning to do,
and how bad was it that Janelle felt the need to warn him? His
phone vibrated one final time.

DON'T FUCK UP.

"Is there an emergency at the shop?" Kenya asked. "You should probably go in."

"Mack and Javier can handle it," he said, powering off his phone. "I want to focus on you."

"I'm okay."

"Are you? Are you really?"

She sighed. "No. Probably won't be for a while, but I think, I think you could be."

"Don't."

She looked up at him, her gaze dull and flat. "Don't what?"

"Whatever you're thinking," he answered. "Don't do it."

She chuffed out a laugh. "You don't know what I'm thinking."

"I know Janelle's blowing up my phone. I know there's a twisted feeling in my gut that won't quit. I know I really want you to talk to me about whatever is so heavy on your mind."

Her lips parted, then closed. She sighed as she sank onto the couch. "I wanted to wait. I wanted us to have a mini-vacation somewhere, just the two of us, before . . ."

"Before what?"

She started to speak, stopped, then looked away. He picked at his fingernails, his anxiety pegging hard in the red zone. "You gotta tell me, KeKe, because my mind is jumping to a bunch of conclusions that I hope like hell are wrong."

"I need to ask you something."

With the urgency of Janelle's texts imprinted on his brain, he drew in a slow breath to brace himself. "Go ahead."

She slid her hands down her thighs, grasped her knees. "That night when Jessa came to the shop, you said you owed me and my parents too much to let me walk away from the show. You said that you owed me most of all. Did you mean that?"

Not a question he'd thought she'd ask, but his answer came easily. "Every word. I feel like y'all saved my life. You especially, because you offered me friendship even when I acted like I didn't want it. I'll never be able to repay y'all for what you did."

Her bleak expression wasn't the reaction he'd expected. "So you've been giving and doing and helping all this time to pay off a debt you think you owe us?" She clutched a hand to her heart. "Owe me?"

Uncertainty swirled inside him as he tried to gauge her mood. Usually he could, but today she'd locked down so completely he couldn't get a sense of what she was feeling or thinking. "When you put it like that, it doesn't sound right, like you're twisting it into something it's not."

"What else is it?" she asked, her tone too soft, too full of something that sounded like pain to be a demand. "I'm going by your words, what you just said. Based on that, it sounds to me like they were right."

She didn't mean the words were right, she meant people. "Who were right?"

"Jessa." She choked. "My parents."

"Your parents?" His hand flailed out in search of a chair, because he could no longer hold himself upright. He sank down, disbelief weakening his knees. "Mr. and Mrs. D . . . they think the same way Jessa does? That you're using me?"

Her shoulders bunched as she stared at the carpet. "Yes."

Breath rushed out of him, his gut clenching as if from a physical blow. Jessa's bullshit he could fend off, but her parents? Not only did they think that she was using him, but they had also *told her so*. "What exactly did they say to you?"

Reluctance pulled down her expression, and he knew that whatever they'd said wasn't complimentary. "Please, KeKe, I need to know what they said. We can't talk through this if I don't know what they said about me, about us."

She retracted her hands into fists, then looked up at him. "They think I depend on you too much, that I count on you to support one wild idea of mine after another. And because you needed to be needed, you gave me anything I wanted instead of convincing me to use my degree and get a real career."

A sound too hard to be a laugh broke out of her. "I mean, they were grateful that you promised them you'd look after me in high school, but apparently they thought you'd grow out of it once we graduated. That we'd grow apart and you'd finally have the space you need to have a real, full life without me. Instead, you're still looking out for me, even if it hurts you and the shop."

So much made sense now. Why she'd looked so defeated when she'd returned home that night. Why she'd offered to quit the show. Yet it didn't explain why she was so closed off now, why she wanted to have a talk with him after they took a getaway. "You believe them?"

"They're my parents." She spread her hands. "They've been together longer than we've been alive."

He rubbed his fingers together, trying to keep anger and a healthy dose of fear at bay. They knew. They knew how he felt about Kenya, and now they were trying to split them up? Cold realization twisted in his chest like a knife. "They don't think I'm good enough for you."

Another hollow laugh. "Flip it around and you'll be right. I'm the problem child. I've always been their problem child. They think I've gotten so comfortable with you always there to save flighty old me from myself that we don't know anything else other than me using you and holding you back."

"That's bullshit!" he shot back, flipping to full anger. "You're not holding me back and you're not using me!"

"But they—"

"I don't care what they said! I don't care how long they've been together. That just means they know what works for them. We know what works for us. And I know one thing for sure: I'm going to always help you whenever I can with whatever you need. Period."

Her shoulders dropped. "Because you feel like you owe me."

"No, I—"

"You just said it, Cam. You said you felt like you still owe me. Even after everything you've done for me over the years." She poked herself in the chest. "If you feel like that, don't you think I feel the same about what I owe you? Don't you think I want—I need—to pay you back so this isn't lopsided between us?"

She rubbed at her forehead. "I wanted the prize money so you could invest it in the shop. I know you want some new equipment to land bigger contracts. I do the books, I know how much that prize money would have meant to the business. Since I didn't win the prize, I'm going to do the next best thing I can do, which is transfer money out of my savings to you."

"No." He slashed his hands through the air. "I told you from the start I didn't want the money. I sure as hell don't want you to empty your savings account!"

"You built me work space in the shop, Cam!" she exclaimed as she shot to her feet. "Valuable space, and I know you didn't make it out of stuff that just happened to be back in the stockroom. I have to reimburse you for that."

"Fine!" He made an effort to swallow his anger and try to see things from her perspective. He wasn't angry at her, but at the situation, and hated that she felt like she owed him, or that things were unbalanced between them. "You can give me a couple of hundred bucks for the new materials if it will make you feel better, but I'm not going to take your entire savings! Besides, I consider it an investment for the shop. You're gonna need that space based on the interest you're getting from being on the show."

Her wince put him on instant alert. "What?" he said.

"I . . . I'm not going to be able to use it," she finally said. "At least, not full time."

He summoned all the calm he had left. Difficult to do when the hits kept coming. "Why not?"

"I have to switch to a career in my degree field, so I asked Janelle to see if there were any openings in her company," she explained, misery lining every word. "I won't be able to work at the shop."

"Have to," he repeated. "You keep saying that. Why do you have to do these things, when it's clear as damn daylight that you don't want to?"

"Because . . ." She swallowed audibly, twisting her fingers together. "That's the deal I made with my parents when I told them I had entered the competition. If I lost, I would have to give up trying to monetize my little hobby, get a real job, and go back to school. I was so sure I would win that I agreed to do it. But then . . ."

He clapped his hands to his head, squeezing his brain, trying to cope with all the verbal grenades she'd launched his way. "What else?"

Visible struggle tightened her features. Whatever it was, she didn't want to tell him. That meant it was really bad. "KeKe, please."

She raised a hand to chew on a fingernail, stopped, then collapsed onto the couch, hunching over and hugging herself in a clear defensive gesture. "Then the Great Gauntlet Incident happened. I flipped out from the stress and you swooped in like the hero you are to save the day."

She looked up at him, because she needed to see him as she

spoke her truth. "I realized how much I loved you. No, I realized I was in love with you, in deep."

He rocked back on his heels. "You're in love with me? For real?"

"Yes." She smiled because the relief at finally telling him overcame everything else. "I'm in love with you, Cameron Lassiter. For real. My heart grew three sizes that day because it needed more room to feel all that I felt. Then Jessa showed up."

Misery crept back in like a fog bank, smothering her joy. "Honestly I was more worried about you coming back into the middle of that than anything she had to say about me. But some of what she said stuck and all of these emotions were burning through me and I couldn't just go home and wait so I went to my parents."

She shook her head. "I should have known better, but I needed to talk it out. I told them what happened and that's when they said all that other stuff . . . and it made me feel guilty and ashamed."

The room blurred. It hurt to rehash the conversation with her parents. It hurt even more to know that she was hurting Cam, too. "I—I tried to deny it. I told them that we loved each other, and they said—they said—that you might think you love me, but it was more that you needed to be needed after your mother died, and I needed you. They said that the best thing I could do for you was to give you the chance to live your life without having to look out for me all the time."

Silence dropped like a hydraulic hammer. She dug into her back pocket for the travel pack of tissues she'd tucked there. His bloodless expression was exactly how she felt inside, a twisted mess of shell shock, devastation, and a soul-deep hurt that would take years to heal. "I'm so sorry, Cam."

"For which part? For your parents telling you to walk away from everything you love to go sit in a cubicle somewhere? Sorry for them also thinking my life should be torpedoed because they think I'm delusional about what I want and what I feel? Or are you apologizing for believing and agreeing with them?"

That final question, launched with the precision of a guided missile, scored a direct hit on the dam barely holding her emotions in check. "I didn't want to, Cam, please believe that! I was overwhelmed, thinking about how much you do for me, big things and small things. As much as I didn't want to believe it, what they said made sense. I wasn't sure if you did things for me because you love me or because you were so used to helping me out since high school."

Blinking rapidly, she drew in a ragged breath, but couldn't choke back the tears, the regret, or the guilt. "When you said you owed me, that you still owed me, I thought there was no way I could tell you how I feel until I leveled up with you. Everything depended on winning the competition and when I didn't, I didn't have any other options. I called you my hero, my knight in shining armor. You're always doing stuff for me, and what have I done in return? What have I given you to thank you for everything you've done for me? How can I not feel like I owe you? How can I not feel like all I've done is take and take and not given you anything back?"

"KeKe." Her tears propelled him out of his chair and over to the couch where he hauled her into his arms. "How can you say that when you've given me so much? When you're the reason behind everything I've done, every success I've had? I'm more than happy to count the ways. Will you listen?"

He held her closer, breathing a relieved sigh when she nodded and rested her head on his shoulder. "On day one, you gave me your friendship and half your lunch. Then you shared your parents with me. You're the reason I graduated high school. The reason I went to college. You helped me decide what kind of work I wanted to do.

You helped me dream up my own shop. You helped me find it, fix it, make it ours. You help me run it, you helped me keep going during those lean months when I questioned everything and was close to giving up. You pounded the pavement with me, finding customers willing to take us on. Everything I am is because you believed in me and didn't give up on me. You're a partner, not a coworker. Do you not remember all of this?"

"I remember," she confessed, "but I never ticked them off like that before."

"Well, you should. That way you can see that you're a pretty important part of my life. You're my rock, KeKe. You held it down with me in those first couple of years when I was convinced I'd made a huge mistake. You are always there for me, and I'm so grateful for that. But I will never forget that you're the reason I was able to keep going when my dad died."

He swallowed hard. "When I found him, the first call was to 911. The second call was to you. Not your parents, not my old therapist. You. Do you remember what you did?"

"I came home."

"You did more than come home." He huffed out a hollow laugh. "You were on a girls' trip. You got in a car and drove five hours home, burning up your minutes to talk to me the entire way. Why did you do that?"

"Because you needed me."

It was that simple and that deep. "You make it sound like that's something that anyone would do, and that's not true. But you did that. You ran through the front door and wrapped your arms around me and I was able to breathe again. You were with me every day after that, giving me your strength, your comfort, dishes to break when I needed to rage, hugs when I needed to cry, laughter when I needed a break. You were like a beacon, lighting my way. I already loved you, KeKe, but that moment? That was when I fell in love with you."

"Really?" She gasped. "Why didn't you say?"

"How could I say? We were nineteen. I didn't want you or your parents to think it was a reaction to losing my father. I wanted to be sure myself. And you were seeing somebody then."

"We broke up soon after that. He didn't understand why I spent so much time with you, and I didn't want to explain, yet again, why I needed to be there for you whenever you needed me. Any potential partner of mine needed to know I wasn't giving you up, and they needed to be okay with that. I didn't realize what that actually meant, and I'm sorry I took so long to realize it."

He gave her a grateful squeeze. "You know I went to therapy after that, back to the same therapist that helped me when I lost my mom. But what you don't know is how much I talked about you, about us, in those sessions. I wanted to be sure of how I felt about you."

"Are you still sure?" She raised her head to stare at him, then gestured between them. "After everything, are you sure now?"

He caught her hand and her gaze and her heart with the simple truth in his eyes and his words and his tone. "The one thing I'm sure of, out of all the things in the world, is that I'm in love with you. Not because I've known you forever, not because I feel like I'm obligated to you or your parents. I'm in love with you because you are the sweetest, smartest, prettiest, sexiest, everything else-est woman that I've ever known. I've dated other people, you've dated other people, but we keep coming back to us. I am sure. So let me ask you: after everything, are you sure now?"

She brushed her fingers over the stubble on his jaw. "I'm sure I'm in love with you. Not because I've known you forever, not because of what you do for me. I'm in love with you because you are kind, caring, supportive, sexy, gorgeous, smart, and funny, and there's that super sexy secret smile thing you do that makes my heart do this little bunny hop thing. I can't imagine life without you."

"You don't have to." Determination arced across his features. "Now that we're here, I need to let you know that I'm in this for real and forever. Is that a problem?"

"Forever is a mighty long time . . ." Her heart did that bunny hop thing as she smiled. "But I like the sound of that."

"Okay." He sighed in obvious relief. "Then there's just one thing left that I have to do."

"What's that?"

"Beat the boss level."

Resolve chiseled his features as he grabbed his phone. Her eyes widened when she realized he'd initiated a video call with her father. "Cam?"

"We're in this together, right?" he asked, challenge and daring coloring his tone.

"Right." That didn't stop her heart's attempt to leap out her throat.

"Cameron?" Her father's image appeared on the screen. "Is Kenya there with you? We haven't been able to reach her since y'all went to LA."

"She's here with me, and we're back home," Cam answered. "Is Mrs. D there with you? We'd like to talk to both of you."

"Of course. Let me get her."

Kenya took Cam's free hand, entwining their fingers while she watched her father locate her mother. "Sweetheart, it's Cameron and Kenya. They want to talk to us."

Her mother stood next to her father, concern wrapping her features as she stared at the screen. "Kenya, why have you not answered our calls? We were worried about you."

"I'm sorry, Mama," Kenya answered. "We just needed some time."

Her mother frowned. "You don't look fine. You look like you've been crying."

Of course she did. Crying was a natural reaction when you thought your world was ending and you were breaking two hearts in the process. "I'm fine now. I—I told Cam about our conversation and the deal we had."

"Did you now?"

"She did," Cam confirmed. "We're calling to let you know that she's not taking the deal. If she wants to go back and get her master's, that's her choice. If she wants to quit her position at the shop and work elsewhere, that's also her choice."

He squeezed her hand. "But if she wants to continue as a working partner at Make It Worx, that's her choice too. I'm going to support her no matter what she wants because I love her and that's what a partner does. You may not believe that what we feel for each other is real, but you don't have to. We believe in us."

Kenya leaned in. "I love Cam. I'm going to stay at the shop, work to increase our business, and one day I'm gonna marry him."

His hand trembled in hers. She looked at him, and for a moment his brilliant smile was all she could see. He then cleared his throat and returned his attention to the screen. "We're not asking for your permission, but we would appreciate it if we got your blessing."

Her parents exchanged glances. Her father spoke. "Are both of you sure about this?"

Kenya and Cam looked at each other, bumped shoulders. She glanced back to her parents. "We are."

"Definitely."

"Then I suppose there's only one thing to say," her mother began.

Kenya tensed, aware of Cam tightening his grip on her fingers. "What's that?"

"You were robbed!" Outrage rang in her father's tone and expression. "Unbelievable!"

Her mother nodded in agreement. "I mean, really! Did you see those costumes? How could they possibly take first place and win over your amazing work and attention to detail?"

Shocked, Kenya listened as her parents continued their critique of the final show until Cam interrupted. "I appreciate y'all, but Kenya and I still have some stuff to talk about."

"Of course," her mother said. "Now that the show's over, we expect to see you both for Sunday dinner."

Kenya heard the question, and accepted it as the olive branch it seemed to be. "We'll see you then."

Cam disconnected, put the phone down, then covered his face with his hands, leaning against the back of the couch. Thinking his reaction was due to the call, she patted his knee. "That went better than I had hoped."

He slid his hands down his face, then slapped his thighs. "I am furious with you right now."

She drew back, surprise and hurt heating her ears. "Why?"

"Why?" He gestured between them and his phone. "You almost threw us away over that!"

The accusation, right as it was, stung. "You weren't there! You didn't hear what they said and how they said it. You don't know how they pressured me from the start of the competition."

"You're right. I don't know, because you didn't tell me." He speared her with a heated look. "How could you keep something so huge from me?"

"I thought I could handle it," she admitted. "I thought we would win and that ultimatum would be dead and buried and we'd move on to the next level. I'm sorry for keeping this from you. I know I should have told you what was going on."

"Yes, you should have."

"So you could ride to the rescue again?" Guilt pricked at her, the emotional whirlwind bringing tears to her eyes. "Yes, I should have told you, but you know my parents. They were far easier on you than they would have been on me. It's why I turned my phone off while we were out in LA. I didn't want them to pressure me to leave. I didn't want you to feel obligated into doing something you weren't ready for just because you think you owe me."

"Ah, KeKe." He hauled her into his lap. "I'm sorry for saying I owe you. 'Owe' is the wrong word. It's just that, doing things for you, helping you? I do those things because I love you and want you to be happy, and being able to help you makes me happy. But if you want me to dial it back, I will. I don't ever want you to feel like you owe me anything, or that you're obligated to do something for me, or that I expect you to. Okay?"

"Okay." She wiped the last of her tears away, then smiled. "Okay."

He pulled her closer, wrapping his arms around her and resting his cheek on the top of her head. "Tell me again."

She knew exactly what he meant. "I love you."

"One more time?"

Smiling wider, she placed a hand over his heart. "I'm in love with you, Cameron Lassiter."

He shuddered. "You don't know how long I've been waiting to hear you say that, how long I waited to put Operation: Win Kenya's Heart into action. I didn't realize that your parents were the boss level."

"Let's not think about that anymore. Let's think about something else instead."

"Like what?"

She moved back from him, stood, then held out her hand. "What do you think about kissing and making up knowing that we both really love each other?"

He put his hand in hers. "You always have the best ideas, KeKe."

CHAPTER TWENTY-NINE

Welcome back to *Good Morning Atlanta*. I'm your host, Theresa Foster, and with me in the studio are Kenya Davenport and Cameron Lassiter from the hit competition show *Cosplay or No Way*, where contestants created costumes for a chance to win $100,000 and the chance to work on the production of a blockbuster movie. Although our hometown favorites, affectionately known as Team KenCam, didn't win the grand prize, these two best friends who fell in love with each other sure won the hearts of Atlanta with their skills, their relationship, and that hot-pink hair that sparked a hashtag and a new fashion trend among teenaged girls, my daughter among them! Kenya, Cameron, welcome to the show!"

Kenya dipped her head in greeting, her signature pink bangs falling into her eyes. "Thank you for having us."

Cam perched next to her on the edge of the couch, both of them too nervous to settle back fully. "We're glad to be here."

"It's been a couple of days since the finale, how are you guys doing?"

"Not going to lie—it still stings a little bit, but it's also a huge relief that it's over," Kenya said. "I'm proud of the work we did on the project and look forward to doing more—with a less stressful timeline!"

"So the show was a costume competition, but cosplay is a bit more than that," Theresa said. "Let's start with a basic question for those who may not know. What exactly is cosplay?"

This was one of the expected questions, a softball meant to help them relax and one Kenya could answer with ease. "It's costume playing," she answered. "Basically people take their favorite characters from a book, movie, video game, or anime and dress up and act like them. Some people try to be exact, and others will do their take on that character."

"You mean like the folks we see marching down Peachtree Street during the Dragon Con parade?"

"Exactly," Cam said. "Some people buy pieces to create their costumes and others make theirs from scratch, or with a combination of bought and made pieces."

"We have some pictures of you from different conventions," Theresa said, gesturing at the giant wall of monitors. Several of the photos they'd submitted to the show flashed across the screens. "You have made some incredibly detailed and creative designs."

"Thank you," Kenya said, smiling at the compliment. "We worked really hard on our costumes. I think that came through on the show."

"How did you get on the show?"

"It was Cam's idea." Kenya squeezed his knee. "He heard about the casting call and suggested that I audition for it."

Cam covered her hand with his. "She's been cosplaying since we were in high school, and she's a wiz at coming up with design ideas and costumes, especially mashups. When I heard about the show, I knew it would be a perfect way for Kenya to showcase her talents."

Theresa leaned forward. "You sound proud of her."

"I am." The sincerity in his voice rang clear as his fingers tangled with hers. "I've known Kenya half my life, and she continues to amaze me every day."

Her heart softened to a fuzzy bunny, then hopped in her chest. "The feeling's mutual."

"Whew." Theresa fanned herself with a laugh. "Anyone who doubted this was real should see you two in person! You're definitely more than friends."

"Yes, we are," Kenya said, gazing at Cam. They'd kissed and made up multiple times over the course of the night. Every last doubt and negative thought had been obliterated in a blaze of orgasms. "Working together these last few weeks, overcoming all the obstacles thrown at us, just brought us closer together and showed us that we're awesome apart but even better together."

Cam's gaze was as soft as his words. "Maybe we didn't come in first place, but I won this woman's heart, and that's the best prize I could ever have."

"Cam." She could have melted into his arms right then and there, but instead blinked rapidly to dry the moisture threatening to overspill her eyes. How this man made her feel so much so deeply continued to rock her, but she knew he'd be there to catch her. Besides, she never wanted to take the sensation, or him, for granted.

"So, does this mean that wedding bells are in your future?" Theresa asked, leaning forward.

"Uhm . . ." Kenya blushed and stammered at being put on the spot.

Cam laughed. "We haven't talked about a date yet."

That caught Kenya's attention. "Hard to do when we haven't gotten engaged yet."

"You're the one who told your parents you were going to marry me," Cam reminded her. "From that moment, I considered myself engaged. But you deserve a special ring and a special proposal. I'm working on it."

Kenya could only blink in astonishment as the interviewer laughed. "Well all right now. If marriage isn't happening soon, what's next for Team KenCam?"

"Getting back to work," Kenya said, smiling at Cam. "We've gotten a lot of interest in projects at Make It Worx, and we've got some leveling up to do."

"First, though, we're going to have a getaway, just the two of us," Cam said. "And the only tool within reach will be a bottle opener."

"Oh yeah, I like the sound of that!"

They all laughed together, then the anchor said, "Well, you may have to postpone that getaway for a little while."

Kenya stared at Cam. He shook his head, as confused as she was. "Excuse us?"

"We have someone who would like to talk to both of you. Can we go to the video screen?"

They turned to the wall of monitors. A Black woman with a riot of curly golden hair appeared. *Oh my God, is that . . . ?*

"Hello, Kenya and Cameron," the woman said, waving at the camera. "This is Regina Cahill, the costume designer for *Anubis Rising.*"

"Oh my God, you're Regina Cahill! *The* Regina Cahill! Hi!" Kenya flipped into fangirl mode. "You are so awesome! We love your work. We watch *Anubis Rising* all the time. The costumes are amazing!"

She rattled off other projects the award-winning designer had worked on until the legend herself interrupted. "Thank you for being a fan of my work," Regina said with a laugh, "but I called because I wanted you to know that I'm also a fan of yours and Cameron's."

"What?" she and Cam said in unison.

"That's right. My team and I watched the cosplay competition from the beginning. I admire the way you met every challenge thrown your way with grace and creativity. We especially enjoyed seeing how well you and Cameron work together. We were rooting for you."

She looked at Cam, almost unable to process what she'd heard. *Oh my God, Regina Cahill watched the show. Regina Cahill admires us! She knows who we are!* "Oh my God, thank you so much!"

"We're honored that you even know who we are," Cam added, his delight illuminating his face. "Thank you for supporting us."

"You're very welcome. I said some things I can't repeat when you didn't win, but maybe that's a blessing in disguise."

Anxiety ramped her pulse up to warp speed. Cam squeezed her hand with the hope she didn't dare let herself show. She nodded at him and he asked, "What sort of blessing?"

"Well, it's—actually, there's someone else here who'd like to say hello."

Regina moved back as a man joined her. "Hello, Cameron. Hello, Kenya. I'm Will Peters, one of the executive producers on *Anubis Rising*. We'd like to invite you down to Dogwood Studios to meet with Regina and her team. We'll also introduce you to the cast and crew."

"Really?"

"Yes, really," Regina said with a nod. "We can talk shop, and y'all can get an idea of what it's like to work on a major production. If it's something you think you might like to do, I can also talk to you about joining the guild."

Kenya's mouth dropped open. Becoming a professional? "Are you serious right now?"

"We don't joke when it comes to our show," Will said. "Especially when our show is getting a movie."

"What?" they asked in unison again.

"*Anubis Rising: The Dawn of Time* has been greenlit," Will explained. "You're hearing it here first. We're a few months away from production ramping up, and we're still finalizing our crews, including costuming and props."

"That's why we'd like to have you down," Regina added. "We want to know more about your shop and the things you do in the hopes that we can work together on some one-off props we need. How does that sound?"

Kenya and Cam looked at each other with barely suppressed excitement before turning back to the monitor. "That sounds amazing!"

Will and Regina laughed. "Great. We'll get your contact information and set something up. Talk to you soon."

The screen went blank. Kenya covered her mouth. "Did that just happen?"

Cam sank back against the cushions. "I think it did."

"It most certainly did," Theresa said with a light laugh. "It might not be the happy ending you wanted, but perhaps it's the happy ending you deserve?"

Kenya held on to Cam's hand, her heart full of love, happiness, and all the things. "No," she said softly, "this is definitely the happy ending I wanted."

ACKNOWLEDGMENTS

Writing is a solitary endeavor, but bringing a book to life is a team *effort*! I'd like to thank my agent, Jenny Bent of The Bent Agency, for always believing in my ability to tell a story, and my editor, Kristine Schwartz, and everyone at Berkley for not only understanding what I wanted to do with this story but enthusiastically helping me make it happen.

I also want to thank Lillie A (@lillie_80 on Twitter), who not only answered my cosplay questions but pointed me to some great resources on YouTube; the hashtag #28DaysofBlackCosplay; and so many awesome Black cosplayers for their creativity and inspiration.

THE
LOVE
CON

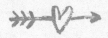

Seressia Glass

DISCUSSION QUESTIONS

1. Kenya has to select a partner to compete with in the finals for *Cosplay or No Way.* Who would you select to compete with you in a challenge like this?

2. Kenya's parents are upset that she is pursuing a career in a creative field instead of in engineering, where she received her degree. Do you think the world sees careers in STEM fields to be inherently more important than creative fields? Why?

3. In order to follow her dreams, Kenya has to go against her parents' wishes. Do you agree with her decision? Was there another way for her to handle the situation?

4. Cam and Kenya are friends long before they start a romantic relationship. How did their friendship impact their romantic relationship?

5. For their famous duos costume, Kenya decides that she and Cam will cosplay Iron Man and Thanos. If you were a contestant

on *Cosplay or No Way*, what famous pop culture duo would you want to cosplay?

6.   Kenya struggles with the pressure to represent multiple communities on the show. Is it fair for her to put that pressure on herself?

7.   Between Cam's gummy worms and Kenya's stress cooking, our hero and heroine use food to de-stress. What are some of your comfort foods?

8.   What are some ways Kenya must work against the stereotype of the "Angry Black Woman" and the microaggressions from people like Rebecca? Do you also feel like you have to change your behavior to avoid stereotypes?

9.   Both Cam's ex and Kenya's parents tell her she leans on Cam too much. Do you agree? How does she work to make their relationship more equitable?

10.   If you were to look five years into the future after the end of the book, what do you see Kenya and Cam doing? What kind of projects would they be working on?

Photo by Porsha Antalan of Fempua Productions

Seressia Glass is an award-winning author of romance and urban fantasy. She lives south of Atlanta with her husband, son, two attack poodles, and a bulldozer of a Cane Corso. When not writing, she likes to collect purple things and jewelry, and spends way too much time watching K-dramas and anime.

Ready to find
your next great read?

Let us help.

Visit prh.com/nextread

Penguin
Random
House